GARDA ~ WELCOME TO THE REALM

STACY EATON

NITEWOLF NOVELS

GARDA – WELCOME TO THE REAL

Destiny ~ Desire ~ Death

There is a place that lies between heaven and Earth, it is called The Realm. Within this place, the Guards of Peace, known as Garda Síochána, learn to guide and protect the ones that live below until they are called home.

Officer Corey Hamilton is dedicated to being the best that she can be, in uniform and out. Her loving nature, compassionate thoughts, and warrior strength make her the perfect candidate to join the Garda Síochána and spend her eternity protecting and guiding others.

Just before Corey dies in a line-of-duty accident, she meets Officer Mitchell O'Reilly. Her feelings for him may change her destiny, but not for the better, as she falls in love with this married man. Brock, Corey's personal Garda, will bring her home to The Realm and attempt to train her for her future, even while she still fights for her past.

Will Brock be able to direct Corey down the right path, or will she cross the line and fall from grace?

Join Corey, Mitchell, and Brock for an emotional and heart-pounding adventure that is sure to make you wonder if angels are really guiding us in our everyday lives.

PART 1

The Meeting

CHAPTER 1 ~ MITCHELL

The smell of rotten garbage tickled my nose, and I exhaled to clear it. Walking lightly in the dark shadows of the alley, I peered around the corner of the large commercial dumpster, my gun drawn, heavy in my hands and pointed low. A rat scurried away. I moved on. The target I wanted could be classified as vermin, but he was larger, much larger.

I had been directed to stay put at the end of the alley near the road in case he came that way, but after debating with myself, I left my post in search of the suspect. A nagging voice inside my head told me I should have stayed where I was, but I continued to ignore it.

Sirens in the distance and the just-audible chatter over the radio kept me in tune with where everyone else was. The suspect, who was wanted for aggravated assault, had fled from police after a brief struggle. Now he hid among the dark alleys of the small city.

The sound of footsteps pummeling the ground reached me, and I moved towards the sound. A second set could be heard moving just as fast, if not faster, behind it.

Static from a radio echoed around the corner, moving closer. The pounding on the pavement grew louder, and I peeked around the brick wall, the back of my shirt snagging on the rough brick behind me.

The suspect was heading this way, his arms pumping hard, close to his body, his feet beating the trash-strewn alleyway while he tried to outrun the person behind him.

The size of his body blocked most of my view, but I heard the telltale sounds of a radio and the clapping of metal on metal as cuffs banged against each other with each downward motion. I knew the sounds of one of my own.

I braced myself to step out and intercept the subject. My timing was crucial: If I went too soon, he could avoid me, too late, and he could ram right into me before he saw the barrel of my forty-caliber Glock pointed at him.

I glanced around the corner one last time, sucking in a quick breath. I pushed off the wall and pivoted into the path of the oncoming fugitive, my gun pointed straight out in front of me as he closed the gap between us.

Surprise registered on his face. He straightened, trying to halt his forward movement, his feet skidded on the damp asphalt. The knowledge that he was now trapped between two cops crossed the features of his sweaty face, and the whites of his eyes grew large. My mouth opened to speak just as his body pitched forward, a pair of small arms wrapped around his broad chest from behind. He slammed to the ground, hard.

A grunt of pain was expelled into the air. I was not sure if it came from him or the person on his back. My gun now pointed down at the subject, I blinked at the sight, twice.

Now on her knees over the suspect, the pursuing officer grabbed one of his hands from above his head, yanking it hard to the center of his back. The guy's face came off the ground, wincing in pain from the quick movement.

"Give me your cuffs," she called out.

I holstered my gun, grabbed my cuffs from the pouch on my duty belt, and handed them down to her. Quite mesmerized by the scene playing out in front of me, I did nothing more than continue to watch her.

This woman dressed in a police uniform, probably half the weight of the guy on the ground, had not only chased him down, but had tackled him face first to the ground. Okay, that was kind of hot. No, that was smoking hot!

"I didn't do anything!" the apprehended subject screamed.

I watched as she pulled his other arm behind his back just as roughly as she had the first, her chest still heaving from her foot pursuit.

She looked up at me, her face covered in shadows, "You mind?"

Broken out of my admiration by her words, I moved to her side while she climbed off the suspect's back. Together we pulled him to his feet.

"Man, you made me hit my head! I'm bleeding!"

"Sucks to be you, huh?" Her face lifted to the suspect, then she glanced at me before she looked down at her radio microphone clipped to the front of her shirt.

"Twenty-nine Paul Six, one in custody, alleyway south of Ridge Avenue."

As she yanked the guy forward, he stumbled, and I realized she only came up to his shoulder.

"Copy Twenty-nine Paul Six, do you need a car for transport?" the radio crackled to life.

"Paul Six, yeah, and the suspect will also need EMS attention, laceration to the head from a fall."

"Twenty-nine Paul Six, copy EMS." The dispatcher paused and then continued. "Twenty-nine Paul Six, also, when you are clear, you have a domestic pending."

"Paul Six, I copy, I'll be clear soon." She pulled the guy's arm harder which forced him to walk faster. With my hand wrapped around his other elbow, I peeked around the suspect's body to her. She was almost as tall as my five foot seven stature, not petite, but not wide. From what I had just observed, she was in damned good shape. A section of long light-blond hair that had pulled out of the neat knot at the back of her neck lay along the side of her face, hiding her features from me.

Tires screeched to a halt at the end of the alley. Flashing lights from a patrol car bounced off the brick walls. I turned to her again. She pushed the hair behind her ear, her jaw was locked, and a muscle twitched in the side of her cheek while red and blue lights reflected off her clear skin.

"You guys alright?" a voice I recognized called out from the street.

"Hey, Joe, can you take it from here? I need to get going, got another call," she yelled down the alley.

"Sure, I got it. Good job, thanks for your help." My partner, Joe Corby, jogged over to us, taking the guy's arm as she stepped away.

"No problem, you need anything else from me?"

We stepped out of the alleyway. Under bright street lights, other police cars were pulling up to our location. I couldn't pull my intent gaze from her as she backed away; the hair she had pushed behind her ear fell forward as she turned. The urge to reach out and tuck the shiny lock back made my hand twitch.

"Just a supplement from you. Who took him into custody?" Joe asked her as he pulled open the rear door, prodding the suspect into the back. I let go, never looking away from her.

"Get my report to you later. Ask your partner, he was there." She smiled and for the first time made direct eye contact with me. Her step faltered and her eyebrows came down just the smallest amount. Her smile faded, and her mouth opened just the tiniest bit into an O shape.

Two very dark eyes bore into mine for three brief seconds. A bolt of electricity zipped through my body, straight to my heart. She stopped moving backwards, cocked her head, and slowly smiled again.

With a quick turn, she spun on her heel and started jogging down the street in search of her patrol car that she'd ditched to pursue the subject on foot.

I watched her until she turned the corner a block away.

"So, what happened?" Joe asked after he closed the back door.

"Who was that?" I countered his question with one of my own.

"Who, the bozo you just arrested?" He started making his way to the driver's door.

I rolled my eyes at his back, "No, I know who he is. The woman—who was that woman?"

Joe smiled at me over the roof of the car, "Ah, yes, amazing isn't she?" He climbed into the driver's seat, putting down the passenger window. "You getting in, Mitch? Or do you plan on walking back to the station?"

I pulled open the door, sliding my wide frame into the tight passenger seat.

"She tackled him." I laughed, for the first time replaying the scene in my mind of her diving onto his back and going down to the ground fast.

Joe laughed beside me as the prisoner yelled from the back, "Hey, it's not funny. That hurt!"

"Yeah, yeah, yeah, I'm sure it hurt. Now you know what the guy you assaulted feels like," Joe barked over his right shoulder.

"He deserved it."

"Yeah, well, so did you," Joe responded while peeking in the rearview mirror.

I turned around in my seat to see the suspect shake his head and look out the window. A thin line of blood ran down the right side of his face from his impact with the macadam.

"So, who was that?"

"Seriously? You really have no idea who that was?" He glanced my way before pulling onto the road.

"If I knew, do you really think I would ask?" I threw back.

"Wow, I thought everyone knew her." He shook his head while he laughed. "That was Corey Hamilton, the woman with a face and body of an angel, and a heart to match. Seriously, you've never seen her before?" The incredulousness in his voice stood out.

"I've heard of her. You all talk enough about her, but I've never seen her face to face." Oh, and what a face. He was right, the face of an angel, although with her gear on I couldn't really tell what kind of body she had.

I wasn't sure about the heart thing, not with the way she tackled him. I didn't think that kind of aggressiveness would go over too well in heaven.

The memory of her staring back at me played over and over like a tape on loop mode. The zap that had sung through my heart in that moment, had she felt the shock, too?

"Yeah, well don't get too excited about it. She's out of our league." Joe pulled up to the police station, letting our dispatcher know where we were. I climbed out and heard Corey's voice over the radio saying she was on location of her call.

How I had never taken notice of her voice before amazed me. Now that I'd seen her face, her voice vibrated through my skull.

"What do you mean, out of our league?" I pulled open the rear door, waiting for the prisoner to climb out on his own power.

"Man, first of all, did you see her? She's amazing! Not that we are bad to look at, but she needs to be with a Greek god of some kind—although she was married to a Ken doll before, and that didn't work out."

Joe grabbed the guy's other arm once he was out, and we marched him into the station. "She's married?"

The suspect glanced back and forth between us, apparently interested in our conversation, too.

"Was married, divorced now." Joe unlocked the door to the processing room. We sat the guy down on the bench, cuffing his leg to the metal post.

"And that's the other thing about us, we're married. She won't look at you twice once she knows that. That's why she's divorced, Barbie boy cheated on her."

The suspect snickered from the bench, "Barbie boy," he muttered.

We both gaped at him and Joe blurted out, "What are you laughing about?"

"Nothing, you guys are just funny, that's all." He chuckled again.

Her voice reached my ears as it played in stereo over our radios. She was telling the dispatcher her status was alright. Strangely enough, I felt relief without having known I was worried.

Another officer walked into the processing room, behind him the EMS crew crowded in to assess the suspect. We walked out as they entered; too many people in one small room.

"Does she date cops?" I questioned as we entered the squad room.

He laughed, "Why you so interested, Mitch? I already told you, we're out of her league, man."

"I'm not interested, I just—" I thought about it for a second, "Well, I'm interested, but not like that. I was just flat out amazed at how she handled that guy. I stood there with my mouth hanging open while she took him down and cuffed him."

I dropped down into one of our swivel office chairs, leaning back.

"She might look like an angel, but she fights like the devil. I'd do anything to have her on my side." He grinned over his shoulder and rolled his own chair up to the desk. "Second degree black belt, I think." He reached for the mouse, waking up the computer with a quick shake.

Second degree black belt, nice! I thought back to the exchange on the street again, her actions lingering in my mind.

"Let it go, man," he chortled as he started typing into our report system.

He was right; I needed to let it go. I was a married man, so no matter what little burst of energy had raced through me earlier, it didn't matter. I pulled myself up to my desk, putting her face out of my mind as I pulled my own report up.

CHAPTER 2 ~ COREY

I pulled into my station, backing my patrol car into my usual spot out back. My mouth was still dry from running after that guy. I unscrewed the cap and drank long gulps of the lukewarm water. I tossed the empty bottle to the floorboard of the passenger seat and climbed out.

For the first time since I'd left the city, I looked down and realized my uniform pants were a mess. Dirt and some other substance coated my dark blue tactical BDU pants from the knees down. Yuck. I should send the suspect my dry cleaning bill.

A low-level beep hit my ears as I pressed my key fob up to the magnetic pad, unlocking the door to the station. I stepped inside, smiling to myself. I had nailed that guy! Face first into the ground! A bubble of laughter erupted as I remembered glancing over at the officer who had stood there. He had given me that last edge to put the guy down, making him slow up just enough for me to catch him.

On my travel to the ground while piggybacked on the bad guy, the other officer's eyes had expanded to a large circumference. I snickered to myself, remembering how he'd stood there gaping at me until I had called him out on it.

I didn't know who he was, but I didn't know several of the newer guys down in the city. Until last week, I had worked a different rotation, having moved to this one when someone else went out on injury.

I grabbed a towel, wiping at my pants to get the worst of the grime off. I had no idea what it was, and to be honest, I didn't really want to know. Luckily, my shift would be over in a few hours.

The city got dispatched to another call while I was finishing my hasty cleanup; a husky male voice answered the dispatcher. I leaned over to the computer on the desk to pull up the roster for the city. Was that his voice?

Only one officer showed assigned to a call, Mitchell O'Reilly; the rest of the officers' names I recognized, so that must be the one who had helped me.

His voice came through the speaker clipped to my chest; a shiver went down my back. Nice voice, deep, husky, and sexy, I thought to myself —very sexy.

The sound matched what I had expected to come from him. The wide shoulders, the strong arms, the way he held his body straight. If the expression on his face hadn't been enough to give me pause as I left, his voice would have.

What had been in his expression? Wonder? Amazement? Lust? I was used to the lustful looks I got from men. God had blessed me with beauty and I knew it, although I did not take it for granted or use it to get ahead.

I sat back in my chair, swiveling myself left and right with my toes, my head resting on the back of the seat. I waited till I heard his voice over the airwaves again. Lowering my eyelids, I pictured his face. The wide strong forehead and cheekbones, the light color of his irises, blue, or were they green? I had been too far back to know for sure.

The phone ringing in the station snapped me back to reality. I reached out to pick it up, letting go of the image in my mind's eye.

I answered the caller's questions quickly and disconnected, moving over to the computer to complete my reports. The radio got quiet as the night progressed to early morning, most people sound asleep in their beds, which was a good thing.

With my report finished, I carried the copy to my car, typing a message to Joe on my in-car computer. I waited, but no response came. The guys hung out on station a lot at this time of night, he was probably there. I put my car in gear and turned right to head back to the city police station.

The township I worked for was large and densely populated. Out here, Middle America neighborhoods were popping up around the horse farms, taking over the countryside with postage-stamp, fenced-in yards and wooden swingsets. It would not be long until our population doubled.

I wound down the country roads until I came to abandoned industrial buildings. It was amazing that such dilapidation could be less than a mile away from the beauty of the township. I drove past them, my attention straight ahead, not wishing to depress myself tonight with the poverty.

I pulled up to the station moments later. All the patrol cars were backed in. The visitor spot was open. I turned my car off and tucked my key into my belt.

The girl at reception buzzed me back to the squad room with a smile. I stepped around the corner to say hello, asking about her family. Our conversation finished, I turned to step out of the room. A foot came into view just as I was setting my foot forward. I halted, rolling up on my toes to keep from stepping forward again.

The incredible light blue color glimmering behind soft brown lashes was the first thing I noticed as he turned in my direction, stopping six inches in front of me as if he had hit a glass wall. Had I not stopped, we would have collided. Surprise crossed his features, a smile lifting over his full lips, the corners of his eyes crinkling.

Oh, those eyes! They were like the summer sky: bright, warm, and welcoming. I wanted to crawl into them and revel in the beauty. My gaze stole to his lips, full and soft. Did I just lick my lips? Heat rushed into my cheeks. My heart slammed against my chest while I rolled back off my toes to stand flat, separating us by a few more inches.

"I'm sorry, I didn't see you coming," I mumbled.

"No, it's my fault," he peeked at my mouth as he spoke. My heart beat erratically.

Movement to my right caused me to glance away from his handsome face. I stepped back and smiled up at Joe, who stood about eight inches taller than I.

"Hey, Corey, did you get the report done already?" He glanced at

Mitch, a smirk on his face, and I wondered about his expression. Mitch's attention was on Joe, but I saw him glance in my direction for a brief moment.

"Actually, I do have it done." I stepped towards him, which put me within five inches of Mitch. His musky cologne filled my nasal passages and made my knees weak. I moved away from him before my body could override my mind and move closer.

At the same time we focused on each other, inches apart, my gaze went from his eyes to his lips and back again—oh, damn.

Joe took the papers from me, "Thanks. Did you meet Mitch?"

"Not officially. Hello, Mitch, I'm Corey Hamilton." I put my hand out to shake his, not even thinking about what might happen.

"Hello, Corey, Mitch O'Reilly." His right hand found mine, his fingers sliding gently over my palm. Tingles rippled up my arm. The shake was a brief pump, but neither of us released our grip right away. The heat from his hand seared into mine, while his blue irises sucked me in further. The urge to lean into him was stronger than I had ever felt, like two magnets being drawn together.

A throat cleared, breaking the moment, and I pulled my hand back quickly, smiling at Joe. The smirk on his face told me he had noticed the length of the handshake.

"Well, I better get back, shift is almost over." I moved to slide past Mitch. He stepped out of my way. "You guys be safe," I called out over my shoulder, afraid to turn to him again.

I pushed open the glass door, thankful for the cooler night air. My body felt hot, my face on fire from the blush that had colored my skin.

What the hell was that? Never had a man blown me away like that. With just the touch of his hand, he had caused my knees to shake and my body to respond. Not even Matt had had that effect on me when we'd been married.

I stopped by the side of my car, inspecting the moon, attempting to compose myself before I got in. The three-quarter moon was bright in the cloudless sky.

"Your eyes are the color of the night sky," the husky voice from the radio had me turning. My heart sped up.

Mitch stood two feet away. So lost in my own thoughts, I hadn't heard him approach—dangerous, very dangerous. "Funny, I was just thinking how yours are like the summer sky."

He took a small step forward, changing his weight from one foot to the other in a nervous manner. I almost laughed. If he was one bit as nervous as I was standing next to him, I knew how he was feeling. I fought the urge to do the same and forced myself to be still.

"I didn't thank you for earlier," I said quietly.

The smile on his face lit up all his features, and my heart skipped a beat. "I should be the one thanking you. Your body slam was pretty amazing."

We both laughed.

"Yeah, well, if you hadn't been there, the body slam might have been just mine." We locked gazes again, a small flame burning between us that I knew we both felt. "I better go." I moved towards my door, and he side-stepped me and reached with his left hand to pull it open. Around his left ring finger, I noticed a platinum band. The fire instantly went out and my heart sank.

Not meeting his intent observation of me, I thanked him and climbed inside. He pushed the door shut. I turned the car on and put it in reverse while he stepped back, watching me.

I could tell he was attracted to me, but he was married. Anger progressed through me slowly. He was just another man who only wanted to get me in bed for some fun. I pulled out of the parking lot, stepping on the gas harder than I needed to, pushing the image of him from my mind like I did the pedal under my foot.

CHAPTER 3 ~ MITCHELL

The skin of her hand was softer than I had imagined as I held it in mine. Instead of releasing it after shaking, I pulled her closer, staring at her lips as they moved towards me. My hand moved to her waist, above where her duty belt should be, but wasn't. Her chest came in contact with mine; a small gasp left her lips as I targeted them.

We stood at the same height, and I was lost in the depths of her midnight blue. I moved forward, daring anyone to stop me from tasting her. My heart beat in double time as I leaned in that last inch.

Beep...beep...beep...I jerked out of my dream with the annoying blare of my alarm. Slamming my hand over my clock, I dropped back to the sheets. What a freaking time to wake up! Why couldn't I have had just a few more seconds, one more measly minute to complete that kiss?

Groaning, I threw back the covers and stepped from the bed to stretch. The door opened behind me, I kept stretching.

"I thought I heard your alarm. Did you sleep good, honey?" Beth spoke from the doorway. I scratched my chest with one hand, adjusting my partial erection with the other.

"Yeah, fine." I kept my back to her, walking to my dresser to pull out clothes for work. I needed a shower and some relief.

"I put coffee on for you," her soft voice sounded hurt, but I wasn't sure how to make that better. I pulled out boxers, socks, and my Under Armour T-shirt, clutching them over my groin as I turned and moved to the bathroom.

"Thanks, I'll get some when I get out of the shower," I replied before closing the door. After putting my clothes on the counter, I braced my arms on the sides of the beige sink, hanging my head down.

A freaking dream! If it was only a dream, then how come I could feel her breath over my lips? Pushing myself off the counter, I jerked my toothbrush from the cup, applied paste, and brushed my teeth with a vengeance.

My eyes locked on their reflection, they were so opposite of hers. I closed my lids to break the visual comparison.

I spit the paste out and rinsed the sink before I turned the shower on. The hot water ran over my back, while I leaned my arms into the cold, white tile wall. The water cascading over my skin heated my core, making me rock hard with memories of her voice echoing in my mind.

Reaching between my legs, I grasped myself just as the bathroom door pulled open.

"Hey, Dad! Can we play ball before you go to work?" I groaned mentally at the interruption, but chuckled at my son's excited voice bouncing off the walls of the small room.

"Yeah, Chase, let me get my shower and we can play for a few minutes." I grabbed the plastic bottle of shampoo, squeezing some into my hand while he ran out of the room yelling for his mother.

While rinsing the lather from my hair, I felt the presence of someone in the room. Wiping the water off my face, I tried to focus on my wife through the cloudy glass.

"You need something?" I picked up the soap, waiting for her answer.

"Chase has been waiting all afternoon for you to get up. I bought him that new glove he's been talking about." I heard the medicine cabinet open and close after she put something in it. "I picked you up some lunch meat. Do you want me to make you a few sandwiches for work?"

"No, don't bother, it's cheesesteak night. I'll just order with the guys." I rinsed off my body, my erection gone now with the mundane chatter from my wife.

16

I heard the sigh over the sound of the water. I gritted my teeth.

"It's not a bother you know. I'd be happy to do it."

I turned the water off and slid back the door, grabbing the towel from the rack. "Beth, I said no, but thanks anyway." I rubbed the towel over my short hair, quickly drying it.

"Fine." She raked her gaze over me, then turned and left.

I glanced at my watch, forty-five minutes until I needed to leave for work, not soon enough. I got dressed and made my way to find my son.

Chase and I threw the baseball around the backyard. He tried hard to catch it, but most of the time it bounced out of the glove he wore, the leather too stiff for his small hand to control.

Beth sat on the porch watching us, her steady glare making me more frustrated by the second. I twisted my wrist, checking the time again, fifteen minutes. I was leaving early; I couldn't take the eagle eye anymore.

"Okay, Chase, Dad has to get to work. Come give me a hug then go put your gear away." He scurried over to give me a half hug.

Over his head I watched Beth walk off the porch. "You're leaving early." She crossed her arms in front of her.

"I have an errand to run before I get to work." I hoped she didn't ask what, because I didn't really have one.

"Are you ever going to talk to me again, Mitch?"

I shook my head, not believing she was going to bring this up again. "Beth, we're talking right now." I walked past her towards the house to get my things.

"That's not what I meant. Don't walk away from me." She followed; I turned when I reached the porch.

"Beth, I'm not getting into it with you right now. I have to go, and this conversation is not something we need to have minutes before I walk out the door."

"When, then?" she put her hands on her hips. Why did women do that?

"I don't know, Beth, but not right now." I walked away from her to get my keys and gun.

I managed to get out of the house without another verbal battle. The last thing I wanted to do was talk about what had happened between us. I just wanted it to go away.

Heading into work, I stopped at the Wawa to grab a cup of coffee. In my rush to get out the door, I had forgotten about the pot Beth had brewed. I parked next to a brand new black Camaro, the windows so heavily tinted that you could not see inside. Nice, I thought as I climbed out of my truck. What I wouldn't do for a ride like that.

"You like it?" a female voice broke into my thoughts and my neck whipped to the front of my vehicle where Corey stood.

"Is this yours?" I pointed at the Camaro to stress the point.

She smiled, "Yep, sure is." She stepped closer, a twenty-four-ounce coffee in her hands. The smell of it mingled with citrus, and I wondered if that was her scent.

"Nice. How long have you had it?" I examined the car as I heard the doors unlock.

"Couple of months, I guess. You ever seen the inside of one?" She reached for the door handle, pulling it open. I shook my head and leaned down to peer in.

"Wow, that's awesome." A smile spread over my face as I turned to her. Her dark Oakley shades blocked the color of her eyes from me. I wanted to take her sunglasses off.

"Have a seat; I'll start it up for you." I didn't hesitate while she walked to the driver's side and climbed in. I watched her close her door and put the key in the ignition after she set her coffee cup into the holder. The passenger seat was soft, plush leather. I leaned back, finding it reclined further than expected.

The vibration of the motor tore through me with almost as much force as the smile on her face when she turned. Her face was less than a foot from mine, our arms inches away on the center console. The memory of the dream came back to mind, reminding me of how much I had wanted to taste her lips.

A sweet citrus sent wafted gently over me. Yeah, that was her scent, how perfect for her.

"Like it?" She slid her glasses onto the top of her head.

Liked it? Hell, no, I loved it; right along with the intricate color of her irises and her sexy face.

"Yeah, I like it." My voice was husky. I knew she noticed, when she peeked at my mouth, and the tip of her tongue flicked out to wet the soft skin that surrounded hers.

I needed to get out of this car—and fast.

"I guess you're on your way into work?" I shifted in the seat to get out.

"Yep, too busy to make coffee at home, so I stopped to grab one here. What about you?"

"Yeah, me, too." We locked stares again, her citrus scent attempting to lure me back into the car. A horn from another vehicle in the lot broke the moment. I climbed out.

"Sometime, you will have to take me for a ride." I leaned into the car, resting my left arm on the roof.

"Sure!" her smile was so bright, I needed my own sunglasses to truly enjoy it.

"I'll talk to you later, Corey. Be safe tonight."

"Always."

I watched her put her hand on the gearshift and stood up, closing the door. She pulled her sunglasses back into place and waved briefly before she peered over her shoulder to back out.

I stood at the curb, waiting for her to get out of sight, not able to turn my back on her for one second.

Why did I feel so drawn to that woman? I walked into the store to grab my coffee, excited to be going to work. The possibility of talking or seeing her again tonight was foremost in my mind.

CHAPTER 4 ~ COREY

*W*as it possible to be giddy at the age of thirty-two? The question rattled around in my mind. Giddy? No. That was something teenagers were when they had a crush on someone, not a professional adult, and not about a married man.

"Damn! Why does he have to be married?" I asked myself as I glanced in the rearview mirror to see Mitch still standing on the curb.

"Married—he's married, as in a wife and possibly kids. Let it go, Corey." I reached for the volume knob and cranked up the music, singing out loud to some good classic Eagles.

My shift started out busy, but by eleven the radio was dead quiet everywhere in this part of the county. Not really surprising for a Tuesday night, but it made for a much longer shift.

My laptop beeped next to me, and I absently lifted the heavy silver lid of the Motorola computer to see what message had arrived.

"Busy?" was written on my screen from a city unit. I pulled up the roster, seeing that the call number was assigned to Mitch tonight.

"Bored," I typed back.

"Coffee?" My laughter echoed in my car, a man of few words.

"Sure. You buying?"

"Yep," came a few seconds later.

"*16 oz French vanilla creamer,*" I typed back.

"*K, where do you want to meet?*"

I thought for a second, trying to come up with a good place. "*Behind warehouse on Market—that electronics place,*" I sent to him and he acknowledged. Butterflies wiggled in my belly as I started heading in that direction. It would take him a few minutes to get the coffee, so I did some neighborhood patrol on the way.

I drove to the location, turned the headlights off, and climbed out. It was a beautiful night, a calm soft breeze blowing with warm temperatures, perfect for standing outside to have coffee.

I heard the growl of his engine and the reflection of his headlights on a trash dumpster before I saw his car. The butterflies I had felt earlier took flight. Coffee, this is just coffee, I told myself.

Mitch smiled as he pulled up, turning off his lights and opening his door before he grabbed our cups. I walked over to take mine from him. Our fingers touched, and the butterflies went wild. I walked back to my car, resting my backside on the front driver's side above the wheel.

He did the same on his car, pulling back the lid on his cup to let the heat out; a swirl of steam rose up to his face. I watched it pass his features.

"How's your night going?" Did my voice sound as shaky as I felt?

"Better now," he grinned. I took a sip of my coffee.

"Why now?" I asked after I swallowed the hot, sweet liquid.

"I got to see you." He winked, "You are much better to look at than the bozo guys I work with."

"Oh, come on, those guys are great!" I laughed.

"Yeah, they are great, but," he turned away, "it's nice to talk to someone who isn't them."

"I know what you mean. It gets quiet out where I am. Sometimes there's no one to talk to."

"Somehow I can't imagine you being lonely. I'm sure you get messages all night long from guys wanting to talk to you."

I threw my head back and laughed, shaking my head as I spoke, "Not really. I keep to myself most of the time."

"Why is that?" his voice took on a serious tone.

My shoulders rose in a small shrug, "Don't know, I just like to keep work…work. I don't spend too much time socializing when I'm here. I do enough of that on my days off."

"What do you do when you're off?" He crossed his right foot over his left, then matched his arms that way after setting his coffee down on the hood of his car. His shoulders and chest looked wider than before as he stood there. What would his body feel like wrapped around me?

Whoa, lady! I needed to change thinking tracks because this one was derailing me. I put the coffee cup to my lips again and took a long, slow drink. Think about what I do, that is a much better train of thought than his chest. No, it's not, but it's safer.

"I spend most of my time doing charity work. I volunteer at the cancer center for children, and a couple times a week I work at the women's shelter."

He cocked his head and contemplated me more closely. Was that even possible? I felt like I was under a microscope already.

"Joe said you had the heart of an angel, I guess he was right."

Laughter bubbled up and released as I pictured myself with angel wings. "I'm far from being an angel."

"From where I stand, I think you're wrong." His voice had taken on a sultry quality. A shiver ran down my spine.

"You don't know me, Mitch," I said quietly back to him.

He pushed off his car, "You're right, but I'd like to, Corey."

We stood two feet apart, staring each other down. How badly I wanted to close the gap and touch his lips, feel his chest against mine.

"Why?" I whispered into the air between us.

"I can't give you a real answer to that. All I know is that from the moment I saw you last night, I can't get you off my mind. When I'm near you, it's like there is a rope around me pulling me closer."

He felt the same thing that I did. I swallowed while I thought of a response.

"Mitch, you're married." There, I said it, the dinosaur in the room.

He heaved a large sigh, "Yeah, I am. That doesn't change what I feel right now, though."

"It may not change the way you feel, but it doesn't change the fact that you are, either." I smiled softly, trying to ease the bluntness of my comment.

He leaned back against his car again, picking up his coffee cup. He finished what was inside. I watched him swallow, wanting to touch his throat with my mouth. I laughed at my own thoughts.

"What's so funny?" he smirked while he set his cup down.

"Nothing, sorry," I felt my cheeks warm. "Okay, maybe I feel the same thing you do, but like I said, it doesn't change anything, and I don't go around getting involved with married men, so we need to keep this on a friendship level, alright?"

He studied me for a moment. "Alright."

We spent a few more minutes chatting about work before he got an ambulance call and needed to leave.

The longing we both felt crossed between us like high-tension wires as he climbed into his car.

For about four weeks, we met whenever we could to share our coffee breaks in peace. The mounting pressure grew between us each time we were together. The apprehension, an almost tangible force that surrounded us, crackled in the air when we stood a few feet apart.

We were careful not to talk about what was on our minds constantly, the need that unconsciously pulled us closer. We, instead, shared stories of our jobs, laughed about stupid things we had done growing up, and avoided any talk of his wife and my ex-husband. The more we spoke, the more we found we had a lot in common, and the closer we became emotionally.

There was not a day that went by that I didn't wake up with his face in my mind, or a time I fell asleep that I didn't wish he were beside me. I longed to feel his arms, to taste his lips, but the problem remained between us: He was a married man.

This night, just four weeks after we had met, found us, like many others, standing two feet apart, leaning against our cars, and staring at one another. The sight of him continued to make my knees weak, and I craved the touch of his lips so badly that it was a constant ache.

I broke eye contact and stood up straight, "Well, I should get back to my area. Thanks for the coffee."

He nodded, watching me closely. The expression on his face was a beacon calling me home and I got lost myself in his stare.

"Have you ever wanted to do something, just one time, just to see what it was like, even though you know it's wrong?" I whispered on the wind between us.

He pushed off the car slowly, took two small steps, and stood just eight inches from me. "Every single time I see you."

I could feel his breath on my face. "What do you want?" I breathed out slowly, leaning unconsciously towards him.

He advanced one more step. Our shirts touched over our thick Kevlar vests, our mouths just an inch away. "I want to kiss you, Corey."

"Then do it, Mitch."

There was no hesitation from either of us. The first graze put my mind in a tizzy; the second set my body on fire. His tongue gently touched the sensitive skin of my lips, unlocking the door, and I allowed him in. Softly, slowly, this kiss was a test. Would we pass?

He pulled back, opening up his heavy lids, "Well?"

"My knees are shaking," I whispered.

"Mine, too," he kissed me again. This time it deepened quickly as our mouths and tongues meshed together so naturally. The fingertips of one of his hands touched my thigh, and tingling ignited from my skin all the way to my bone. How could that happen?

My hand slipped into his, intertwining our fingers as his other one came to curl around my neck. I slid my other hand onto his head, finally daring to touch what I had ached to feel before. The short hair tickled the palm of my hand.

No other kiss had affected me the way this single one did. My heart sang, my body ached, and my mind went to war with what I was doing and feeling. I knew my actions were not right, but I wanted him so badly.

The kiss ended, our foreheads touched as we held hands and tried to harness the passion we had unleashed.

"I should go." I pulled back. Heat glazed his face, and I knew the same was mirrored on mine.

Nodding slowly at me, he stepped back. "I'll see you later, Corey." Our fingers slipped away from each other's.

"Be safe, Mitchell." I turned to my car.

"You, too."

"Always," I smiled over my shoulder and climbed into the driver's seat.

I was on cloud nine from the kiss, but found myself falling from the sky as I drove away. How could something that felt so good be so wrong?

CHAPTER 5 ~ BROCK

The night hid me from view as I watched Corey and Mitch locked in a passionate embrace, the tense muscles in my back twitched. I wanted to use my persuasion to end it, but I didn't. I stood motionless.

"I'm surprised you allowed that to happen, Brock." The voice would have startled me if I had not already felt his presence enter behind me.

My arms crossed over my chest, I shrugged my wide shoulders.

"I do hope you don't allow her to continue. She could very easily cross the line and commit the sin of adultery." Out of the corner of my eye, I saw him step beside me. Hidden in the shadows of the building, we could not be seen, but even if we stood beside Corey and Mitch, they would not know of our presence unless we let them.

I scoffed at him, "You know as well as I do, she could commit all seven deadly sins and be accepted into our group with a simple apology. The Maker has waited a long time for her to join us."

"So have you."

I slowly turned my head to the man beside me. Montgomery was my Garda, my guardian, since before I joined the Realm, the place that was between heaven and Earth where those of us who worked as guardians could move between the two levels of life and death. We were the elite, warriors of a special type trained to guard the others that would walk among us or were destined to make a huge difference on Earth.

"Of course I have waited, she is my charge." I turned back to the scene in front of me: Their foreheads resting together, content in this moment they shared.

"If you say so, but somehow I believe you have more invested in this guardianship than her just being your charge. There is the story, you know."

"Whatever, Montgomery. Did you need something, or are you bored today?"

"Yes, I do need something, actually not me, we are being summoned for a meeting. I was sent to find you since you tuned yourself out when you entered this side." He stepped back.

"Fine, I'll be there in a moment." I watched her walk away. I just wanted to make sure she got in her car and left.

"Brock, you know she is fine tonight. Come, we have business. She will be with you, I mean us, soon enough."

I turned to glare at him over my shoulder, but he had already phased. I watched her car drive out of sight and turned to consider Mitch again.

There was a very tightly-woven connection between them. The stories of soul mates whispered in my mind, but I pushed it aside. If they were, then I wouldn't stand a chance.

I watched him until he climbed into his car, wishing I could talk to him, but now was not the time.

I closed my eyes and phased back to the Realm.

PART 2

The Death

CHAPTER 6 ~ MITCHELL

*T*he taillight of her car disappeared around the corner and with it a piece of my heart. I looked down at the cracked pavement. What am I doing?

Since the day I had met her, I had wanted to kiss those lips. I had dreamed of doing it a thousand times, not just dreams, but fantasies. She brought about feelings that I never knew could exist.

Were these just hormonal fantasies because of an unhappy marriage? Was it just because I thought she was beautiful? No. I meant yes, she was beautiful, but that couldn't be the reason.

I took our empty coffee cups over to the trash bin. Inside my car, I stared out the window, my head resting on the seat back. I closed my eyes.

I had never felt a kiss so deeply in my life. It wasn't just one of passion, but one of possession. The moment we touched, she owned a part of me—or maybe we swapped a part of ourselves with each other. Did she feel the same way that I did?

The radio broke me out of my mental conversation, and I put my car in drive to go assist one of my other units.

As I climbed out of the car to help Joe, I could still feel her lips on mine, her citrus scent strong in my nose. Would anyone else be able to smell her on me? I scanned my uniform: nothing noticeable.

We finished with our incident, and I walked back to my car. It had been thirty minutes since she had driven away, yet I somehow missed her. How was that possible?

Flipping up the laptop cover, I cycled through the waiting messages on my computer. The last one was from her, a simple *"How?"* typed on the screen. How what? How did this all happen? How did we end up standing in the parking lot kissing? How did I feel like she had sucked a piece of my very essence out of me with that first touch of her lips? How the hell was I supposed to know!

"I have no clue," I typed back. I cleared the call I was on and pulled out onto the road to drive around. I glanced up the road that led to her township as I drove by the intersection.

"Me neither," came to my screen a minute later. My fingers hovered over the keyboard, and I pulled into a dark parking lot.

"Do you regret it?" I typed. I almost backspaced to erase the message, but sent it before I chickened out. I pulled into a space near the back of the store lot, so I was facing the roadway, pretending to watch traffic.

The response that came down made my stomach flip anxiously, *"No, you?"*

I smiled, *"No, no regrets."* I released a breath I didn't know I had been holding.

We moved away from the topic then. In between calls, we chatted about different things for the rest of the night. As always, we kept the conversation of my marriage out of our chats.

Even with all that had happened between Beth and me the last year, I never really thought about the fact that our marriage could be over. Was it now?

I never believed in cheating on my spouse, I took my marriage vows seriously, and even when things weren't great between us, I had never stepped over the line. Hell, I barely even flirted with anyone in the eight years Beth and I had been together.

Now, all I could think about was Corey, the feel of her skin under my hand, the elegant color of her eyes, and the softness of her lips. I was in so much trouble.

I leaned my head back against the headrest. What was I doing? Guilt tried to coil around my insides, but I pushed it away. I should not feel guilty, not after what Beth had done to me.

Was I justifying my feelings for Corey because of the wrongs that Beth had done against me? Feelings? Did I really have feelings for Corey?

Yes—undeniably so.

I craved her in a way I had never wanted another person, not just physically, but mentally. I wanted to see her, watch her face, hear her laughter, and talk to her for hours. Hell, we never had to have sex! I just wanted to be with her. Okay, so sex would be good, too, but I could live without it—maybe.

My fingers wiggled over the keyboard as I tried to get the courage up to ask her something. Three times I started typing and backspaced to erase the words I had written. Just as I was typing one more time, my computer beeped. I deleted the message I had typed and pulled up the one I received.

"I still owe you a ride in my Camaro," Corey wrote. How did she know I was trying to suggest just that? Ironically, over the last few weeks, we did that quite often, typing the same words or feelings to each other at the same time. It was eerie how often we thought the same things.

"Name it," I typed back quickly.

"What are you doing Thursday morning?" the bright white letters appeared on my charcoal screen.

"I have court at 8:30, but after I'm free," I responded.

She sent me her cell phone number and told me to text her when I was done with court. The thought of being able to spend some time with her away from work excited me more than it should have.

With the dawn starting to crest the horizon, we said goodbye on the computer. All at once, I missed her. We had spoken for hours while we worked, and after tonight, I missed her more than I normally did when we said goodnight.

I picked up my cell phone and typed in the cell phone number she had given me. Saving it, I typed a quick text to her. *"Here's my number."*

I put the car in drive and moved back to my station. My shift was ending soon, too. As I climbed out of the patrol car, my phone vibrated in my hand.

"Got it! Thanks! Sleep well and I will see you on Thursday."

"Enjoy your day off. I'm gonna miss not chatting with you."

"You have my number. You can chat with me anytime you want."

"I don't want to bother you," I typed back.

"You are never a bother. I'm here anytime you need me." I could feel the smile in her words. I wanted to type back that I needed her now, but instead I just said goodnight and forced myself to delete the chat from my phone.

Thursday rolled around and my court case couldn't get done fast enough. I held off sending her any messages until I got to court. I was proud of myself for not sending the dozen messages the day before that I had started to type. We set up a place to meet, and I told her I'd let her know when I was clearing the courthouse.

An hour later, I drove my Harley into the parking lot near the mall. Her blacked out Camaro was backed into a spot just where she said she would be. I saw her sitting behind the wheel through the windshield as I pulled in.

My eyes swept over her as I climbed into the car. The turquoise tank top that she wore made her eye color appear lighter than normal and showed off her tanned skin. How would she react if I leaned over and kissed her right this second?

The Cheshire smile that crawled over her lips had me wondering if we were once again sharing the same thought. She looked out the front window and seemed to shake her head a bit.

"You have to promise me something," she said as she put the car in drive.

"Sure, anything," and I would promise her anything.

"Promise me that someday you will take me for a ride on your motor-cycle," she grinned as she pulled away.

"You like riding?" the thought of her arms encircling me from behind was a heady feeling, and one I had better put to rest before I got uncom-fortable in the seat.

"Don't know. I have never been on one."

"What? You've never been on a motorcycle before?" Disbelief

resounded in my voice. I was amazed; I had been riding motorcycles for so many years, I sort of figured everyone had been on one.

She laughed, "I have never trusted anyone enough to allow them to drive me around."

"So you trust me, huh?"

Her face took on a serious tone for a moment. "Yeah, I guess I do." She glanced at me before directing her attention back to the traffic in front of her.

I would do everything I could to protect her. That is what police officers do, they protect, although my need to protect her seemed to be for a totally different reason than as described in our profession. I had feelings for her that grew deeper with each moment we spent together.

"I'd keep you safe," I winked at her when she glanced my way again.

"Okay, deal, next time you do the driving."

We settled into some small talk as she drove about an hour north of where we both lived. We were far enough away that the chances of running into anyone we knew were slimmer. While we had never discussed it, I was sure that was why she had picked this location.

We climbed out of her car in a dirt parking lot and made our way towards a path that ran beside a large rushing creek. The sounds of the water relaxed us even further as we walked in silence for a few minutes.

She stopped to point out a large bluebird. "He is almost the same color as the center of your eyes," she whispered.

I tucked her hand into mine, the texture of her skin soft as I ran my thumb over it. We continued until we came to a large rock near a small waterfall.

She led me to the rock, and we sat down with our legs dangling over the edge. Peace filled me as I sat by her side. We didn't need to talk, the small glances we gave each other said enough. Just being beside her was enough. Well not exactly, I wanted more, I wanted to pull her into my arms and kiss her.

She turned to me as if I had voiced those words aloud. I pulled her to me just seconds after the vision crossed my mind. I slid my hand to her neck and led her lips to mine.

The kiss blazed an electrical path through every nerve ending in my body, and I pulled her body as close to mine as I could, but even that wasn't enough. I needed more.

She seemed to agree because she shifted and broke the kiss apart to move back from the edge. She moved back into my arms immediately and we lay down on the hard stone side by side, my right arm under her head to support and protect it from the stone ground.

Her arm wrapped around my back, holding me close. Urgency was building within us, a need that was identical in both of us. She moaned into my mouth, and I swallowed it. I wanted to touch every inch of her body, feel every muscle move, and hear her cry out my name.

The kiss slowed, softened, and then she pulled back, her eyes glazed, her breathing fast.

"I don't understand how you can make me feel this way," the words slipped off her swollen lips.

"I know. I feel it, too." I ran my finger over her soft pink lips.

"This scares me, Mitchell," she whispered.

"What? What we are doing? We can stop. I don't want to scare you, Corey." I moved up on my elbow, giving her some space.

She shook her head, "No, not this. The feelings I have for you." The touch of her hand caressing my cheek was like a slice of heaven.

"They scare me, too." How could they not?

"Mitchell," she hesitated before touching my lips with her fingertips, "I'm in love with you, and I can't seem to stop falling more each moment I see you."

My heart swelled. "Corey, I love you, too." There was no hesitation, no conflict in these words; they were the truth straight from my soul.

I didn't know when I had fallen, maybe the first moment we saw each other, or maybe the first time we had coffee. It didn't matter. All I knew was that I loved this woman more than I had ever loved another woman, including Beth.

That thought sobered me slightly. Beth, my wife, the one to whom I had made a vow. I looked away. I had no right to tell Corey I loved her, not when I wasn't free to do anything more about it. Guilt crashed over me like an angry wave.

"It's alright, Mitch, I know." Her soft voice reached me, and I embraced her tightly. When she pulled away, I let her go, but it felt like she took another piece of my humanity when she did.

She sat up and we took a few minutes to dwell on our own thoughts.

"I'm so sorry I have put you in this position. I had no right," she whispered, her arms resting on her bent knees.

I reached over and pushed a soft lock of her hair away from her face, desperate to see her features.

"Don't be sorry, Corey. Who would have ever thought that we could have this kind of connection, and so quickly? I know I never saw it coming."

The sound of her laugh warmed my heart. "I know." She shook her head, "It blindsided us, didn't it?"

"Yeah, it did." A few minutes later we got up and started heading back to the car. Our walk was peaceful but tense as we were both lost in our minds.

Before she unlocked the door to her car, she stopped next to me. Her flushed face revealed unbridled passion that ignited heat inside my body.

She stepped into my arms, and I pushed her back against the car, our bodies lining up so perfectly together. She pulled away from the kiss, lifting our entwined hands to study them.

"We fit so perfect together. Even our hands fit like puzzle pieces meant to be interlocking."

I couldn't argue with her words, so I did the only thing I could, I leaned in and kissed her one last time.

The ride was quiet on the way back to where I had parked, the music playing around us on the Bose stereo inside the cabin of her car.

Was it ironic that the song that played was one that talked about needing someone so badly, but not being able to have them?

CHAPTER 7 ~ COREY

*T*he kiss sent shivers down my spine and brought tingles to parts of my body I never would have thought could tingle. Emotions roared through me that I could not control.

How was it possible to feel so much for a person so quickly? How was it possible to feel like our spirits were twisted together as if we were one being?

I wanted Mitch so much that I was tempted to offer myself to him right there on the rock with the stream rushing past us like the blood in our veins. There was no thought to anything, except for the single word that rotated through my confused mind: Beth.

Like dashing cold water on a roaring flame, it dampened the heat without taking the fire away. I pulled away from Mitch's hold only to be overtaken with emotions again by the heated expression in his summer-sky eyes—not just passion, but a yearning I had never seen before.

I wanted him to love me. I wanted him to know that those words flowed within my heart even though I fought against them. Had I fought hard enough? Of course not! If I had, I would not have been wrapped in his arms, lying on the rocks under a sunbeam sent straight from heaven.

I knew he felt the same. I sensed it just like I sensed the same need in him to kiss me and hold me.

The kiss we had while standing next to my car was almost like a goodbye—bittersweet.

As I drove back to his motorcycle, reality broke in, and the depths of my feelings and the passionate words that we spoke rushed back over me. Guilt accompanied them.

God, forgive me! I was as bad as my ex-husband! I had always sworn I would never prey upon a man who was married. I knew what it felt like to be cheated on, and here I was doing it to another woman. Anger and guilt were new feelings for me. Dear God, how do I deal with this?

Let go.

I know. I needed to let him go. I needed to send him home, let him lead the life he was supposed to live, not one of lies and deceit. What must he really think of me? What would he think of me someday in the future if our relationship did grow into something more? Would he always wonder if I would stray?

No. For his own good, and for my sanity, I needed to let him go. I glanced at the passenger seat. His head was turned towards the window, but the dark tint offered me a brief reflection of the soft frown on his face.

Just as I knew he wanted me, I knew he felt the same distress at our situation.

I parked my car beside his Harley, the dark paint and shiny chrome were almost ominous in the fading daylight. We sat quietly for a moment, both trying to come up with the words we knew we must say.

I shuttered myself, willing the strength to come to my mouth.

"Mitch," I picked at a tread on my steering wheel, afraid to voice my thoughts.

"Corey, don't say it. Look at me, please." He spoke quietly and I responded to his plea. "Don't say it. I know, I know." His left hand cradled my cheek. I leaned into it, willing back the tears that threatened.

"I'm so sorry," I whispered as the first tear rolled down my cheek.

"Corey, please...please don't cry. Oh God, Corey, you are tearing me apart." He wrapped his fingers behind my neck and pulled me close. Our lips met in an emotional kiss that did not last long enough. A lifetime would not have been long enough.

With our foreheads together, we touched each other's faces, memorizing the planes one last time.

"Go, Mitch." I swallowed, "Please, go before I won't let you leave." My voice begged for two different things, for the right thing and the wrong one.

He was stronger than I. He pulled away and opened the door. He hesitated in the open doorway, and mentally I begged him to turn back to me.

He did turn back, but only to lean in to speak. "Be careful, Corey."

"Always, Mitch." I smiled as another tear slid down my cheek.

He closed his eyes and stood up, stepping back to close the door. I didn't wait for him to climb upon his bike, and I didn't trust myself enough to even peek in the rearview mirror as I drove away.

I held myself together until I walked into my house. The lights in the kitchen ceiling were so bright against the stainless steel and granite that I turned them off. Leaning back against the metal fridge, I allowed my body to slide down to the floor as the tears took over.

How I could cry for a relationship that had never existed did not make sense. I didn't understand it. I only knew that my hope of true love, of being with the man who was the yin to my yang was over. No matter what, I could not come between a husband and wife. It did not matter what kind of a relationship they had, I would not do that.

My head knew the right thing, but my heart broke in ways I didn't think possible. Had I cried this hard when I knew my marriage was over with Matt? No. I had gotten angry, shrugged, and walked away, wishing him the best.

I would not force someone to be with me if he didn't want to—so maybe that was why this hurt so much. I knew Mitch wanted to be with me.

He wanted me, yet I could not have him, and I knew that. The tears slowed, and I wiped at my face with the backs of my hands. A peace stole over me as I sat there surveying my dark kitchen.

I had to let him go. No matter how much I cared about him, or how right I thought we were together, I could not keep him. He was not mine.

I finally stood and walked to my room. I pulled a nightgown from my dresser and entered the bathroom to shower. As the water ran, I stood outside the shower letting the memories wash over me.

I turned off the faucet and stepped away. I wasn't ready to wash the last remains of him from me yet. I took off my shorts, undid my bra and slipped my arms out of it without taking my tank top off.

Climbing under the sheets, I stared at the ceiling, wondering how long it would take for my heart to mend. Within minutes, I felt my body relaxing and slipping off to sleep.

I woke early to get ready for day shift. Filled with mixed emotions, I got up and went to get my coffee. As I walked by my desk, I noticed my phone blinking. I picked it up to find a text message from Mitch that had come after I had gone to bed.

"I hope you are sleeping better than I am. I forgot to tell you I was off on Friday. Be safe at work. I will text you if I can."

I read over the message a few times before deleting it. So he wouldn't be at work today, at least I would not have to worry about running into him on a call.

I got ready with a heavy heart. I knew that although the temptation would be lessened, a part of me had hoped to at least see him at a distance.

My shift moved quickly, with one call after another. Even if he had been at work, our time to chat on the computer would have been hampered from endless ambulance, animal, and domestic calls from my dispatcher. At least something was keeping me busy and my mind occupied.

At the very end of my shift, as I was heading back to my station, a vehicle caught my attention. I recognized the blue Ford truck that was pulled into the ice cream parlor by the emblem on the rear license plate. That particular emblem could only be used by sworn police officers.

As I was stopped at the intersection, the door to the store opened and a woman walked out holding the hand of a small child. Behind them was a man licking an ice cream cone. Our gazes met over his partially-eaten treat, and he stopped walking.

Both of us directed our attention to the child in front of him as the boy reached up to open the door handle of the truck.

He had a son.

The light changed color, and I turned to head towards my station without looking back. I needed to see that. I needed to know. He had never told me. Why?

I pulled into the station and parked my car. Slamming my hand against the steering wheel, I wanted to scream. Does it even matter why? Dammit!

I picked up my phone and scrolled through my contacts. Finding Mitch's name, I deleted it from my phone.

Fool! I was such a damn fool! I knew there was a wife. How did I not know he had a child? Of course, I never asked. Wait, he should have told me. He should have said something.

The anger I felt for myself switched directions. I got out of my car, slamming the door as I walked towards the station.

When I got home, I changed clothes and walked down to my basement. Forty-five minutes of kicking and punching on the weight bag didn't lessen the anger. It wasn't until I was well into the next forty-five minutes of Tae Kwon Do forms that I felt my body start to relax and focus on my slow, smooth movements.

The next day, I spent time at the station catching up on paperwork. Saturday mornings were relatively quiet and a good time to sort through things that needed attention.

My phone jingled a tone that told me I had a text message. I picked it up without thinking and glanced at the glass screen. My fingers began to tremble when I saw the phone number and the message, *"Can you talk?"*

I was tempted to ignore it or type back, I don't talk to liars, but I wasn't that kind of person. *"Sorry, not right now, working on something."*

"Okay, when you have time, let me know."

I set the phone down next to me and tried to focus on the report I was working on. Yeah, right.

Pushing away from the desk, I stared out the front window of our station. The road was quiet this early in the morning. Okay, dispatch, you can send me a call. Anything would be better than being stuck with my thoughts.

The microphone at my chest beeped with three tones and called the city officers for a robbery in progress. Okay, so I wasn't dispatched, but I would head that direction to see if I could help. They only had a few guys on this time of day, and I knew they always welcomed the help.

As I walked to my car, I told myself I was going to search for the criminals, not try to get a glimpse of Mitch. I snorted to myself because even I knew that was a lie.

I listened to the description of the suspects while I drove down to the city streets at a good clip. One of the officers got on the radio and gave out a general direction of travel, and I set off that way, advising my dispatcher when I was in the area.

I saw two cops jump out of their vehicles and take off into an alley on foot. Where did that alley come out? I accelerated and drove around the corner, barely checking to see that the road was clear as I turned. I made another turn and stopped quickly at the end of the alley exit just as the subject ran out and slammed into the side of my patrol car.

It gave the pursuing cops a chance to catch up and put him face first onto the hood of my car.

"Corey, go back into the alley, about halfway through, he tossed a gun. Can you go find it?" Joe called out to me as he cuffed the guy up.

"Sure, Joe." I took off jogging into the alley, the heavy weight of my belt bouncing on my hips. About a quarter of the way down, I slowed and started searching. It didn't take long.

Beside a large brown trash receptacle lay a black Smith & Wesson semi-automatic pistol. I turned to call down the alley and found myself staring at an approaching Mitchell. Damn.

His light blue uniform shirt fit tightly over his protective vest. The equipment spread out evenly over his duty belt around his thick waist. A waist I had wrapped my arms around. I blinked to clear the memory.

"I got it." I examined the gun, half expecting it to get up and walk away. I felt more comfortable observing the weapon, deadly or not, than trying to face him.

I heard Mitch get on the private side channel of his radio and call Joe to tell him the gun was located. He stepped up beside me. The heat from his body spread over me even with the seven inches between our arms.

I shifted to move away from him. "You got this?" I glanced his way, but did not make eye contact.

The feel of his hand on my arm made my knees weak. I locked them to stop the quivering.

"Corey, we need to talk." I lifted my vision from the dirty pavement in front of me to his worried expression.

One second was all it took for my resolve to start to shatter. The stress outlined on his face and the pleading in his eyes made me step closer to him without thought.

The fingers of his hand slid down my arm to my hand. All thoughts of the instrument of crime on the ground were forgotten as the urge to kiss him roared through my body.

So focused were we on each other that neither of us heard Joe walk up and clear his throat.

I pulled my hand back and spun around, flushing as I met raised eyebrows.

"Okay, you guys have this, right?" the fact that we had been caught in an inappropriate position made my words come out in a nervous rush.

"Yeah, we got it." I watched him stare down Mitch for a moment before he turned to me, "Thanks, Corey."

"Yep, you got it." I walked away as quickly as I could without appearing like I was running, even though in my mind, I was.

One look! One simple touch and I was putty in his hands! Dear God, please give me strength! The blue sky above me, normally so serene, only reminded me of how much I loved to peer into his face. I shook my head and climbed back in my car.

CHAPTER 8 ~ BROCK

There were many things to do in the Realm, and time moved differently here. It could be a minute or several days. Like a finger on the fast forward, we could control the speed. The only thing we could not do was reverse.

If we could have gone back in time to change things, I might have gone back to the night of the foot pursuit and changed the outcome of their meeting. So many lives were going to be affected soon.

We were not supposed to control free will, but there were times when we used it to change a destiny slightly, to protect someone from an outcome that would cause so much pain. I should have used persuasion to change the events of their first meeting.

I stood back against a tree, watching them kiss on the hard rock near the running water. I considered the area and had to admit the setting was the perfect backdrop to a seduction, but I wasn't going to let that happen.

I invaded her thoughts with one simple word, but a word strong enough to cause her to pull back. She was not the only one feeling guilty about her actions, but I reminded myself that she had a different destiny and I was only trying to protect her for that.

I didn't have to hear their thoughts to feel the pain in the car ride back. I could have eased it, but I knew the timing was not right. Another simple thought, so easily put into her mind, changed her direction. I knew she would need to get used to the idea of letting him go before she actually did it, if she was even able to before her time was up.

While she sat on the kitchen floor, I finally allowed my presence to be felt and helped to ease her pain. I allowed peace to flow over her before I left her to rest for the night.

She had appeared so heavenly lying on the pillow, her hand snuggled up under her cheek as her breathing slowed. I allowed my body to come through, and I ached to brush a piece of hair off her cheek. Only fear of an unknown connection kept me from doing so.

I had stood watching her as she did roundhouse kick after roundhouse kick on the blue and white weight bag. I hadn't been present when her anger took hold, but as I viewed her brutal workout, I realized she had held the anger long enough and I could have helped her to calm down, but she managed to do it quite well on her own as she moved slowly and fluidly from one stance to another in her martial arts form.

Her shoulders squared, her back straight, she focused with an almost deadly stare as she moved from a back stance to a double knife hand block, turning to do a quick spinning roundhouse kick and then a reverse punch.

The left side of my mouth lifted. She was a warrior. The Maker had chosen her well.

Now standing at the mouth of the alleyway, watching them with just their hands touching, I could feel the connection between them.

When the other cop walked up, I flashed over to the other side of them and watched him approach. He was eyeballing the two of them and his line of sight kept going down to their fingers gently touching. A slight grin touched one side of his lips before he stopped it. I kept my presence from the other officer; we would meet again, soon.

CHAPTER 9 ~ MITCHELL

Since the moment I stepped out of her car, I had thought of nothing but her. Neither of us needed to say the words of what was right. We both knew that this relationship could go no further—not until I made a decision.

Could I continue on in a relationship that felt more like the proverbial ball and chain example of marriage, or could I step away and be with the woman who occupied every thought and breath of my life?

I knew what I wanted.

I wanted Corey.

I wanted to feel the serenity that surrounded us when we were together. I wanted to embrace the laughs and smiles that we shared, and I wanted to partake in the touches and kisses that set my internal passion on fire—but could I destroy my family?

I paid for the ice cream that Chase had begged me for and we turned to go back to the car. It had been an impulse stop to reward Chase for his great playing on the baseball field today.

I'd had mixed emotions about stopping at this particular ice cream parlor, but Chase had begged for the blue cotton candy ice cream that they made right here. How could I say no?

With Beth and Chase in front of me, we walked out the door. I never expected to see Corey sitting at the traffic light. The moment I saw her behind the wheel of the white and blue patrol car, my head turned to Chase. I had never spoken of him. I had always meant to, but we tried to stay away from my married life, and somehow it had never come up.

When I turned back to her, she was passing directly by, staring straight ahead. I groaned inwardly at my stupidity.

"Let's go, Dad!" Chase broke me out of my stupor, and I pushed the key fob in my hand to unlock the truck door. I was going to have to speak to her as soon as I could and try to explain. How was I going to explain that I had a son and just forgot to mention it?

I wanted to toss the mint chocolate chip ice cream that was slowly dripping down my cone out the window. No longer did I want the creamy treat. I only wanted to figure out how to explain this to Corey.

The urge to slam my hand on the steering wheel was so great, but it would only bring unwanted questions from Beth who was already examining me out of the corner of her eye.

For over a year now, things had been so difficult for us. Ever since my brother had passed away seven years ago, my world had spun out of control. I glanced in the rearview mirror. The only reason I had stayed was because I loved that kid sitting in the back seat sucking on the top of his cotton candy treat.

If I loved him so much, why hadn't I told Corey about him?

I ground my teeth and forced myself to finish my ice cream, my inner thoughts in a swirling turmoil as to what I could say and how she would react to my words.

Would I lose her?

The thought brought out a gasp and earned me a quick glance from Beth.

"You alright? You sound like you're in pain."

"I'm fine. I just remembered something I was supposed to do at work," I mumbled.

Her sigh could have been heard in the car behind me, even if they had their window closed. I fought the urge to roll my eyes.

The next morning, I couldn't get out of the house fast enough. All I could think about all night was trying to find a way to explain to her why

I hadn't told her. The worst part was that I hadn't come up with a good explanation.

Once I got to work, I sent her a message. While her reply had seemed cordial enough, I felt the soft rebuke of her anger in it. I would find a way to talk to her. I had to.

Another major incident brought her down to the city to assist, and Joe didn't have to tell me twice to go help her find the gun the suspect had thrown during the chase.

I could have easily tripped right over the firearm as I approached. My interest was only in her. When she turned, my knees threatened to collapse under me.

Her eyes opened wide and traveled down my body. Like the night we first kissed, my body gently shook at her nearness. She turned her attention to the ground where she had found the weapon.

She was about to turn and walk away when I reached for her. The little barbs of electrical impulses raced up my arm at the touch of her skin, and the look on her face made me realize what I stood to lose if she would not listen to me.

"Corey, we need to talk."

The expression on her face was a mixture of pain and sadness tinged with a tiny bit of desire that had her draw near me. I slid my hand down her arm to grasp her hand. I wanted to pull her close. The fact that we were in the middle of a crime scene was the furthest thing from my mind, until Joe approached us.

Corey took off at a pace that would have made me seem incredibly guilty if I had attempted to follow. I watched her leave and realized Joe was oberserving me intently.

"What the hell are you doing?" he threw at me when I finally faced his way.

I shrugged, not sure what to say.

"Mitch, what's up with you and Corey?"

I turned away from him to view the gun. "Nothing. Did you bring the camera and a box for this?" I bent down and inspected the weapon more closely, like I was trying to figure out the exact make and model.

"Dude, don't blow me off like that. We're friends. Is something going on with you two?"

The heavy stream of air that came out of my mouth hinted at my frustration level. I stood back up and pierced him with a glare. "I don't know, okay? I don't want to talk about it right now, alright?"

He watched me closely for a minute, realized I was close to losing my cool, and then grinned out of nowhere. "Okay, I'm here when you're ready to talk."

I ignored his comment and saw that his hands were empty. "I'll go get the camera and gun box." Without another word, I walked away.

When I got to my car, I popped the trunk and pulled out the things I needed. Setting them on the trunk lid, I pulled my phone out of my pocket and sent her a text.

"Can we please talk? I love you, Corey. Please let me explain."

She didn't reply until I was back at the scene and the gun was stored in the container.

Her single worded response of *"Later,"* was all I needed to calm the tension coursing through me: Later. At least her reply wasn't a no.

The Saturday day shift turned into a constant one-thing-after-another for me, and while I was busy, I noticed that Corey was getting dispatched to her own array of back-to-back calls.

As shift change got closer, I had not heard from her, so I took out my phone and sent her another message.

"Can we meet after work?"

I paced around the parking lot, waiting for her reply and finally got a *"Where?"* response.

"How about down at the creek, the entrance near the walking bridge?"
"Fine."

While her reply was short, I released a sigh of relief. At least she was going to give me a chance to explain.

I paced at the foot of the walking bridge, waiting for her car to pull into the parking lot. When I saw the black sports car pull in, my heart sped up to triple time. The dizzy sensation that passed through my body when it released the adrenaline made me shiver. She kept her focus off me as she approached. I took the advantage and allowed myself to suck in her image and savor it, just in case this all turned out bad and she never spoke to me again.

She finally met my gaze when she stopped three feet in front of me.

"Mitch," her voice cracked with emotion and I was thankful I was not the only one nervous.

"Thanks for meeting me, Corey. Do you want to sit down over on the bench or walk?"

She glanced over at the bench, then to the bridge behind me. "Why don't we just stand up at the top of the bridge?"

I nodded and followed her up the slight incline to the crest.

With both of us resting our elbows on the wooden railing, we stood in silence with only the sound of the water running softly under us.

"Why?" She spoke so quietly that if I had not been listening to her every breath, I might not have heard her.

"I've been thinking about almost nothing else since last night. I don't have an answer to that, Corey, and that's the God's honest truth. I don't know why I didn't say anything. All I can say is I'm sorry."

With my voice directed down towards the water, I watched her from the corner of my eye as she rested her forehead down on her now-folded arms.

"Not good enough, that's not good enough, Mitch." She pushed back from the railing and turned to walk away.

I grabbed her arm, "Corey, please, please just listen, please."

She focused on my hand wrapped around her arm, then met my pained expression. Her midnight blue irises were watery and she blinked back the wetness as we stood locked in place.

"Why should I listen? What difference does it make, Mitch? You're married, you have a son. I'm happy for you, and I'm sorry if things aren't great at home and you had to come find something else, but I can't be that person for you. I care too much about you to share you with others."

She lowered her head again, and I watched tears drip to the ground. The sadness she felt reached through the space between us and pulled me in. I wrapped my arms around her, pulling her as tight to my chest as I could. When her arms wrapped around my back and her body shook, I wanted to cry myself.

I was going to lose her completely if I didn't explain the rest of it, but I had never told anyone and I wasn't sure how to begin. I might still lose her after I explained, but as I stood there and thought of a life without her, I realized there was no way I could walk away from her.

Right here in her arms was where I wanted to be, now and forever.

I kissed the top of her head, the side of it, and then leaned in and placed my lips on the soft skin of her neck. I felt her body shiver at my touch, sending sparks through my nerve endings. I kissed the spot again, feeling her head fall further to the side to grant me access to the tender area.

"Corey, I love you." Taking her face in my hands, I kissed her lips. The salty tang of her tears touched my tongue, and our mouths meshed together. Her arms curled up and over my shoulders, holding me, while our kiss turned intensely passionate.

If kisses could be considered indecent exposure, we should have both been locked up right then and there.

When we pulled apart, we were panting and holding on to each other as if we were a drowning couple who knew that the only hope we had lay in each other. Maybe that was true in my case.

"Corey, I love you, more than anything. This is the first time in my life that I feel totally complete, and the thought of losing you is killing me. Please, just listen to me and hear what I have to say."

She leaned back and we stood almost eye to eye. "I love you too, Mitchell, and I can't imagine not having you in my life. It's like I'm not whole unless I'm beside you, and I barely know you. We barely know anything about each other, and there are so many obstacles in our way, especially on your side."

"Shh, Corey, we will figure it out together. I don't want to be without you. Promise me that we'll talk about this and figure it out together."

"I promise, but you can't keep secrets from me."

"I won't, I swear to God I won't." I hugged her tightly again. "Why don't we go sit down? This next part is kind of intense, and I think it would go over better if we are sitting."

The quizzical regard that she gave me said she was interested in what I was going to say even if it scared her. I took her hand and led her to a wooden bench on the other side of the creek.

When we sat down, I pulled my hand away, needing to distance myself from her slightly before I spoke. She sat back with the patience of an angel. I smiled when I thought about that. She was an angel, she was my angel.

With my eyes closed, I tried to figure out the best way to say it and soon discovered it would just be better to blurt it out.

"Chase isn't my son."

"What?" She leaned forward.

"No one knows this, but Chase is actually my nephew."

CHAPTER 10 ~ COREY

*H*is nephew?

"Did you adopt him?" If he had adopted him, that wouldn't be a bad thing, would it? It would just show how wonderful and caring of a man he was.

"No. Up until last year, I thought he was my son." He turned to me, stark pain on his face. "Beth and I have been together for nine years. Right before we got married, Beth had an affair with my brother. The last time they slept together was the week before we were married."

"Oh, my God. Oh, Mitch, I'm so sorry—and you just found out last year?" My hand went to rest on the tight muscles bunched on his back. There was no way I could avoid reaching out to him. The pain was so evident on his face.

"Yeah." He leaned back on the bench and put his hand on my knee. I squeezed it tight.

"How did you find out? Did she tell you? Does your brother know?"

"No, she didn't tell me. I found out myself. He was killed in a car accident about seven years ago." My right hand flew to my mouth, but he continued before I could speak. "I went down to his place in South Carolina to clean out his house. There was a box of mementos and letters that I found, but at the time, I couldn't bring myself to read them." I watched as he shuttered his emotions, reliving some pain that was deep inside.

"About a year ago, I decided to clean out my attic, the box was up there, and I sat down and started going through it. Inside were two letters to him from Beth."

"So he knew?" I turned on the bench so I could put my arm around his back and hold his right hand with mine.

"Yeah, he knew."

I didn't know what to say. There were no words.

"When I found out, a lot of things started to make sense. Before we got married, he hung out with us all the time, then shortly after Chase was born, he moved away and rarely came back. When he did, Beth was always tense, and the relationship that I had had with him while we were growing up was strained. I didn't understand it until I found the letters."

"Do you think he loved her?" My hand was rubbing the back of his neck, trying to ease the tension there.

"From what I read, I think he might have." He shook his head to clear it.

"For the last year, I have been trying to figure out if there was some way to get past the lies that Beth told me. For over eight years, I thought that Chase was mine, then I find out he's not. That lie was hard to deal with. It's still hard to deal with."

"But you love him, right?" He had to love the child.

"Of course I love him." He shook his head. "He didn't have anything to do with this, and he will never know that I'm not his father. It's Beth that I can't seem to forgive. The lie she had me believe all these years, it tore down any bit of trust I had for her."

We sat quietly for a little while. "For the last year, I have wanted to walk away, but I wasn't sure where I wanted to walk to."

He turned to me, a hopeful gleam in his eye.

"Is this what you want, Mitch? This? Us?" I whispered, praying he would say yes but scared that he would.

"Yes. I know now that this is what I want. You are what I want."

Mitch had kissed me slowly and then we watched the sunset. We walked to our cars shortly after darkness descended. No promises were made, no other words were spoken, but in our hearts, we both knew that what we had was something unique and special, and we both wanted it.

My sleep was peaceful that night. I had found what I had been searching for, the second half of me, the one who held my heart above all else and completed me totally. I had found my soul mate.

The sky reflected my mood as I drove into work the next day. The sunrise, brilliant in the bright blue sky, mirrored perfectly one of the things I loved most about him. I could not wait to hear his voice on the radio or to see him after work. Nothing could destroy the happiness I felt as I put on my gun belt and signed on to my computer.

Sunday mornings were generally very peaceful. I spent some time having coffee with a friend at a local coffee shop and then traveled through the neighborhoods, stopping to talk with residents and letting kids check out the inside of the patrol car.

Mitch and I had spoken a few times via computer, but the city appeared to be busier than usual this early in the day. Around lunchtime, I stopped off at my friend's café and grabbed a roast beef sandwich to eat on the outside porch.

As I was finishing up the last of my meal, I listened apprehensively to my radio. Mitch was being dispatched to an armed robbery, with the subjects fleeing. They had a full squad and some extra cars on the street today, so I knew I would not be needed right now.

I watched three kids cross the busy street and head into the café, the oldest about nine and the youngest about six. I rolled up my deli paper and squeezed it into a ball in my hands.

"Subjects just got into a black Nissan sedan. Heading east on the highway. I'm in pursuit." The muscles under my skin tensed at Mitch's words coming through my speaker.

Pursuits never ended well, so often one or more of the cars involved would crash into innocent people or other motorists. Most departments had a policy against traffic pursuits. Unless a violent felony had occurred, you did not engage in a pursuit. You obtained the most information you could about the vehicle and called it out for others to watch for. This one met the criteria where most departments would allow for it, as long as you made the pursuit as safe as possible.

"We're turning right on Main." His voice was tense, the sounds of the siren almost as loud as his voice. Other patrol cars were joining in on the chase now. I listened, the tension in my body growing by the moment. If the car made one more right onto First Avenue, they would be coming my way. I stood up and threw my trash away, intent on getting to my car and ready to jump into action if they came into my township.

Just as I was about to climb into my car, I heard a yell and a thump. I spun around to see that an elderly woman had fallen onto the ground and lay still.

I ran over to her and dropped to my knees just as Mitch called out on the radio, "Right on First Avenue."

Damn.

I bent down to the woman who was lying unconscious, a little pool of blood under her head. I spoke into her ear, trying to rouse her.

"Twenty-nine Paul Six," I called out over the radio, dreading that I was tying up airtime while the pursuit was going on.

"Twenty-nine Paul Six, priority only." Yeah, I know that!

"Paul Six, I need ambulance and medics to Carol's Café for an elderly woman who fell and is unconscious."

"Copy Twenty-nine Paul Six." As soon as he cleared the radio, Mitch's voice came back over.

"We are now south on Riversdale."

Crap! They were coming this way. I could hear the sirens in the distance and they were moving fast, multiple sirens, too many to count, some running in different pitches.

My hand gripped the wrist of the woman. Her pulse was strong and steady.

The door to the café opened and the three kids came out. The sirens grew closer.

The kids moved toward the road, one of them looking both ways. Finding it clear, he urged the other two on. The sirens continued to grow louder.

I released the woman's wrist, standing to watch the kids. I saw something drop from the youngest one's hand, but he didn't seem to notice. They all kept moving.

The sirens closed in, and I started towards the road.

"We are approaching Snyder Boulevard." Mitch's voice was hard, solid, steady.

The kids made it to the edge of the road and I released the air I was holding. All the kids stood on the side of the road waiting to see the action as it came speeding past.

I started to turn when the youngest glanced down at his hand and noticed he had dropped his piece of candy. He turned to the roadway. The green and pink wrapper lay in the middle of the street right beside the double yellow line. He stepped back into the road.

"No!" I yelled and started moving towards the road.

The older boy tried to reach out for the child, but the kid ran into the street. I ran towards him. The sirens almost on top of us, I entered the road and saw flashing lights coming my way from the corner of my eye.

The child bent to grab his candy and stood, turning to the side. There was no way he was going to make it. I heard brakes start to squeal, more than one pair. I was so close, I could save him.

I threw myself at him with outstretched arms, my palms out to push him with every ounce of force that I had in them. I felt him lift off his feet from my shove. My alarmed glance met the frightful one of the older boy in the second before the black Nissan slammed into me.

The impact of the car struck me in the ribs as I flew forward. I heard a snap, felt my body thrown into the air. Screams were coming from around me while sirens blared everywhere.

Pain radiated from every inch of my body as I rolled down the road, finally coming to a stop, but the pain did not.

The sirens and the screams continued around me for a moment, and I fought to open my eyes and stand, but I was numb. Someone screamed a word, but just as my mind started to process it, there was nothing but silence.

CHAPTER 11 ~ BROCK

I watched the scene in front of me. Corey was bent over the woman on the ground, assessing her injuries, but her head was not there. Her thoughts were anxious, and her adrenaline started to spike as the kids moved towards the road.

She stood and stepped away from the woman. I was powerless to stop her. This was meant to happen. I had a decision to make now, a decision that would affect many lives.

The child moved back into the road and Corey did as the Maker had said she would. She ran to the child, throwing herself at him. He almost made it out of the road before the car slammed into Corey. The bumper had come in contact with the child's leg; he would heal.

Corey went airborne and rolled over and over down the hot asphalt. I now had to make my decision. A man's voice broke into my thoughts when he screamed her name. I turned to see his pale face as he stood outside of his patrol car, his hand gripping the metal of the door, holding him upright as he realized who had been struck.

My decision made, I stared at her intently and brought her home.

"No, Brock! It's not time."

Montgomery put his hand on my shoulder, and I turned to glare at him.

"I made my decision, this is the right time."

Montgomery shook his head and dropped his hand.

I turned back to the scene. She stood with her back to me, silent, watching what was in front of her. Calm surrounded her like all that crossed over.

A glance past her found my stare locked with another. Tension ran like a lightning bolt between us, but I smiled a slow winning smile and turned my attention back to her.

"Welcome home, Coralenna," I called out softly. Her shoulders tensed slightly and she turned to face me.

CHAPTER 12 ~ MITCHELL

$\mathcal{M}$y mind felt refreshed when I woke up. The feeling that a weight had been lifted off my shoulders, a burden I had carried for so long alone, was a relief. Telling Corey about Chase and the lies that Beth had told me for years helped me deal with my anger.

Knowing that Corey and I would find a way to make this work, that I would have the woman I loved by my side, an incredible woman who cared about me and would not lie to me, filled my heart with hope. Would I finally have what I had always wanted?

With a spring in my step, I left for work and stopped on the way into the station to pick up the Sunday morning donuts. Yeah, everyone gave us cops a hard time about eating them, but nothing was better on a Sunday morning than a cup of coffee, a Boston crème donut, and banter with the guys—well, maybe one thing, but I could wait for that.

Something was in the air today. The calls were coming in faster than normal for a Sunday morning, and my time to chat with Corey was limited. That was alright, I knew that I would get to see her after work.

Just before I went on my meal break, I got dispatched to an armed robbery in progress with possible shots fired. The subjects were seen running from the scene and getting into a black sedan. I drove around the area, while Joe, who was closer to the business, stopped to get more information.

The sedan peeled out around a corner just as I rounded another one. I accelerated and took off, calling out our location. Game on!

The feel of the gas pedal under my foot engaging and the hard surface of the steering wheel kept me grounded. My right hand was on my microphone so I could call out our movements as needed. A quick glance in my rearview mirror showed more of my cars catching up, three right now.

We moved forward at speeds not safe for these city roads. The sedan wove in and out of traffic. I held my breath that it would not clip anyone. The thought of the amount of paperwork I was going to have to complete blinked through my mind for a split second.

When we made the turn onto First Avenue, I briefly thought about Corey. I knew that if we entered into her jurisdiction, she would jump into the fray. I didn't recall her being on any call before this, so, knowing her, she was already moving towards the action.

I was focused on the vehicle, praying that it would not strike any other vehicles. When we turned onto Riversdale, I knew we were totally out of the business district. As long as the cars stayed out of the way up near the café and store, then we would be out in straight county roads where it would be less likely the robbers would crash into someone else, more likely they would lose control on a turn and crash themselves.

A quick glance into my mirror showed at least five other cars behind me, some crossing the double yellow to get a view of what was ahead of us, our spacing safe for the speeds we were traveling. I glanced down at my speedometer: seventy-five, damn.

I glanced up as the brake lights on the car we were chasing lit up, its tires locked up, and the car started to fishtail. I slammed on my brakes as the cars behind me did the same. The sirens were competing with the sounds of the tires trying to find purchase on the road.

I watched in horror as I realized the sedan had struck someone. A person had flown in the air in front of the car. I could only see the legs. Dark navy pants and heavy tactical boots lay on the roadway, completely still. My heart, which had already been beating at an accelerated level, now surged forward into my throat.

I slammed the column shifter up into park and threw open the door. As my line of sight came around, I saw the white and blue patrol car in the parking lot. The realization of the victim's identity stabbed me in the chest like a knife.

My knees gave out and I grabbed the door to hold me up as I saw her lying on the ground, not moving.

I don't remember saying anything, but the scream that echoed through my mind must have come from my own mouth.

I heard feet pounding on the ground behind me. Sirens were being turned off, car doors were closing, more feet.

I watched Joe run past me. Two other people ran to the sedan and pulled the driver and passenger out of the car at gunpoint. I stood staring down the street.

Joe bent down beside the still figure. A few other people ran to her, civilians who were trying to help. I took a step forward, barely able to lift my foot, another. I had to get to her, had to see that the body was not hers.

It couldn't be her. Oh my God, please don't let it be her.

Joe spun in his crouch towards me, his face intense, his jaw locked. Our lines of vision met and then broke as he considered something behind me. No. No! I moved faster, and he stood up to come to me.

I was almost there when he threw himself up against me, holding me back.

"Mitch, she's gone."

I pushed at him, I needed to get to her. She was alright. She had to be alright! "No! Let me get to her, Joe!"

"Mitch!" He grabbed me by the shoulders, stopping me, and put his face into mine. "She's gone, man, she's gone." His voice softened as the words exited his mouth.

I shook my head, my knees threatening to give out under me. The sound of an ambulance siren reached my ears, and I turned to it.

"No! The ambulance is here! They can help her! Move, Joe, I need to get to her."

"Mitch! Her neck was broken, she's dead. She's dead man…she's dead."

The words did not reach me, but the appearance of pain and anger in his face did. No longer could my legs hold me up. I staggered, and Joe put his arm around me and pulled my arm around his shoulder.

He walked me back to my car. My lungs burned, and I couldn't breathe. I felt like my life had just been sucked out of me.

"I killed her. Oh my God, I killed her," I mumbled as Joe stood me next to the hood of my car.

"No, you didn't, Mitch, they did."

There was no voice of reason I would listen to. I knew in my heart that I had killed her. I buried the heels of my hands into my eye sockets and bent over. I choked on the spit in my mouth and started coughing. The coughing turned to a strangled yell, and I dropped to my knees. With my hands on the ground in front of me, I hung my head as the tears began to fall.

PART 3

Part 3 ~ The Realm

CHAPTER 13 ~ COREY

*L*ights flashed around me and people ran past. All of their faces displayed shock of one degree or another. A woman held her hand over her mouth while she tucked a child's face into her stomach. A man dressed in dark blue pants and a light blue shirt ran past to a body lying on the ground. The items wrapped around his waist made him wider than he was. He seemed familiar, but I couldn't recall his name.

My attention turned from the familiar man to the person lying on the asphalt. Who was lying there so still? There were too many people around, and I could not see the face. As I stood there, I felt like I should be doing something, yet I had no idea what.

I panned the area; cars with flashing lights were parked haphazardly on the roadway and shoulder. I realized then how quiet the area was. The people before me appeared to be talking or even yelling, yet no sound came to my ears. It was disconcerting to know that I should be able to hear something, and yet the only sound that came was a deep husky voice from behind me.

"Welcome home, Coralenna." The sound shocked me; I spun to face the voice.

Two men stood about twelve feet away. One of them was about fifty with gray hair and a friendly but concerned expression on his face. His shoulders were broad, and his body displayed a solid athletic build.

Intense light green eyes stared back at me from the other man who appeared to be in his thirties. I had the distinct feeling that I should know him, but again I could not place him. He was shorter than the other man, with wide shoulders and short, wavy light brown hair.

"Do I know you?"

"Not really." His deep voice was calming, although I felt tension coming from him even at the distance where we stood.

"Then how do you know me?"

"Because I have been watching you for years," his voice was smooth and very masculine.

"Stalking me?" I glanced to my side as someone ran past.

"Protecting you. My name is Brock, this is Montgomery." He motioned to the older man beside him. I glanced at his companion and nodded.

"Coralenna, come with us, and we will explain everything," the older man said.

"Why are you calling me that?" I cocked my head to the side as I spoke.

"It is your God-given name at birth. Come, we have much to teach you." His voice was soft and kind. He held his hand out to me, but I wasn't ready to go just yet.

I turned to study the scene behind me. "How come I can hear you, but I can't hear anything else?"

"You are on the other side now. You will learn to hear them again soon; it is one of many things we will teach you."

A tremor passed down my spine as I realized what he must mean, "I'm dead." I spun back to the younger man, his fierce sea foam gaze observing me closely.

"Yes, you are."

I swallowed and turned away. I watched a man fall to his knees, the pain on his face so evident that I wanted to comfort him. I felt like I had to help him, and I took a step forward.

Brock materialized in front of me, blocking my path. "Not now, Coralenna. We must go."

I jumped back into a fighting stance, my arms up, my hands lightly fisted. "How did you do that?"

A small chuckle came from behind me before Brock answered, "I just can, you will be able to soon, too. It is time to leave."

"Where are we going?"

"Home, Coralenna, we are taking you home."

Montgomery stepped up beside me and smiled pleasantly. Without thought, I returned his easy smile, feeling at peace until I glanced over the scene again.

"Did anyone else die?" I watched people running around. The man was now on his hands and knees, his head bowed as if he were crying. Was he crying for me? Why?

"No, you saved the child," Montgomery answered. He pointed to the side of the road where people sat around a young boy who was crying and holding his leg.

I nodded, "Okay."

Montgomery took my arm gently at the crook of my elbow and turned me. A feeling of happiness and contentment passed through me at his touch.

"We have been waiting for you for a while, young lady. You are going to love it here." He winked.

I glanced over my shoulder one last time. The man that had run past me earlier was now bent down next to the other man, his lips were moving and I thought he said, "No, you didn't Mitch, they did." His heated look rose to where we all stood.

Who was at fault for my death? Should I be angry for being dead? I felt only peace and some minor confusion. The man's glare met mine, and I wondered if he could see me. No one else seemed to be able to, but as our view seemed to lock together, his jaw tightened before he moved his attention to Brock. Brock stepped closer to my side, and the three of us turned and walked away.

Not four steps were taken when the scene disappeared, and I found myself in a room. It was neither hot nor cold, nor too bright or dark. The soft sky blue of the walls pulled at me and reminded me of something, yet I could not figure out what.

The room had floor-to-ceiling glass windows along one wall, beyond it a vast yard. Water could be seen way off in the distance. Was it a lake or an ocean?

Around the large room were small sitting areas. Plush couches and chairs in soft fabrics and muted colors filled each area, and the scent of flowers reached my senses, although I didn't see any in the room.

"Where are we?"

Montgomery sat down on the nearest couch. "You are home, my dear," he said with an easy smile. "Come sit, let us talk."

Part of me was hyper, and I didn't want to sit, but the place was so peaceful that maybe I would calm down if I did. I walked to the chair beside him, the cushion hugged my body as I leaned back, and I sighed at the comfort.

"They are nice, aren't they?" Montgomery chuckled.

I glanced around the huge room again. "This can't just be my home. How many people live here?"

"There are many. I believe each hall holds over two hundred. There are three hundred halls, although we are a bit low in numbers these days. The temptations of life have driven our numbers down."

"Numbers for what?"

"Gardaí," the voice of Brock came from behind me. I had forgotten he was with us. He stepped around the chair and sat on the couch opposite Montgomery.

His glower kept hold of mine as he moved. He reminded me of a tiger stalking its prey with his smooth lithe movements.

"Gardaí?" I looked away from Brock, he won the staring contest.

"We are called Garda Síochána, or Guard of the Peace translated into English. You will be trained to be a Garda, or a guard as you might think of it."

While Brock continued to be a man of few words, Montgomery seemed more than willing to answer my questions. I directed the next one to him.

"What language is that?"

"It is Irish, have you ever heard of the Irish Police?"

"Yes. We're like police?" I asked hesitantly.

Both of them chuckled, and I glanced at Brock, the small grin on his face and the way the skin crinkled around his eyes were familiar and way too attractive. I frowned at the thought.

"No, we are not police, although it is our job to protect the living." Montgomery crossed his left leg over his right and waited for my attention to come back to him. Brock's smile had disappeared, and he had resumed the stare down.

"Were one of you my Garda?" My question encompassed them both with a glance.

Montgomery turned his head slowly towards Brock. I noticed Brock tense.

"You are my charge." The husky tone of Brock's voice implied more than that.

"Well, if I'm dead, you must not have done a good job." I'm not sure why I wanted to piss him off, but the fact that he hadn't taken his glare off me the whole time irritated me, attractive or not.

His eyelids lowered just the tiniest amount, but I saw them. Montgomery threw his head back and laughed.

"This was your time," Brock said, sounding angry, and Montgomery stopped laughing and considered him with a raised eyebrow.

"Yeah, we will have to discuss that later," Montgomery replied.

As interesting as that sounded, I needed to figure a few things out before I started digging around. "So why me, how did I get picked to be one of these Garda people?"

"Because you're strong, you have the heart of an angel, and you are a fierce warrior fighting for what is right. You also believe."

"Believe? What, like in God?" I could see Brock staring at me from the corner of my eye, and I met his gaze head-on for a moment before Montgomery responded. I wanted to tell Brock to stop. He was making me nervous, even in the peaceful setting.

"Yes, you believe in God, heaven and hell, in the good and bad, and you lived most of your life that way."

"What do you mean most of my life? Did I do something wrong?" I watched the two men as they exchanged a glance.

"No," Brock's answer was short. He clenched his teeth tightly, and I saw a muscle tick in the side of his jaw.

"How come I can't remember my life?" I returned my attention to Montgomery.

"You don't remember anything?" He studied me while I thought about it. Other than the scene I stood in at my death, I didn't remember anything or anyone from my life. A chill passed over me as I thought about the man on his knees. Did I know him?

"No," I shook my head with my answer, "I don't." Should I be distressed that I could not remember my life? I wondered.

"You will, be patient. It can be very confusing for people when they pass over. Most go straight to what you would call the gates of heaven. You are in the in-between, so it is a bit different. It takes a little while for the memories of life to come back to us here."

"So I'm not really in heaven?" The thought that I had died and not gone to heaven bothered me, and I sat up straight in the chair.

"You're in heaven, don't worry, my dear. You are just in a place that we call the Realm. Those of us here can travel up to heaven or down to Earth." He sat up and put his elbows on his knees, watching me carefully.

"Only the strongest of people can be in the Realm. Only the strongest and most valuable souls can be a Garda," Brock's voice was soft as he spoke, and our gazes locked.

Once again, he stared me down, making me feel almost naked in front of him, like he was examining me, straight into my heart and being.

The sound of footsteps moving closer broke the connection, and I turned to the newcomer in the room.

"She's here already?" the tall blond man asked as he entered.

I saw Brock shake his head back and forth slightly, and Montgomery tried to stifle a laugh.

"Yes, she is." The tone of Brock's voice implied there would be no further discussion. "Coralenna, this is David. David will help you get acclimated to your surroundings here."

David glanced between Brock and Montgomery, his eyebrows rose at the tone of Brock's voice, before he turned his attention to me.

"Hello, sweet Coralenna. It is wonderful to have you here with us. We have been waiting some time, although I thought it might be a bit longer." He smiled at me as he spoke and turned to glance at Brock as he finished.

"A pleasure to meet you, David." I reached out my hand to shake his.

"No formalities here. Come on, let's get you away from these guys and get you settled in." He ignored the hand that I held out and waved me to follow him. I dropped my hand uncomfortably to my side.

"Don't worry, Coralenna, you'll be fine. Get settled and then we will talk again." Montgomery smiled and stood.

I nodded and let my view fall on Brock. The light shade of his eyes sucked me in for a moment, but I shook myself and walked away without saying a word.

David stood at the threshold to the room waiting for me to step up beside him. "Let's show you your quarters first, then I'll show you around the grounds."

David stood about a foot taller than I did; his shoulders were wide, but nowhere as wide as Brock's. His hazel irises sparkled with friendship.

"Sounds good," I replied as we turned together and moved down the long hallway. On the left were doors and archways to other rooms, and to the right, another wall of windows that overlooked a beautiful garden.

"Wow!" amazement glazed my exclamation as I took in the view of flowers and stone paths outside the glass.

"Beautiful, isn't it? You won't find anything here that isn't beautiful." The grin he gave me seemed to have another message in it, but I turned away from him and took in the gloss of the hardwood oak floors.

He pushed a button on the wall that revealed the entrance to a glass elevator. We stepped in, and I moved right to the glass, resting my hands on the gold-plated railing. The sight before me took my breath away.

As far as I could see, there was only raw beauty. Gardens full of bright flowers and a stream running through the center were off to my right. To my left, I could see the large body of water again. Sand along the shore sparkled white next to the glorious blue waves lapping gently.

"Wow," was all that came to my mind as I took in the sight before me.

"Told you," David laughed. The elevator rose, and I continued to stare. "You have one of the best rooms here. It's on the top floor, and your balcony wraps the building so you can see both sides."

I glanced up at him with a huge smile on my face. "How did I get so lucky?"

His face grew serious for a moment, then he replied, "Because you're special, Coralenna, very special."

I shook my head, "I'm not special." A nervous laugh escaped me.

"But you are. Trust me on that." He winked just as the door slid open behind me, and we both exited.

The hallway was just as luxurious as the one downstairs with polished oak floors and elegant side tables set along the length of it. The hallway went on for what seemed like forever.

"What floor are we on? I didn't even notice," I asked as we walked to the far end of the hallway past more doors than I could count. There were no numbers on any of them; the only difference was the knocker in the center of each. I saw a sailboat on one, a flower on another, and one had a lightning bolt. Quite a few had animals: dogs, cats, tigers, and even an elephant.

"We are on the fortieth floor. Your room is at the end."

"Why does everyone have a different knocker on their door?" I asked as we passed by a door with a brass eagle.

"The markers mean something to the people who live inside the rooms. The eagle we just passed, that was my room."

"You're up here, too? Does that mean you're special?"

He laughed, and I couldn't help but grin at the sound of it—so jovial and fun as it bounced off the walls.

"Yeah, I'm special." He stopped in front of a dark oak-stained door. The knocker on it was silver with a yin-yang symbol in the center.

"This is your room."

I stared at the symbol, drawn to it, but not sure why. "Should that have meaning to me?" I pointed at the knocker.

"Yes, and it will again very soon." He reached for the doorknob, and I realized there were no door locks on the doors.

"No locks?" I asked as he turned the knob.

"There are no thieves here in heaven, Coralenna. We have everything we could ever want, so no one takes from others." He pushed the door in, and we stepped through the threshold.

My breath got caught in my throat as I stared around the elegant room, not elegant in the formal sense, but elegant in the simplicity of it.

The living area was simple, with black and white furnishings, black leather couches and white throw pillows. Soft white carpet under my feet covered the entire room from the door to the glass wall of the balcony.

I walked straight to the balcony and opened the door. A soft breeze blew the scent of the flowers from below up to me. The sounds of the waves gently striking the shore rose to meet my ears. An eagle flew overhead, and my heart filled with happiness to see it all.

"This is absolutely amazing," I whispered from the railing.

"Yes, it is. You have the view of both, I only have the view of the gardens." David stood beside me and leaned down onto the railing with his elbows.

We were both quiet for a long time as we embraced the beauty in front of us. He spoke the words I was thinking.

"I could stand here forever and just behold the tranquility."

"I was just thinking the same thing, and yet I feel slightly agitated, like I should be doing something."

He turned to meet my dark blue gaze with his hazel ones, and I watched them sparkle brightly. "I know exactly what you need. Come on."

CHAPTER 14 ~ MITCHELL

"*M*itch, come on man. You gotta pull it together," Joe said quietly beside me. "Come on, let's get up."

I leaned back on the heels of my boots. With my body shaking heavily, I allowed Joe to help me to my feet. While I could feel my body quaking, I could not feel anything else.

Joe led me to a patrol car and opened the door, holding it open while I climbed inside. I fixed my sight on the windshield, yet I saw nothing other than a looped video showing the incident.

The rush of adrenaline during the chase, the bright red of the taillights in front of me, the sight of black boots flying through the air and rolling over the hard macadam—over and over again, the loop played.

Corey was dead. How the hell did this happen?

"I don't know, Mitch, just the wrong place at the wrong time, I guess. It's not your fault." My face snapped to the left, I didn't realize I had spoken out loud until Joe answered me.

"It is my fault! If I hadn't seen that car and chased it, she'd be alive!" I practically shouted at him as he drove away from the scene.

"Dude, you gotta get a grip on yourself! Man! I understand you're upset and you feel like this was your fault, but trust me, this was *not* your fault." I watched him shake his head with more anger in his voice than I expected.

"How can you say that? If I wasn't chasing that damn car, she wouldn't have gotten hit!" I slammed my hand down onto the dashboard.

"Mitch, look dude, there are higher powers at work than you know." He shook his head again.

"What, like God? What the hell kind of God would take a person like Corey away from her life! She was so good! She helped everyone, went above and beyond what she had to do. She was a walking angel, dammit! She shouldn't have died!"

I stopped my tirade when I realized that Joe had growled quietly. "Did you just growl?" I asked him.

His jaw ticked then locked down, and I watched him grind his teeth. He didn't answer me, and I let it go, too upset by what had happened and knowing that the world was no longer as wonderful as it had been when Corey had been in it. I turned to watch the landscape pass as we made our way back to the station, my gaze flicking over the buildings, cars, and people but not really seeing any of it.

At the station, I stepped out of the car and stared at the large brick building. People were coming and going, some smiling, some appearing stern. None of these people were affected by what I had just done. None of them cared.

I watched the ground as I moved to the station door. Joe stepped beside me as we walked and held the door open for me as we entered. I went straight to the locker room, ignoring the glances from the other officers in the station. I didn't want to see the accusation on their faces. Every one of them had liked Corey.

I sank down onto the wooden bench, listening to the soft whoosh of the hinged door closing to separate me from the squad room. I hung my head, now so heavy I could barely hold it up.

Tears prickled behind the lids as I thought about the first time I had seen her beautiful face. Flashes passed through my mind of our first kiss, the sight of her laughing with her head thrown back, her tough stance when she was dealing with a suspect. They moved quickly like a movie on fast forward, never stopping long enough for me to savor.

I heard the door open slowly and tried to sit up. I couldn't move. I was frozen in grief. Just yesterday I had realized that she was everything I wanted, everything I needed, and today I had lost her, forever.

"Hey, Mitch, you okay?" Joe shuffled over to me, taking a seat next to me on the bench.

I shook my head, clasping my fingers together in front of me, squeezing my hands tightly to hold myself together. My heart felt like it was about to rip apart.

"Hey, I know how it feels to lose someone you care about." His voice was soft next to me. "You'll get over it."

I turned to him. "Get over it? Jesus, Joe! She just died and you're telling me to get over it! Insensitive much?"

A smile crossed his lips quickly before his face changed to solemn again. "No, I'm just saying, I know it hurts now, but it will get better."

"I don't want it to get better. I deserve to feel like this," I muttered to the ground, noticing that my boots needed a cleaning. Strange thing to think about at this moment, but mundane thoughts helped stress. Muted words filtered to my ears. "What did you just say?" I turned to him.

He stood up, moving away, "Nothing. I didn't say anything."

Funny, I could have sworn he'd just said, "F-ing Brock." I let it go since I had no idea why he would say that name, and at that moment, I didn't really care.

"Look," he turned back to me at the door, "the chief wants to talk to you."

My shoulders slumped as I sighed deeply yet one more time. I knew I was going to get called into his office, but not quite so quickly.

"Did you love her?" Joe asked from beside the closed door.

I didn't want to answer him so I kept my head down.

"Did she love you?" I turned my head to him as he reached for the door handle. We stared at each other for a moment, and I knew the answer to that question showed on my face.

"Sorry, man, that sucks." His comment shocked me by the amount of insincerity it carried. I watched him shrug and walk out of the room. What the hell was his problem?

I examined my boots again and knew I was about to get plenty of time to clean them. I stood up and made my way to the chief's office.

When I entered his outer office, I could hear him talking on the phone. I stopped to give him time to finish his conversation.

"Yeah, I know. She was a good cop. We will make sure she gets the best funeral that's possible." He was quiet for a moment, listening to someone on the phone. "Yeah, I know, I'm waiting for him to come to my office now." Another pause and then he said a terse goodbye, and the sound of the plastic phone hitting the base reached my ears. I stepped up to the door.

"You wanted to see me, Chief Hensley." The older man sat at his desk, his hands resting over the rotund belly of his navy blue golf shirt. His gray hair parted over to the side, appearing windblown. Today was Sunday; he wasn't supposed to be working.

"Come in, Officer O'Reilly." He leaned back further into his chair briefly before leaning forward and putting his elbows on his paper-strewn desk. He nodded at the chair in front of his desk, and I took it.

"What happened?" His dark gray eyes dug deep into mine. His sixty-something face was intent on what I had to say, although not harshly.

I broke eye contact, trying to figure out where to even start, how to describe the horrible nightmare that I just wanted to fade away, but every moment was ingrained in my memory.

"Start with when you saw the car."

In as strong a voice as I could manage, I proceeded to explain how I had seen the car and then attempted to stop it. The vehicle had fled, I pursued. The first part was easy, but I started to hesitate when I got further into it.

"I know this is hard, Mitchell, everyone really liked Officer Hamilton, just tell me what happened." I tunneled my vision past him and out his window. A car drove by, a person walked the opposite way, life moved on.

I cleared my throat and continued to explain that the car was heading towards the café area and I saw children on the side of the road. I never saw her until it was just her feet flying through the air around the side of the sedan I had pursued.

The room was silent for a few moments; I stared at the pen holder on his desk, the one that sat beside his brass name plate.

"You were close to Officer Hamilton?"

I met his gaze. "Yes, we were friends," my voice was husky as I answered.

He nodded to me, "I'm sorry, Mitch. It is very hard to lose a brother or sister in blue, and to lose one you considered a friend is even harder." He paused for a moment. "My understanding is that she ran into the road to save a child. Is that correct?"

I shrugged, "Sorry, sir, I don't know." I hung my head, "I kind of lost it at the scene and have no clue what happened or even where the guys are that I was chasing."

"No worries about them, they're locked up and they will be charged with homicide by vehicle, I can guarantee you that."

Knowing that someone would be punished did not make me feel better. In my heart, I knew the crash was still my fault.

"It wasn't your fault, Mitch," the chief addressed my thoughts. "You were doing your job, she was doing hers. You both signed up to serve and protect, that is what you were both doing. It is a shame that it had to happen the way it did, but she will receive a hero's funeral for it."

My eyelids closed of their own accord. I couldn't bear to think about burying her. Oh, God! Hold it together, just a little while longer, Mitch. Do not break down in the chief's office.

"I think you need a few days to deal with this," the chief said in a soft voice.

I blinked back the wetness and nodded to him, "Thank you, sir." I moved to stand.

"Officer O'Reilly, we will need an official statement before you leave, and then you can go home to your family and take a few days to deal with this. It will get easier."

My family—the breath that left my chest was like someone slugged me in the gut. They were the last ones I wanted to see right now. "Yes, sir, thank you."

He stood up and moved around his desk. "Go see Sergeant Bryant. He will take your statement."

I nodded once and he stopped beside me, resting his hand on my shoulder. I bit back the tears that threatened to fill my vision again.

"It won't ever go away, what you saw, but eventually it will get better, son."

I gave a quick nod to him and turned, not trusting my voice. In the hallway, I stopped and regained my composure. I knew I had to give this statement and give it in detail. I swallowed hard and went in search of the sarge.

I put on my business face and locked down my emotions. The interview took over an hour, and when I was done, I walked to the locker room and changed into jeans and a T-shirt. Grabbing my keys, I made my way through the squad room. Once again, I ignored all the knowing glances from my fellow officers.

I climbed onto my motorcycle and cranked it over, revving it harder than necessary. I pulled out of the parking lot but didn't head towards home.

I found my way to the park we had been in the night before and sat on the bench for hours, remembering every second of the time I'd had with her.

The anguish of knowing I would never see her again made my heart want to implode. What was this world going to be like without Corey in it? I couldn't fathom not having her in my life.

How do you lose part of yourself and still go on? How do you survive when part of your soul is missing? How could I possibly go back to my home, my family, and pretend like I hadn't just lost the most important thing in my life?

CHAPTER 15 ~ BROCK

$\mathcal{I}$t didn't matter that I was staring at her as if I wanted to eat her alive. She was here and knowing that I could reach out and touch her, that I could see her true inner beauty radiating off of her like rays of sun, kept me in reverence of her being. She was more beautiful now than she had been in her living life.

I knew she had no memory of her time on Earth, but eventually it would come back. I would worry about that later.

I saw her take a step closer to him, and I knew I had to stop her. With no thought, I blocked her path and startled her.

As we walked away, she peered over her shoulder one last time. I glanced back and saw the heated look. I pierced him with one of my own and walked with Coralenna through the gate Montgomery opened.

To know that she was here, with us, caused emotions I had held hidden for so long start to surface. It had been quite a few years since I had stood among the living, and I had never missed the waves of raw feelings that could stop a man cold, the emotions that held Mitch in their grip.

I watched as she studied the room and helped Montgomery to explain what she now was. There would be many more talks, but she needed a chance to get settled first.

As if on cue, David had walked in. I knew I was going to take flak for her being here now. I expected it. I just didn't want that to happen in front of her so I would have to explain it, not yet.

When she left the room, Montgomery and I stared each other down. He raised his eyebrows, waiting for me to speak.

"What?" I sat up and rested my elbows on my knees, pensive.

"You know what." He shook his head at me. "Why on God's earth did you decide to take her now? You know as well as I do that this was only to be the beginning, not her final end."

I stood in a huff, walking away from him towards the windows. "Yes, and you know that what was planned for her was not fair. I decided to take her now so that everyone can move on with their lives."

I crossed my arms over my chest, unusually tense. Yes, I knew she should have stayed on Earth longer, but I could not handle waiting.

Laughter made me turn and glare.

"Don't tell me you are getting soft, Brock! You, the man who has held all his emotions in check since the moment he arrived; the one who never shares anything of himself. You forget, I know your story."

"I am not getting soft." I turned back to the glass and ignored the comment about my past. I was not proud of it and often wondered how I had gotten the privilege of coming to play on this team and not the southern one.

"It doesn't matter, she's here, and it's done."

I shrugged.

"I expect that you will be summoned soon."

I hung my head. Yeah, I knew I would be summoned to the Maker, although he already knew exactly what I had done and why I had done it my way. I would be reprimanded; my summons would be to explain my punishment for not following out his plan to the letter.

I just hoped that my punishment would not take me away from being Coralenna's Garda. Even though she was training to be one, I was always to be connected with her in a way no one else was, just like the connection I had with Montgomery. He could find me no matter where I was, and he was the one I went to for guidance, except with Coralenna.

From the moment she had become my charge, I had kept my thoughts silent from him. When I had learned of the paths her life would lead, it took everything I had to keep my thoughts and feelings to myself. I was frustrated and wanted to change where her life would take her, but I feared she would be pulled from my protection.

A warming of my essence called me to the Maker, and I took a deep calming breath before I turned to Montgomery, "Wish me luck."

"Luck is not what you need; I think you'd be better off going to pad your pants with tissue because you are going to get one swift kick in the rear."

We both chuckled, and I phased from the room to meet the Maker.

CHAPTER 16 ~ COREY

*D*avid pushed away from the balcony and led me back to the front door. I took a second to consider the room as we walked through. A chrome, black, and white kitchen stood off to the right. Anything and everything I could imagine appeared to be on the counters and behind the glass cabinet doors.

"We eat?" I asked as we reached the door.

"Sure, we eat! The best part about it is we can eat whatever we want now. If you had food allergies, you won't have them here. If you were ever worried about gaining weight, you don't have to now. You can enjoy whatever you heart desires." He winked at me, and I caught his innuendo and smiled.

We climbed back onto the elevator in silence, and again I stood exploring the beauty of the land.

When the door slid open behind me, I followed David down the hall, "This is one of the exercise floors. No matter what you like to do, we have it here. He pointed to a door that was open. Inside, hundreds of weights and machines filled the room. A handful of people were scattered around and a few glanced up and smiled as we passed by.

He kept walking, and I peeked in another door and saw a ballet studio complete with mirrors and a wooden barre around the entire room. Cool.

Near the middle of the hallway, he turned into a room that caused me to pause. The floor was covered in a large red mat; three of the walls were mirrored. Around the edges were targets and weight bags.

"This is the martial arts room." David turned to me.

"Are you going to teach me martial arts?" I stopped by the edge of the mats. Somewhere in me, I knew that I should not step onto them with shoes.

David's laughter filled the large room. "Teach you? No way! You could slaughter me in this room. Girl, you know how to do this."

"I do?" Confusion radiated through my voice and I scanned around the room. I did find comfort here, but did I really know how to do this?

"Yeah, Coralenna, you know how to do this, and to be perfectly honest, you are amazing at it. Come on, let's get you dressed, and you can practice."

I glanced around the room again—practice? I swallowed nervously but followed David along the edge of the mat to a locker room. He told me to go in and grab my uniform and belt out of my locker and get changed.

Inside the locker room, I found closets, each labeled with a name. I found mine about halfway down. Inside the closet were two white uniforms and a black belt. Black belt? Was I a black belt?

Reaching down to unbutton my pants, I suddenly realized that I had on dark navy pants and heavy work boots. A picture flashed of the man running past me earlier. He had been wearing similar pants and boots. Was I like him?

I pulled the boots off and slid the pants down my legs. The soft white cotton workout pants felt so natural. My tight fitting Under Armour T-shirt was quickly replaced with the soft flowing top. As I allowed my hands to slide down the front, the word dobok came to mind. Dobok... that's what this uniform is called.

I reached for the belt and lifted it carefully off the hook. A sense of excitement raced through my fingers, and I slipped them over the cloth. My name was embroidered into it. I touched each letter slowly. It felt familiar, but I still was unsure that I knew what I should do. I wrapped the belt around my waist and tied it without a second thought. When I considered my image in the mirror, a sense of completion surrounded me.

With my hair pulled back in a ponytail, I took one last look in the mirror and walked back to the door.

When I stepped out, I scanned the room, an uneasy feeling passed over me. I don't know how to do this!

"It's alright, Coralenna, you will remember it soon." I turned to see him standing in the corner, dressed in a dobok like me, a black belt wrapped around his waist tightly. He bowed to me and immediately I returned it.

I stepped onto the mat and approached him. "I'm not sure you are right. I don't think I know how to do this."

"Relax, Coralenna. Close your eyes and take a few deep breaths. Feel the room, listen with your heart; it will come back to you."

I did as he said, but I felt no different. I shook my head and just as I opened my eyes, I saw David skip forward and throw a roundhouse kick. I blocked it with a down block and jumped back, instinctively taking a fighting stance.

He spun around and came at me with a side kick. I blocked it and threw a roundhouse kick that struck him in the middle of his back. A pulse of energy traveled up my leg. He grinned.

The sparring continued until we were both dripping with sweat. The moves came to me without thought; they were second nature, like walking or breathing. Each time we made contact with each other, a pulse of energy would travel through the area where we connected.

I wasn't sure what that was all about, but the energy was positive and that felt good. It kept me focused and increased my adrenaline.

He was right. I did know how to do this and apparently so did he —very well.

After knocking him to the ground with a sweep of the legs, I fell next to him and rolled to my back, sucking in air.

When clapping came from the edge of the room, I sat up quickly. Our little sparring match had attracted quite a bit of attention. About fifteen people stood near the door and along the wall. I had been so intent on sparring with David, I had not even noticed. My face flushed from embarrassment.

My gaze roved over the group of men and a few women and stopped when they landed on Brock. My heart beat faster as our eyes met. The expression on his face startled me. "Feel better now?" David said as he stood up.

The group started moving towards the door slowly, all but Brock.

I brought my attention back to David. "I feel fantastic. I didn't realize I knew how to do all that. It just felt so natural." I stood up next to him.

"You know a lot more than that. I told you it would come back to you. Why don't you go back up to your room and relax a bit? Take a shower, get dressed, and then I will show you around the grounds."

"Sounds good." With one last glance over my shoulder, I saw that Brock was no longer there, and I made my way back to the locker room, stopping to bow off the mat before I stepped off. With my earlier clothes in hand, I left the exercise room and made my way to the elevator at the end of the hallway.

A few people smiled as I passed them and said, "Welcome." I didn't know what to say, so I simply smiled back.

Back on my floor, I entered my room again and examined it closely. Yeah, the black and white fit me perfectly, the yin and yang of life.

I walked down a hallway I had not noticed before and found myself in a large room. A huge bed dominated the center, draped with soft gauzy material. Unlike the living area, this room was done in pastel colors of the ocean. Soft blues, beiges with touches of pink and purple like the sunset, were scattered around the room.

I grinned as I took it all in and walked to a door that I assumed to be a closet, the inside of which was full of every possible type of outfit I could imagine.

Near the back were fancy dresses and blouses. I touched the soft silk of one of the blouses, it felt heavenly. I moved through the clothes, so many colors and textures, reaching out to finger some until I settled on a black T-shirt and a pair of jeans.

Another door on the opposite side of the room led to a bathroom. A shower big enough for eight people covered the far wall and a large soaking tub was situated beside the windows. I could sit in the tub and stare out at the beauty, awesome.

I opted for a quick shower and found that the six water jets worked wonders on my tired muscles. Bottles of my favorite soaps stood in a row on a shelf; I hummed a nameless tune while I lathered away.

After drying off with the softest lilac towel I had ever felt, I slipped on my clothes and brushed out my long hair. I found a hair dryer under the sink and started drying my long locks.

I only dried it about halfway, wanting the air to finish the job and give it some natural curl. No makeup was needed; I had never liked to wear it anyway. Satisfied with my appearance, I turned and walked back to my living area.

I stopped mid-stride when I entered. My senses picked up someone in the room. Through the glass, I saw Brock standing on the balcony. I frowned. People might not steal here, but what about privacy?

I walked to the sliding door, stopping at the edge with my hand on the frame. "What are you doing here?"

Brock must have been lost in thought because he spun quickly as if I had startled him. His eyes landed on mine and then flowed slowly down my body and back up. I suppressed a shiver at the hungry look in his face.

"Did you enjoy your workout?" he asked when he finally met my gaze again.

I stared him down this time, feeling stronger. "Yes, I did, thank you. Now tell me why you are in my room."

He broke the eye contact this time and turned towards the balcony, resting his hands lightly on the railing. "I'm just checking the view."

"What, you don't have a view in your room?" I stepped out of the door, drawn to the railing and the lush scenery beyond it.

"Everyone has a view, but some are just more beautiful than others." His voice was husky and soft as he turned to face me; a chill wanted to run down my neck, but I suppressed it.

"Why are you here, Brock?"

His lips twitched for a second, and I found I wanted to see them turn up into a smile, but they didn't. "I'm dead just like you, that's why I'm here."

Hearing that word, sadness crept into my mind, and I turned away from him. "That's not what I meant."

"Relax, Coralenna, I'm just checking to see if you need anything."

He turned sideways and rested his hip against the railing, crossing his arms over his chest. "Why did you think I was here?"

I shrugged and let my attention wander out to the water. A sailboat was barely visible on the horizon. I realized that I wanted to sail, let the wind blow in my hair, feel the sun on my face, draw in the scent of the salty ocean.

I saw Brock reach out as if to touch me, but he pulled his hand back before it got too far away from his tightly-coiled body.

"I guess I have everything that I need, thank you," I answered him quietly.

He stepped closer to me, his chest within inches of my back. I squeezed the railing with my hands, afraid they would shake if I did not.

"Not everything," he whispered near my ear, the soft caress of his breath sucked the air out of my lungs.

"Coralenna, you ready?"

I spun around to find David standing in the doorway, and Brock was gone.

"Doesn't anyone knock around here?" I blurted out, unbalanced from Brock's last words. Where did he go?

"You alright?" David asked as he stepped out on the balcony.

I took a deep breath to settle my heart and nodded. "Yeah, I'm fine. Let's go. Show me more of this beautiful place."

He stepped aside and let me pass back into the room.

As we rode down the elevator, I was still thinking about what Brock had whispered in my ear. "David, can I ask you something?"

"Sure, anything."

The elevator door slid open, and we walked out a door I had not seen before. A stone walkway led towards the water. I fell into step beside him, trying to figure out what I really wanted to ask. He was patient and waited for me to speak again.

"What's Brock's story?" I finally spit out as I scanned over the horizon. The sailboat appeared much further out from here than it had from my balcony.

"Okay, anything but that," he laughed and shook his head.

"What do you mean, 'Anything but that'?" I stopped and stared at his back as he continued to walk. When I didn't catch up right away, he stopped and turned.

He contemplated the ground as if debating what to say. "Coralenna, I can't tell you about your Garda. Only he can tell you about himself."

"Don't you know anything about him?"

"Sure, I know a lot about him, but I've been working with him for a long time. Unlike on Earth, we don't gossip about people here. If you want to know about someone, you have to ask him or her. Sure, we'll tell you some things. For example, see that guy over there?"

I turned and followed his line of sight. A shorter man with very dark olive skin stood by the ocean, his arms held wide and above his head.

"That guy is Tash. He helps to take pain away from people. Right now, he is helping one of his charges at a funeral. I know what Tash is able to do, but I don't know his story. He has never shared it with me. He might have shared it with others, or maybe he doesn't remember it, but he has never graced me with his story if he does know."

"Wait, back up. You guys don't ever talk about each other?"

"Nope."

"If you guys never talk about each other, then why did you all know about me?"

He burst out laughing and started walking again, waving his hand forward to encourage me to follow. I did.

"I told you before, you're special."

"Do you guys know my story?" I asked as I caught up to him.

"Some of us do. Only Brock knows your whole story. I know about your martial arts training, I've helped to guide you, encouraged you over the years, but I don't know much about your personal life or your life before you started studying Tae Kwon Do."

"Why is that?"

We reached the edge of the beach, and I kicked off the leather flip-flops I had slipped on. David kicked his off, too, leaving them next to the path, and we stepped out into the sand.

He shrugged, "That wasn't my purpose. My purpose was to make sure you were strong, that your mind and body were one—that you have the perfect yin and yang." He gave me a lopsided grin, "I must admit that I did a good job."

"You're not allowed to gossip here, but you're allowed to be vain?" I laughed.

"Not vain, just humoring you," he laughed along with me for a moment, and then we both quieted as we approached the edge of the water.

"Were there others that helped me?" I crossed my arms over my chest and stared out over the gentle waves.

"Sure. There have been a lot of Gardaí who have watched over you, although Brock has been with you for several years almost all the time."

I shivered to think about him watching me. That fierce gaze with which he pierced me made me uncomfortable.

"What's wrong, Coralenna?" David asked from beside me.

I hesitated to answer him, not sure I even knew what to say. I shook my head and turned to walk along the edge of the water.

"I don't know. Brock just puts me on edge. The way he stares at me, the way he moves and just shows up places, it gives me the creeps."

Almost instantly, David appeared in front of me.

I jumped back, "You can do it, too?"

He laughed so hard, he had to lean over and put his hands on his knees. I stepped around him and kept walking down the beach, not seeing the humor in it.

"Wait," he called out between laughs, "wait, Coralenna, I'm sorry, it was only a joke."

I didn't stop. He ran up to me and grabbed my arm to stop me. A sizzling burst of energy raced up my arm, and I jerked it out of his hand.

"What the hell was that?"

He smiled down at me. "That was not any part of hell. That is a piece of our heaven."

"I noticed that when we were sparring and we made contact, I felt the same energy then. Is it just because we, you and I, are touching or does that happen to everyone?"

"Different types of current will flow between different people. What did you feel when Montgomery touched you?"

I thought about it. While it seemed only a few hours ago, it felt like weeks had passed since he had taken my arm and led me from the accident scene.

"Compassion, strength, serenity—he made me feel calm."

"Not surprising, I feel the same thing from him. He helps people to calm themselves. What about when I touch you? Other than the energy shock, what does it remind you of?"

He reached out and gently touched my arm with his palm; soft energy flowed from his hand and straight to my heart, not in a tugging way, but in a soft caring way, like the way a friend would hug you when you were feeling down.

"I feel friendship," I smiled.

"Good. That's good! You and I are going to be great friends. Now what do you feel when Brock touches you?"

"I don't know." I shrugged and started walking along the sand again.

"What do you mean you don't know?" He caught up.

"I have no clue what I feel when he touches me. He's never done it." I peeked up at David and saw both of his eyebrows arch high over his lids.

"Wow, okay, so when he does, you let me know," he sounded like he actually giggled beside me, "because I think it might be like an explosion." He threw his arms up in the air as he made the sound of a bomb exploding. I shook my head at his antics. Was an explosion good or bad? I wondered. Either way, I was afraid to find out.

CHAPTER 17 ~ BROCK

$\mathcal{I}$t had not gone as bad as I had expected. He had understood my decision, although the Maker had stressed that his plans were for a reason. He decided that I would not be given any particular punishment at this time, but that I would have to deal with the change in the situation.

I had no idea what that meant, and he didn't feel the need to explain. His innuendo made me think that it had something to do with Coralenna and her past.

I phased back to the Realm and reached to feel where she was. David had her working out intensely, and I phased to the basement and the martial arts room.

Inside, thirteen people stood and watched the fierce sparring match. Coralenna and David held nothing back, and I could feel their energy trying to burst through the walls.

With one last sweep, she knocked him to his back and fell next to him. So intent was she on her partner that she never noticed anyone else. She would have to change that. She could never let down her guard.

I left her to take a walk by the water, dwelling on what the Maker had told me.

He stated that since I had taken Coralenna from the Earth early, she had unresolved business that needed to be dealt with. Before he could send her out on a true assignment, she would be given a chance to clear some things up and, depending on her choices, she would continue to train as a Garda or she would move out of the Realm and into heaven.

I had no idea what she would have to do; the Maker didn't feel it necessary to explain further. It would be told to her and if she wished to speak to me about it, she could. I could not imagine what business she had left unresolved unless it had something to do with Mitch.

I stopped and stared out over the water. Dammit! It had something to do with Mitch—it had to, but what?

With the memory of her in his arms, I phased up to her balcony, feeling the need to be close. I knew she was in the shower, so I stood at the railing, staring out over the land, lost in memories of her from the past several years. I was trying not to think about the intense longing that had grown inside of me as she had lived through that part of her life.

"What are you doing here?" her voice wasn't angry, but she wasn't happy with finding me here. I turned to find her inner beauty hugging her so brightly that it broke the seams of her clothes—oh man, how nicely it hugged her.

The urge to pull her close to me and touch those curves was powerful. I reined in the feeling. "Did you enjoy your workout?"

"Yes, I did, thank you. Now tell me why you are in my room." Her back was straight, and she faced me for the first time with the intense strength that I knew she had within her.

She unnerved me, and I turned from her. "I'm just checking the view."

"What, you don't have a view in your room?" She stepped up beside me.

I had no power over the husky tone in my voice when I spoke. "Everyone has a view, but some are just more beautiful than others."

"Why are you here, Brock?" The regard she gave me was intense.

"I'm dead just like you. That's why I'm here." I knew that was not what she wanted to hear, but how could I tell her that I couldn't stay away now that I could finally speak with her?

"That's not what I meant."

Was that pain in her voice? I didn't want her to feel pain. "Relax, Coralenna, I'm just checking to see if you need anything."

"Why did you think I was here?" I watched her as she faced the water, her inner beauty could outshine the sun. My fingers itched to touch her and moved on their own towards her, but fear of what would happen held me back. What if the connection wasn't what I had pictured it would be?

"I guess I have everything that I need, thank you." Her voice was soft and carried over the light breeze to me, pulling me towards her.

"Not everything," I whispered gently into her ear, so tempted to lean in and kiss her sweet lobe. I saw the shiver just as I felt David's presence and phased away.

Damn David and his timing! Back in my room, I dropped onto the couch, throwing one arm over my face, the other lying over my stomach. My body ached to touch her, to know if what I had dreamed of since first seeing her would be there.

Would that all-encompassing passion sweep through us? Would we be unable to deny the feelings that electrified us when we touched? I had seen it before: two Gardaí who could touch for the very first time and instantly be entwined in their destinies forever. They were rare, but they did happen. Would she be mine as I had dreamed?

CHAPTER 18 ~ MITCHELL

*T*he hour was late when I pulled my motorcycle into the driveway and turned off the engine. The effort it took to lift my left leg to climb off was almost painful.

All of the lights were off in the house except for one in the upstairs hallway. Enough light fell into the foyer down the stairs that I could walk into the living room and collapse into a chair without bumping anything.

I wanted to sleep, but fear of being dragged back to the scene in my dreams kept me wide awake. The creak of the floor above alerted me to someone walking around. I listened to the soft rustle over the carpet as Beth descended the steps and came towards me.

I wanted to get up and run away from her, but I couldn't move. She stopped in front of me, and I fixed my eyes on the window, her shadowed body standing just to my side. I did not want to see her face.

Her hand touched my arm, and it took all my willpower not to push it off.

"Mitch, I heard about what happened today, I'm so sorry." Her voice was kind and soft, yet it angered me.

"Who told you?" the words left my mouth tensely.

"Joe stopped by to check on you. He left just a little while ago. He thought maybe you had gone out to one of the bars, so he went to find you. I should go call him and tell him you made it home."

How nice of Joe to stop by and worry about me, I thought sarcastically. For some reason, that pissed me off more than Beth's talking, maybe because of some of his earlier comments, or maybe because I didn't trust Beth around him.

I shook my head as I heard her step into the kitchen and lift the phone off the wall. Like I have anything to say about Beth's past! Please! Wouldn't she be surprised to find out I was in love with another woman, a woman whom I had killed today.

I closed my eyes quickly, trying to block out the visual that came with that thought.

I heard Beth talking softly in the kitchen and the sound of her bare feet on the wooden floor in the hallway.

"Joe wants to know if you want him to come over."

I ground my teeth, "No."

"Are you sure, Mitch?"

I slammed my arms down onto the armrest of the chair and stood up quickly, "Yes, I'm sure. I just want to be left alone."

I knew my voice was harsh, and she took a step back. I shook my head and walked to the stairs while I heard her whispering into the phone again.

With shorts in hand, I walked into the bathroom and turned on the shower. With my arms resting on the counter, I hung my head and stared at a dollop of mint green toothpaste stuck to the bottom of the ceramic sink near the drain.

I shouldn't have growled at her, I knew that. I just didn't want to be here—with her.

The squeak of the bed reached me, and I knew she was climbing in to wait for me.

I pulled off my shirt as tendrils of steam started to fill the small room. My jeans and boxers fell to the floor. I stood as still as a statue under the hot water and wished to just be washed down the drain.

The steamy water rained on me and released the tension in my shoulders and back, but not my heart. My head hung and drops of water fell off the planes of my face, a waterfall of salt-less tears.

Why did I have to see that car today? Why had God been so cruel to put her in my life and so harshly take her away? What purpose was there for that—except to torture me? Anger coursed through me as I questioned a God I had believed in but that I felt had wronged me.

The water grew lukewarm and then cold before I turned it off. The towel felt like sandpaper on my skin as I rubbed myself dry. I felt raw, inside and out. Donning my clothes, I stepped into the bedroom and climbed into bed, facing the wall, as close to the edge as I could get.

Beth shifted beside me, and I hoped she wouldn't say anything. When she did, I couldn't help but sigh.

"Mitch, do you want to talk about it?" I could tell by the sound of her voice that she had propped herself up in bed.

"No."

She gently laid her hand on my shoulder, and I shrugged it off.

"You know I'm here if you want to talk about it, honey," hurt filled her whispered voice.

"I know. I just want to sleep," my sentences were clipped and tight on my tongue.

She was quiet for a moment and then the bed shifted again as she lay back down. I knew she was facing me, but I didn't want her comfort, didn't want to face her.

I stared at the shadowed wall for a few hours, thinking back on the last few months. Finally, my mind started to shut down, and I drifted off into a restless sleep.

When I woke, the sun was bright in the room and the house appeared to be quiet. I lifted my wrist and checked my watch, 3:30 P.M. I had slept longer than I thought I would. Sitting up in bed, I stretched my back and tried to release the stiff muscles.

The sound of little feet running up the stairs reached my ears, and I stood up to go to the bathroom. After finishing my business, I heard Chase yell down the stairs to his mom about not being able to find something.

I opened the bedroom door and smiled down at Chase. "What are you looking for, kiddo?"

"My new baseball glove. I'm going over to Robbie's to play, and I can't find it."

"It's in your closet; I saw it there the other day." I stepped past him in the direction of his room.

"I already looked there, it's not there," he whined behind me.

Stepping over a pile of toy trucks on the floor, I pulled open his white louvered doors and checked on the middle shelf, smiling to myself. I pulled out his glove and handed it to him.

"It's not, huh?"

His face lit with joy that warmed my cold heart, and I reached over and mussed his short brown hair.

"Thanks, Dad! I didn't even see it!" He turned and sprinted for the stairs, yelling that he'd found his glove.

I chuckled as I followed him and made my way down the stairs. The smell of hot coffee permeated the air, and I moved towards it. Beth stepped out the back door and yelled at Chase to be polite and have fun.

I glanced at her back and made a beeline for the cabinet with the mugs. With the mug full of hot coffee, I walked out to the porch and sat down.

I wasn't sure what I should be doing with myself. Normally this was my day off, but those mundane things that I normally would do just didn't seem important, and I soon found myself recreating the events from the day before while my coffee grew cold beside me.

I was so lost in my thoughts that I didn't notice Beth come out onto the porch until she stepped in front of me and sat beside me on the white wicker love seat.

"How are you doing today?" she spoke tentatively, probably wondering if I would snap at her again.

I fought the urge to stand up and move away, and ground my teeth instead for a moment.

"I'm here. What did Joe tell you about yesterday?" I watched a car drive down the street, a woman with a minivan full of kids.

She leaned back further into the couch. "He said you were chasing a car from a robbery, and the car you were chasing struck another officer."

Her voice was soft, caring, and I again got the urge to move away from her, not wanting her to care.

I picked up my cold coffee and took a sip. This wasn't the first time I had drunk cold coffee.

"Mitch, that accident wasn't your fault. Joe said the officer was running to get kids out of the street. You weren't the one to hit her." She turned on the couch and pulled one leg to the flowered cushion so she was facing me.

"I could have called the chase off. I could have never seen the car. She could have lived." My voice trailed off as I finished.

"Were you friends with her?"

I could tell her the truth, but what good would that do now to tell her? No, we weren't friends, she was my soul mate, the love of my life, and I was going to leave you for her. I answered instead with a simple, "Yes."

"I'm so sorry, Mitchell. I can only imagine how hard this must be for you." She slid closer and wrapped her arm around my back. I leaned forward, resting my elbows on my knees, hoping to put some distance between us, but that only allowed her to wrap her arm further around me.

"Joe told me she was a wonderful person. He said that everyone loved her."

I stood up, "You're not making me feel any better reminding me of how amazing she was, Beth." I walked to the white painted railing that wrapped around our small front porch, gripping the wood tightly in my hands.

She approached me from behind, "I'm sorry. That wasn't what I meant to do. I just wanted you to know that you are not the only person hurting, many people cared about her."

Silence filled the air until a bird squawked in the distance and a car drove down the road.

"Joe said they have already announced the funeral arrangements, and they wanted you to be one of the pall bearers."

A shiver ran down my spine as I thought of carrying her to her final resting place. "I don't know if I can do that."

"If she was your friend, then you need to do that. She would want you to do this last thing for her." She rested her hand on my arm, and I turned on her.

"How the hell do you know what she would want? Maybe she didn't want to die! Maybe she wouldn't want me anywhere near her grave because I killed her! You think about that?" I shouted at her, knowing I was being unfair but unable to stop myself as my pain spewed out of my mouth.

I thought she might turn and walk away. I had hurt her, I could tell, instead, she wrapped her arms around me and pulled me close.

"I am sure she would have wanted to live, but she didn't, Mitch. God had other plans for her, and if you were her friend, then you need to honor her by carrying her casket. Be there for her until the end, Mitch. She deserves that."

As she spoke, the tension in my shoulders dwindled, and I felt her grasp on me tighten. I wrapped my arms around her, needing the compassion she was giving me, squeezing my eyes shut to fight back the tears that threatened.

"I didn't know her, but from what Joe says, you cared for her a great deal. You need to give her the love and honor she deserves, for her and for yourself."

The tears came fast with her words, and she held me tightly as the sobs wracked my body and I held onto her with all I had, wishing the whole time she was Corey.

"I'm so sorry. Oh my God, Corey, I'm so sorry," I cried into my wife's shoulder as she held me, and my heart finally split in two.

CHAPTER 19 ~ COREY

*D*avid and I walked a bit further, and he filled me in on a few things about what my position included.

He explained that while we could help guide people into good decisions, we could not take their choices away. We were allowed to inject positive thoughts into the minds of our charges, but we could not change decisions they made.

We were assigned to select people, and those were the ones we helped to guide. We were not to implant thoughts or guide those who were not our charges, as we would not know their full story. Only their own Garda would know the path they should walk.

"How do we do all that? I mean we can't communicate with them from here, can we?" I kicked at a pile of sand in front of me as we stopped, facing out to the water. The sun was perched low on the horizon, reflecting back over the soft waves.

"When you are assigned your charges, you only get a few to start off with, then you are connected to them, and you can feel them when you need to. You will only need to look inside yourself to know what they are doing."

I turned my head to him, squinting in the bright light from the water.

"How many charges do you have?"

He studied the water, "Somewhere between three thousand and three thousand two hundred, I lost count."

"Seriously?" I blurted out. "How do you keep track of that many people and their lives?"

He laughed beside me, "It gets easier the longer we are here. We can feel when people need us. You will feel the frustration or pain they are in when they need guidance. Some people need a lot of your time, some don't." He shrugged.

I shook my head, finding it hard to believe one could watch over so many people and guide them to make good decisions.

"But do you do everything from here? When I died, Brock and Montgomery were there with me."

"When someone needs us or is in pain, we can feel it, and we go to them."

He turned to start walking back the way we had come. I stepped up to walk beside him. "But where do you go and how do you get there?"

"You phase. There is a level just above the living arena where we walk. You will see others like us there, and we watch over and guide from there. We are close enough to reach them, but far enough away that most of them cannot tell we are there."

"Some people know who we are?" I checked out his profile and noticed his right ear used to be pierced, twice.

"There are those who can see further than most. They know we are there. Of course, the Os Malos can see you."

"The who?"

"The Os Malos, the evil ones. We work for God, right?" he turned to me.

"And they work for the devil. Got it," I nodded as we continued to walk.

"See how quickly you are picking up on this? You are going to be a natural!" he chuckled beside me as I slowed.

A tingling sensation rushed through me and took my breath away. I stopped and felt as if I were about to pass out. My mind buzzed and voices came to me, but not David's. These voices were far away and pulling at me. I stared down at the sand as I felt my body shifting.

"Coralenna, look at me!" I faintly heard David yell. "Coralenna, you have to focus on me, you are not ready for this." His voice was taking on a vibrant urgency, but the sound was slowly fading.

I felt his energy race up my arm, but before it reached my heart, I blinked and found myself standing on the grass in a well-groomed neighborhood.

Two-story homes sat back from the roadway, and I heard voices coming from the house in front of me, a soft blue colonial with a white porch. On the porch, a man stood staring out in my direction. A woman, just a bit shorter than him, stood on the porch as well. My breath caught in my throat as I realized this was the same man who had been on his knees when I had died.

I stood frozen in place as the woman spoke to him.

"Joe said they have already announced the funeral arrangements and they wanted you to be one of the pall bearers."

A stab of pain pierced my heart as he spoke. "I don't know if I can do that."

"If she was your friend, then you need to do that. She would want you to do this last thing for her." The hand that she rested on his arm made me want to move forward. She was only trying to comfort him, yet I felt that I should be doing the comforting, not her.

"How the hell do you know what she would want? Maybe she didn't want to die! Maybe she wouldn't want me anywhere near her grave because I killed her! You think about that?"

The assault of his words gave me pause. I stood only ten feet from the front porch now. My view glued to his features, my mind reached for something, anything that would help me understand who this man was. I knew without a doubt that I should know him.

The woman pulled him into her arms, her love was obvious, and the stab I had felt earlier in my heart radiated through my chest. Why should I feel jealous?

"I am sure she would have wanted to live, but she didn't, Mitch. God had other plans for her, and if you were her friend, then you need to honor her by carrying her casket. Be there for her until the end, Mitch, she deserves that."

Mitch, Mitch...the name vibrated through my mind, a memory of a stream, the sound of a motorcycle, the taste of coffee all flowed over my senses. I took another step forward as he wrapped his arms around her.

His eyes were clamped tightly shut, his body tense.

"I didn't know her, but from what Joe says, you cared for her a great deal. You need to give her the love and honor she deserves, for her and for yourself."

Love...Mitch...love...a kiss, the feel of a hand on my face, the taste of his lips—all the memories of the moments we'd shared breached the wall that held them back and washed over me. Mitchell...I was in love with this man.

I watched him as my emotions rushed forward. The sobs tore at my psyche, and tears blurred my vision. I stepped forward, wanting to go to him and tell him I was right here.

Before I could take my next step, Brock materialized in front of me like a solid wall, and I jumped back.

"How the hell did you get here?" His inquisitive expression bore into my face.

"I don't know! I don't even know where here is!"

"Come on, we need to get you back, you aren't ready to be down here yet."

He stepped around me, and I turned to see David watching me closely.

Over my shoulder I saw that Mitch was calming down while Beth rubbed his back softly. I clenched my jaw.

"Those are not emotions you are allowed to feel," Brock snapped at me, and I spun towards him.

"What feelings? Right now the only thing I feel is totally confused!"

David stepped up to me, "Coralenna, I'm not sure how you did that, but we need to get you back."

All three of us snapped our heads to the side when another voice spoke to us. "Training session?"

Brock stepped in front of me and David pushed me slightly behind him. Um, excuse me, guys, is there something I should know? I almost asked but could tell by the way they held themselves that something was happening and this wasn't a good time to question them.

"What do you want?" Brock spit out at the other man, one I recognized from the scene. He had been talking to Mitch. His face floated in front of me for a second, and realization hit me: Joe. This was Joe and he was my friend, except David had just explained to me that normal people couldn't see us.

I stepped around David and stared at Joe, "You're Os Malos?" I sputtered out.

Joe's gaze flipped to me and he smiled, "Hello there, Corey. Sorry they got to you before I did. We would have loved to have you with us. It's not too late to change your mind, you know."

David pulled me back to his side while Brock sneered at Joe, "You keep away from her, Joe."

Joe examined our little group then directed his attention up to the porch where Mitch and Beth stood holding each other, oblivious to the drama taking place on their front lawn.

"Oh, I will, for now," he smiled and started to turn away. "Nice to see you again, Corey. Hope to see you at your funeral," he laughed, turned, and vanished.

"Where did he just go?" I was baffled at the instant appearance and disappearance.

"Doesn't matter. David, let's get her out of here." Brock stepped forward, and David took my arm, gently pulling me forward. I turned at the last moment and saw Mitch and Beth pull apart.

We ended up on the balcony of my quarters, and within two seconds, Montgomery joined us.

"Why did you take her down there?" Montgomery stared at David.

David straightened his back, "What? I didn't take her anywhere. We were talking on the beach and she just phased."

Montgomery regarded him for a moment then turned to me. "How did you do that?"

I shook my head. "I have no idea!" I spat out, exasperated. "You are supposed to be explaining that to me! All I know is that I was standing there talking to David when I started hearing voices and I thought I was going to pass out. Next thing I know, I'm standing on the grass watching people talk."

I didn't mention to them that I knew who the people were. Obviously, my ability to phase was not normal, so would it be safe to say that my memory coming back so soon wouldn't be either?

Even as I explained myself, I felt pieces of my life filling up my mind. Memories of my years were clicking into place fast, too fast, and I felt dizzy. I swayed, and Brock started to reach for me but pulled away. David's hand landed on me and he moved me to a chair.

I sat down heavily, staring at my knees.

"You aren't hearing voices again, are you?" Montgomery knelt down beside me.

"No, just felt dizzy for a moment. I'm fine now." I forced a smile as I glanced at him and snuck a peek at Brock who had a tight expression on his face. Could he feel what was going on with me? I looked quickly away, feeling guilty.

Montgomery patted my knee before he stood up, "Well, I guess we know who her charge is, don't we?" He watched Brock closely, and I saw Brock shake his head and turn towards the railing.

"I've been assigned someone already? I thought I had to train first." I leaned back in my seat, bending my head back to take in the men standing above me. The sky was dark now, how much time had passed since I had phased?

"Normally, you do have to train, but—" David stopped and turned to Montgomery. Brock turned around and glanced at them and then down at me.

No one spoke, so I finished the sentence, "But I'm special." I nodded, not understanding anything. "Got it." Yeah, not really, I thought to myself and examined my hands in my lap.

Montgomery blew out some air and shook his head, "I don't understand it either, Coralenna, but for some reason, you are special."

I laughed, "Gee, thanks!"

"That's not what I meant, young lady, not what I meant at all. Generally, new guards have to train and it takes them awhile before they are ready to leave the Realm. Teaching someone to phase is hard, but you managed to do it on your own."

"I didn't manage to do anything on my own. I just got sucked out of here to there. I had no clue that I was doing it."

"Well, that will just make it easier for you to learn to control it later. Let's try something. Think about going somewhere, here, not in the living arena, and see if you can get there."

"How do I do that?" I stood up and encompassed them all in a glance.

David stepped up to me and smiled, "Just think about someplace you have been here in the Realm, and then try to place yourself there."

I turned slightly, uncomfortable with everyone watching me and tried to figure out where I wanted to go. I smiled to myself when I picked a place and then focused on it carefully. Picturing the room and the fixtures, my body tingled and my mind darkened just slightly before I felt a wave crash over me. I blinked twice and found myself in the locker room.

I giggled as I took in my new surroundings, but the laugh faded as the three men followed right behind me, appearing in the reflection of the full-length mirror.

David grinned from ear to ear, while Montgomery smiled softly and shook his head. Only Brock didn't appear happy about my ability to phase, and I watched his lips tighten.

"Very good, Coralenna, very good," Montgomery put his hand on my shoulder, and I felt the warmth of this friendship travel through me.

I glanced up at Brock, wondering what his touch would feel like. He stared me down. I wanted to step away, and I decided I didn't really want to know what would pass between us.

"You know, it's nice that you all followed me and all, but I kind of picked this place for a reason." I raised an eyebrow at David.

All three of them glanced around and finally realized they were in the ladies' locker room. David smirked at me, "Yeah, I see that now. Okay, I'm out of here." Before I could smile in return, he disappeared.

I turned to the other two, and Montgomery smiled, "Touché, I guess this means you would like a bit of time to yourself?"

I nodded to him and smiled. "Please."

"Fine, young lady, I think you deserve some quiet time. We are connected, so if you need me, all you have to do is reach in and you will feel me. You can come to me anytime, but I would rather you not leave the Realm anytime soon. There is still much for you to learn."

"I can't promise you anything. I didn't have much control over it the last time, but I will do my best to remain here."

"Very good, I will see you later." He phased away as soon as the last word left his mouth.

I turned to Brock, his full lips still tightly pressed together, his thick arms crossed over his chest. He was only a few inches taller than I, and we practically glowered at each other. I raised my eyebrows at him, waiting.

"Did your memory come back?" he finally asked me while taking a step closer.

I held my breath for a moment and hesitated, "No."

He lowered his chin and stared at me through his thick brown eyelashes, "You do know that lying is a sin."

I swallowed, "Yes."

"Do not go back to the living arena, Coralenna. You are not ready to face what happens there."

"Is Joe really an Os Malos?"

His chin jerked up, "You do remember!" He stepped closer and dropped his arms.

"What? No! You called that guy down there Joe." I shook my head and stepped away from him.

He watched me and stepped closer, I saw his hand twitch at his side before I met his stare again. My breathing accelerated and I wanted to phase away from him but couldn't concentrate enough to do so.

He focused on my lips and I felt them part on a fast heavy breath. Why was it that this guy scared me, or was it something else? Mitch's face flashed into my mind, and I stepped back from him.

"Don't phase down again." Brock stood another two seconds before he vanished from my sight.

I released a huge gush of air from my lungs and sank to the bench.

CHAPTER 20 ~ BROCK

I had phased down to the Earth level to watch over another one of my charges, trying hard to keep a tag on Coralenna as I did. Unfortunately, this charge was walking a very tight line between good and bad and needed some direct attention for a few minutes.

I had just finished mentally convincing my charge that wearing the new clothes she was trying on under her own older clothes was not a good idea when David phased to my side, sheer panic on his face so great that I tensed.

"She phased!" he yelled at me.

"What do you mean she phased?" I asked quickly.

"We were talking, and she just disappeared! I tried to keep her there, but I couldn't." David was shaking his head, clearly worried.

"She's in the Realm, right?"

The guilty expression that passed over his face told me the answer, and I grabbed his shirt and pulled him forward. "Where the hell did she phase to?"

"I don't know! I couldn't feel her in the Realm, that's why I came to find you. She has to be on this level."

Immediately, I tried to relax and listened for her inner voice. Hearing her, I phased and pulled David along with me.

Dammit! I took in the scene around me and the vulnerable concern on her face as she observed Mitch and Beth on the porch. I stepped in front of her before she could get closer. If she could phase so quickly, would she be able to reach out to them? I couldn't take that chance, not yet.

I could feel the confusion racing through her and wondered if her memory was coming back. Jealousy spiked in her, and I needed to get control of the situation before she remembered everything. I couldn't take the chance of touching her now and stepped away for David to take control and lead her back.

When Joe showed up, things only got worse. I wanted to punch him in the face when he spoke to her. I flicked a quick look at David when I realized he must have explained some other things to her about who else walked this level.

I phased to her balcony, and David followed with her. Montgomery felt us enter and came to us immediately, so closely connected to me that he knew what had happened.

All of us were amazed that she could phase out of the Realm, no one had ever been able to do that so quickly. Hell, it took me several weeks before I could phase within the Realm and I was one of the stronger ones.

Something was going on inside her mind, I could feel her heart racing, and she was trying to distance herself. I watched her carefully.

If I had been in the Realm earlier instead of keeping my other charge from stealing, I would have felt her phase out. I felt responsible and it pissed me off. Watching her sit down shakily only increased my agitation.

Montgomery stood beside her and turned to me, "Well, I guess we know who her charge is, don't we?" I didn't want to explain it to him yet, so I turned away.

"I've been assigned someone already? I thought I had to train first." Her voice rose slightly as she spoke, was that fear in her words?

"Normally, you do have to train, but—" We all exchanged glances with each other when David stopped talking, we knew what he was going to say, and so did she.

"But I'm special. Got it." She wouldn't look at any of us.

Montgomery got her to test her phasing, and we were all stunned that she was able to do it her first time. While her location was quite humorous to us all, I didn't care where we ended up. I needed to stay close to her. The thought that I could lose her crossed my mind.

Her dark blue gaze met mine. I felt the pull. Did she?

I waited till everyone left. Should I reach out to her? I wondered, but my fear held me back. What if the connection wasn't what I had hoped for?

"Did your memory come back?" I asked her, sounding pushier than I had intended. The magnetism between us pulled me closer.

"No," I knew she was lying, and I told her so in not so many words. She didn't trust me; I had to earn her trust first.

"Do not go back to the Earth level, Coralenna. You are not ready to face what happens there," I warned her sternly.

"Is Joe really an Os Malos?"

"You do remember!" I stepped closer without thinking, wanting to force the memories away, almost grabbing her shoulders as the words came out.

"What? No! You called that guy down there Joe." She stepped away, but I followed her, wanting desperately to see exactly what would happen if I did touch her. Her lips were so full and they parted as I glanced down. As her breath rushed out of her erratically, I knew that I couldn't do this to her here, not now, not like this.

She ultimately made the final decision when she stepped further away, hitting the back of her knees on the bench. I warned her again and phased away before I could test the connection for which my body yearned.

I ended up on the shore, staring up at the moon. Montgomery stood beside me a moment later.

"Your punishment?" he asked casually.

"Yep," I answered.

I saw him nod from the corner of my eye. "Good one, I didn't expect that. Did the Maker tell you why?"

I shook my head, "Said she had unfinished business with him. She has to finish it."

"Unfinished business? What does he want to do, condemn her to hell through a mortal affair with Mitch?"

My head snapped toward him, "No! That can't be it," but even as I said the words, I knew that was it. This was a test. My head fell forward, and I groaned. I could still lose her to him.

"Brock, does she remember anything?" He turned in the sand to face me.

I lifted my head to him, "I think she does, but she doesn't trust me enough to tell me."

"You need to gain her trust. Stop trying to scare her." He stopped for a moment, "You haven't tried to physically connect with her yet, have you?"

"No."

"What are you afraid of?" He leaned his head forward and studied me.

"I'm not afraid of anything," I shot back and stepped away from him.

"It sure seems like you are, Brock, which I find odd, because you aren't afraid of anything." He moved beside me, and we started walking along the shore.

The gentle slap of the waves should have relaxed me, that was why I came here, but they did just the opposite. The tender lapping roared in my ears instead.

"Are you afraid that the connection will not be enough? That it won't be what you want?"

"I'm not afraid, Montgomery. I just don't want to scare her."

He laughed deeply, "Scare her? Brock, every time she sees you, you frighten her."

I stopped walking. "I know. That's why I don't want to test the connection. I want her to trust me, not be scared by what she will feel."

We took another few steps forward.

"Alright, I agree that does make sense, but with this new situation, you might want to work harder to get her to trust you."

I turned to him, "How?"

"That I don't know, but you need to think of something, and quickly. With the way she is remembering and the way she is able to phase so quickly, I am concerned that she will come amongst her other abilities quickly, and then we might have a very serious problem."

"Do you think she has the ability to walk among them mortally yet?"

"I'm afraid that if she can't already, she will be able to soon." He turned to face the now dark water.

A shiver raced down my spine, "That is what I am afraid of, too."

PART 4

The Funeral

CHAPTER 21 ~ MITCHELL

For the rest of the day, I sat quietly on the front porch and thought about what had happened. Beth sat with me for a while, and I finally explained to her what had exactly transpired with the incident. I figured I at least owed her that.

She left me alone when I was done, bringing me food and only interrupting my thoughts when she handed me the phone. Joe had been calling relentlessly.

"How you doing, man?" he asked after I said hello.

"Numb," I mumbled.

"Yeah, I'm sure you are," he answered, and I heard music playing in the background, sounded like a Led Zeppelin tune.

"I just left the station; the funeral is arranged for Friday. Did Beth tell you I called earlier about it?"

"Yeah, she told me they wanted me to carry." I watched a squirrel run across the road and up a tree.

"You going to? They asked me to carry also."

"I don't know if I can, Joe."

"Oh, come on! You were having an affair with the woman! It's the least you can do."

I sat up straight, tensing, and turned toward the screen door to see if Beth was there. "I was not, Joe, and you need to keep that shit to yourself and not go starting rumors."

"Aw, come on, don't you know everyone knows you two were meeting all the time? Someone even saw you two kissing in the park."

This was exactly what I didn't need. I had never wanted to tarnish her reputation. "Joe, let it go. No one saw anything, and people need to find something else to talk about."

"Whatever, Mitch, you gonna do it or what?" he snapped back at me.

"What the hell is your problem? Ever since Corey died, you have been a total asshole."

He was quiet for a moment, "You're not the only one who is sorry she's dead."

His words were cold, and I wondered why. Was Corey more important to him than I knew? Was he jealous of what I had with her?

"Fine, I'll do it."

He acknowledged my answer and then said he'd call later with the other arrangements.

I set the cordless phone next to me and leaned back on the cushion. Beth walked out the door, watching me closely. Had she heard anything? Had I said anything? I didn't think so, but my head wasn't on exactly straight anymore.

"Your cell phone has been beeping all afternoon. I figured maybe you might want to see who has been trying to get in touch with you." She held out my iPhone, and I took it from her. Had I erased Corey's last messages?

She smiled softly and turned to go back inside. I turned on my screen to find fifteen missed calls, six voice messages, and twenty-nine text messages. Scrolling through the messages, I found that I had not deleted our last conversation. I glanced up at the door, had Beth read it? Damn.

My finger rested over the delete button, but I just couldn't manage to remove it from the device. I knew I would have to, but I just couldn't do it yet.

I skimmed through the rest of the text messages, and sent back a few replies. I wasn't ready to listen to the voicemails yet, they could wait another day.

I lay my head back against the cushion and stared at a tree in the yard. Once again Corey's face came to mind, blocking the view of the foliage. I couldn't believe she was really gone.

CHAPTER 22 ~ COREY

*W*hen everyone finally left me alone, I phased back to my room and giggled as I realized how easy and fun phasing was. I embraced the quiet that filled my room and wandered around the kitchen, checking in the cabinets and fridge. A bottle of my favorite wine stood on the top shelf, I snagged it.

After the day I had just had—I stopped suddenly. Had it only been a day? Time was strange here, I couldn't be sure.

Inside a drawer, I found an opener and then pulled a glass from one of the cabinets. With the crystal filled almost to the rim, I stepped out onto the balcony again.

I sat down in a cushioned glider and allowed my feet to slowly push me back and forth, a gently swaying rhythm that kept time with the sound of the waves lapping the shore below.

The wine tasted heavenly, and I relished the cold liquid as it slid down my throat.

Memories of my life were ticking through my mind: learning to ride a bike, dinners with my parents, graduation from high school, my first kiss with a boy named Steve in fourth grade, and my last kiss—with Mitch.

I heaved a sigh and leaned my head back.

"Pretty heavy sigh, Coralenna."

I whipped my head to the side where Brock stood. I raised my eyebrows. "I thought I was going to get some peace."

He smiled roguishly. "Mind if I join you?" his voice was low and husky. I wanted to say no, but just maybe I could find out more about this daunting man standing before me.

"Would you like a glass of wine?" I allowed my visual exploration to travel over the powerful legs that filled his jeans to perfection.

"Sure, white Merlot, right?" He took a seat next to me in another glider.

I watched him fill the seat before I spoke again, "I assume you know that is my favorite?"

"Who do you think put the bottle in your fridge and the other items in your quarters?" The grin he shared was playful and just a touch seductive.

I fought a shiver and stood to get his wine. As I poured his glass, I wondered why there was such an intense chemistry between us. Did people in the Realm have relations like living people did?

I frowned as I carried his glass outside. The answer didn't matter; I had no intentions of getting involved with him.

Once seated back in my glider, we lapsed into a comfortable silence. The moon shone down on us, and the stars were brighter than I had ever imagined.

"How long have you been here, Brock?" I finally broke the silence.

"Several years. I am one of the newer Gardaí." He sipped his wine.

"Do you like what you do here?"

He turned to me, the brightness of the moon reflecting off of his face, throwing dark shadows over the sharp planes of his cheek. The darkness hid the color of his eyes, but I realized I already had that detail memorized.

"What's not to like? You get to guide people to be better, to make the right choices. You give them an afterlife." His voice was silky and raspy at the same time and it vibrated through my ear canals, down my neck, and right into my chest.

"I guess that's good." I filled my mouth with another taste of wine and swallowed slowly. Brock watched me.

"How long have you been watching over me?" I turned and surveyed the darkened land before me.

"From the moment I finished my training. You were the first one they assigned me to," he laughed. "You were pretty easy to watch over," his voice grew lower, "until recently."

I turned to him, "What do you mean, 'Until recently'?"

I saw him frown as he contemplated my words and waited to see if he would answer the question.

His shoulders dropped slightly, as if a decision had been made that he did not want to make.

"I know your memory is coming back, Coralenna. I can feel it, feel the changes inside your mind. I know you well." He cast a quick glance my way. "You always made the best decisions, always thought before you did anything, until—"

I could have denied remembering, but Brock was right, I should not lie. "Until Mitch?"

He leaned forward, resting his arms on his thighs, and gently twirled his wineglass between his knees with his right hand. His face turned my way, "Yes, until Mitch."

I stood up and tipped my glass back to finish my drink in two unlady-like gulps. After setting my glass down on the table between us, I walked to the railing and leaned on it.

"I know that I made bad decisions, but I couldn't help myself. There was this crazy chemistry between us." Kind of like the zings I feel from you, I thought but did not add out loud. I didn't hear him move up behind me.

"Kind of like what runs between us?" The sound of his voice was so close, it resonated. I allowed it to wash over me.

"What chemistry?" I whispered into the air.

"Coralenna, look at me." While his voice was soft, the power of his command was obvious, and I turned despite myself.

"What did I say about lying?"

I hung my head, knowing he was right.

"You might not want to admit it, but it's there." The sound of his voice swelled around me, tugging me closer, and I stepped forward, meeting his stare, drawn to him.

"Yes, I feel it, but I don't understand it." We were less than a foot apart. He stood four inches taller than I did, and I wanted to run my fingers through his dark hair and pull his face to mine. The thought lasted until Mitch's face flashed through my mind.

I turned from him, suddenly feeling guilty. "But I love Mitch."

He grunted. "If you haven't noticed, he's alive and you're dead."

I spun on him, "So just because I'm not alive anymore, I should forget the way I feel about another man?"

His jaw locked, and the muscle on the right side of his cheek twitched. "Yeah, he's not part of your life anymore. You need to let him go." He contemplated for a moment, "Let him go and find out what we have here." His head turned and his face came back to mine almost pleadingly.

At that moment, I wanted to know what we had, but I couldn't keep the memories of what I had shared with Mitch from invading my mind.

I shook my head, "I can't, Brock."

Anger mixed with hurt as the emotions crossed over his features, "Why?"

"Because I don't know you and because I love him."

He snorted an angry laugh, "You love him? You love a married man who is alive and walking among the living; the same one who was about to cheat on the wife that he vowed to love forever?" He turned away, but his words were like a slap in the face.

"He was going to leave his wife." I immediately cringed as the words left my mouth. I realized how horrible they sounded.

"Yeah, so breaking up a happy family was worth it to you?"

"He wasn't happy with her!" my voice rose. Why was I trying to explain it to him?

"If you had stayed out of it, he would have gotten over it. Now you just made it harder for him to forgive her."

"I did not!"

"What? You think that almost making love to him by the stream didn't make things worse? Or telling him that you love him? Dammit, Corey, you have confused the hell out of him! It's going to take years for him to get over all of this and to forgive himself for what he did."

My jaw hung open, "You were there? By the stream?" The words barely left my mouth, but I already knew the answer.

"Of course I was there! I was the one that guided you to stop." He put his hands on his hips, staring down at the ground.

My face burned at the thought of him watching such an intimate moment. The memory of why I had stopped, feeling that I could not engage in this type of a relationship when he had a wife. He had planted that thought.

"I was also the one that comforted you when you knew you needed to let him go, and I stood beside you when you saw his family. Who do you think eased your pain at night so you could sleep?"

I blinked at him, not knowing what to say.

"You have to let him go, Coralenna. You can't be a part of his life anymore. You have to find a way to give him the peace to move forward and forget you."

"How am I supposed to do that? How can I ease his pain when I feel it so intensely and mirror it in my own soul?" I cried out to him.

"You will have to find a way, or you will be joining the Os Malos."

I jerked back. "What?"

He shook his head and stepped away from me.

"You can't just say that and not answer me." I watched him pace for a moment.

"Coralenna, I can say no more. I should not have said that, but you need to know you walk a very thin line right now. Let him go and come to me." He held his hand out in front of him. "You might not know me as well as I know you, but you will."

His palm was turned up, beckoning me to step closer. My fingers twitched at my side with the urge to reach out.

"No." I stepped back until I felt the railing behind me and crossed my arms over my chest. His hand dropped slowly to his side.

"Bad decision, Coralenna." Emotion tainted his voice.

"I'll take my chances." I lifted my chin higher and squared my shoulders.

"So be it." With those words, he phased away.

My shoulders fell, and my body trembled. How could I let Mitch go when every fiber of my being felt attached to him? I knew the feeling was wrong, and somehow I knew that Brock spoke the truth. My decision could change the course of my afterlife.

Was I prepared for that?

CHAPTER 23 ~ MITCHELL

I finished buttoning the shirt of my neatly tailored and pressed class A uniform with shaky fingers. I stood before the mirror over Beth's dresser and carefully clipped my tie into my collar.

I watched Chase walk slowly into the room through the reflection, "Hey, Dad, can I ask you a question?"

With my tie now straight, I picked up the silver clip to hold it neatly in place, "Sure, son, what's on your mind?"

He climbed onto the bed and studied my duty belt for a moment, "What happens when you die?" His expression was sad as it met mine in the reflection. I turned from the mirror to him and sat down.

"You go to heaven," I responded as his large green eyes looked up at me forlornly.

"Do you ever get to see your family again?"

I cleared my throat, not sure how to respond, "Well, you get to watch over them from heaven, and when the family members die, they join you there."

Chase threw his arms around me, "I don't want you to die like your friend did."

"Chase, I'm not going to die, son." I held him tightly.

"But your friend did, and you could, too. I hear you talk about all the bad people you have to deal with, and what if you get hit by a car or someone shoots you?"

"Chase, we can't worry about when we will die. We have to live our lives to the fullest that we can. No one knows when their time is up, but I swear I have no plans of leaving you anytime soon."

Chase pulled back and his eyes were watery. "You promise?"

"I promise, kiddo." I pulled him to my chest again. "Aren't you supposed to be going over to Robbie's house?"

He pulled away, and I let him go. "Yeah, but I wanted to tell you I was sorry about your friend before I left."

My vision wavered as it misted, and I responded quietly, "Thank you." I cleared my throat, "Now go over to Robbie's house and have a good time."

"Can I take my new video game over?" he asked, using the childlike voice I was used to.

"Sure, go grab it and head over. Mom and I have to leave in a few minutes."

He was already running out of the door "Okay. Bye, Dad."

I picked up my leather duty belt, the eighteen pounds it weighed felt more like fifty. I pulled it around my waist as Beth entered.

"You almost ready?" she asked me quietly, checking over my reflection.

I nodded briefly and went to task securing my belt. With a last straightening to my tie and duty gear, I turned and picked up my dress cap, heading to the door.

I stopped as I approached Beth, expecting her to turn and walk out of the room. Instead she turned her face up to mine, her expression sad.

"I'm sorry you have to do this today. I know it's not easy." She stepped closer and laid a gentle kiss on my lips.

"Thank you." I cleared the hoarse sound out of my throat just as an air horn from a patrol car sounded outside. Her lips tipped up slightly with a brief smile before she turned and walked down the stairs.

For just a moment, I wanted to slam the door closed and refuse to go. I closed my eyes, "Please, God, give me the strength to make it through today."

I walked down the stairs and out the front door. Joe was in his usual patrol car, clean and freshly polished, even the rims.

I watched Beth walk over to her car; she would follow us to the ceremony. Once she was inside hers, I slid into the front seat without a word. Joe nodded, and we drove towards the university stadium where the service would take place.

There were no churches in the area that were large enough to hold the amount of people expected to be present. Hundreds of cops would be there to pay their last respects to a sister of the Thin Blue Line, not to mention the hundreds of people that she had touched in her charity work, her friends, and her family. I knew I would feel humbled to see all those that cared about her.

The thought of carrying her body while all those people watched, knowing that it had ultimately been my fault that she died, tied my stomach in knots. My heart rate sped up, my palms grew damp.

We arrived at the stadium way too soon. People were putting the police cars into a processional line in a separate location from the civilian parking area. I took in the number of cars already there and listened as Joe spoke with someone. Our vehicle was moved near the front of the line.

We received our instructions as to where to stand, and I mindlessly kissed Beth on the cheek before she left to meet up with some other wives. The brothers and sisters in blue would stand together as one, an incredibly sad sight to behold.

The hearse pulled up to the back of the stadium, and my stomach rolled hard enough that I thought I would hurl. I started pacing around the parking area, suddenly wishing I had a cigarette, a habit I had given up years ago. The noise from the stadium grew louder as the minutes progressed.

I can't do this. I can't carry her out there with all these people. I looked at the back of the hearse, knowing that inside that simple wooden box lay the woman I loved with all my heart. Sweat rolled down the back of my neck. A hand landed on my shoulder and I turned, startled to see Tom Barrett, one of the other officers who was carrying the casket and who worked for our department.

"You holding up alright, O'Reilly?"

While absently shaking my head no, I turned to him and strained out the words, "Yeah, fine."

"Mitch, we all know how you felt about her, your feelings were obvious. You shouldn't be doing this, man, why are you?"

I skipped over the first part. Had we been so transparent? I wondered. "Joe talked me into it." I leaned my head quickly in Joe's direction.

"What an ass! Look if you want to step out, I'll find someone to carry for you. You shouldn't have to carry someone that you cared that much for." His hand squeezed my shoulder, and I thought about his words.

"Thanks, Barrett, but I feel like I need to do this, for her." A quick glance back to the hearse showed the funeral home director getting ready to open the back door. God, be with me here, I need your strength, I quickly prayed.

Barrett nodded in understanding and stepped away to give me room to breathe.

Too soon, the director told us to prepare, the ceremonies were about to start. The night before, a private service had been held with just Corey's parents and her close friends. Today's events were for the brothers and sisters in blue and the community she had helped. I could have gone to the smaller event, but there was no way I could say goodbye to her twice.

They pulled her casket out and we gathered around, stepping into the places to which we had been assigned. I stood in front on the left. Joe stood in the back right corner. Barrett stood on the opposite side of me; there was no need for words.

To the right side, the officers of her department stood in a double line, dressed in their Class A uniforms, somber and stern. During the funeral service, other departments were covering their township so they could all be here to put one of theirs to rest. They would follow behind the casket.

A few brief words were said, and I reached down to pick up the casket. I can't do this, oh God, I can't do this! My hands began to shake, and I swallowed bile in my throat.

Yes, you can, a small voice echoed inside my head. *You can do this, Mitchell, for me, you can do this.* That voice sounded so much like Corey's that I gasped slightly and gripped the brass bar tightly as my vision suddenly watered.

I can do this. For you, Corey, I can do it. We stood as one holding the heavy casket and our first steps were made. The bagpipes could be heard from nearby on the stadium field, and we moved toward the sound.

My legs still shook, but they continued to function. The casket stand stood in the field and we made our way towards it. There was silence from the stands and surrounding chairs. Only the mournful sounds of the bagpipes playing and the hollow beat of the drums marked our entrance.

We placed Corey on the stand and stood at attention as a final song was played. I stared out at the crowd. Thousands of people were here, more than I could have imagined. How loved she was. I fought back the tears as we stood ramrod straight, waiting for the final notes to float through the air.

Sixty minutes later, the service concluded. Multiple eulogies had been given about her strength and amazing character. Tears flowed while quiet chuckles were produced by the occasional happy memories recounted.

The time had come to move her to her final resting place, and I stood numbly beside the casket once again, walking back the way we had come. My body continued to move forward, but I could not think beyond the next step. With her safely back inside the hearse, we returned to our vehicles and prepared to follow her to the cemetery. The hardest part was about to commence.

CHAPTER 24 ~ BROCK

I wanted to kick myself for what I said on the balcony. Instead of trying to get her to trust me, I had scared and angered her. I punched a hole in the wall of my quarters.

How could I get her to understand that she should trust me and that she needed to just forget about Mitch? What kind of hold did he have over her? Were they really soul mates? Is that what held them so tightly bound together?

I paced around the inside of my quarters. I could feel her pain, feel her frustration even now. Her tears pulled at me, but I had to give her space. I had to come up with a way for her to trust me enough to come to me, to reach out to me.

What was going to happen if I couldn't get her to see me? Would she destroy her chances of heaven by doing something on the Earth plane while she was being tested? If we had the connection, would it keep her from being pulled by the feelings? Would it protect her from making the wrong decision?

What would I do if the connection wasn't there? Would I be able to deal with the consequences?

Montgomery phased beside me, and I jumped slightly, so lost in my own anguished thoughts.

"How did it go?" he asked with an eyebrow up.

"Not good. I scared her again," I shook my head and plopped down in a large brown leather chair, laying my head back against the cool smooth material.

Montgomery laughed softly and sat down on the matching leather couch. "I'm not surprised."

I considered him, "I don't know how to convince her that she needs to let go of Mitch without telling her what will happen to her if she doesn't."

"It is not your place to tell her that. Why are you so afraid to reach out for the connection?"

"Why are you so sure there will be one?" I threw back at him.

He leaned back, and the leather crinkled in the quiet. "It's written in the stars, and you know that."

"Yeah, okay." I leaned my head back again, staring at the ceiling. Coralenna's face filled my head. I wanted so much for it to be true, but what if it wasn't? What if that dream never got fulfilled because she made the wrong choice?

Even now, I couldn't affect her choices. I couldn't even guide her now. There was no way to put thoughts into her head now that she was one of us. I could feel some of her thoughts, feel her emotions and understand them because I knew her so well, but I couldn't guide her.

As if thinking about her brought the feeling, I sat straight up, "Dammit, she's phasing again!"

CHAPTER 25 ~ COREY

*L*ater that night, I lay upon my bed and stared at the ceiling. Tears leaked from the sides of my eyes as I thought about the words Brock and I had shared.

Was it possible to let Mitch go? Was I strong enough? Could I turn to Brock and find out what this connection was that charged between us? Could I go from one man to another?

As I lay there, I immediately felt the pull. Voices were speaking to me, hundreds of them at once, but one so much stronger and louder than the others. The tug at my consciousness was so intense and demanding that I didn't dare deny it, and I allowed my body to phase.

The sun was high in the sky, and I blinked at the brightness. The voices were everywhere, my name on the tip of their tongues, but Mitch was the one that drew my attention.

He stood beside a casket with five other officers, decked out in their formal uniforms. He filled my vision and I soaked it up. From the dress uniform that fit so perfectly to the shine on his belt and boots, I absorbed everything.

His internal debate was strong and I could hear him fighting for the strength to pick up the casket. I didn't know if I could influence him or not, but I tried. A sense of accomplishment soothed me as I saw him bend to pick up the brass bar.

The officers were taking their first steps when I felt my worried entourage arrive from the Realm. I ignored them and walked along with the casket, engrossed in the concentration of the men carrying my Earthly body.

"Coralenna, I don't think you want to be here for this," Montgomery's concerned voice broke through the silence as his hand wrapped around the top of my left arm.

David's hand quickly slipped around my right arm, effectively keeping me from advancing. Brock stepped in front of me, confusion and hurt on his face.

"How did you get here?"

"I heard them, they called me, and I couldn't ignore it. Let me go." I tried to pull my arms away from them, but they held fast. I knew if I tried hard enough, I could break free, but I hoped they would release me on their own.

"It's not a good idea for you to be here. This is your funeral. It will only cause you pain," Montgomery spoke compassionately beside me.

"More pain you mean? More than I already feel? Who cares? Let me go. They called me here, he needs me here. I want to be here. I need to see this," the words tumbled out of my mouth towards Montgomery before I turned my attention to Brock.

"Maybe it will allow me to let go," I whispered, knowing he would understand the meaning. He appeared to mull over my words. Could I fool him? Was it wrong of me to try?

Yes, but being able to see Mitch was worth it.

"Fine, but I'm staying here with you."

"We will all stay here with her," David said from my other side, and they let go of my arms.

I stepped around Brock and walked forward on the spongy grass, scanning over the sea of faces that stood on the field around me: hundreds of police officers in full dress uniform all at attention, chins up, shoulders back, hands in fists at their sides. All of them were lining the area around the field. Up on the stands, thousands of people, men, women, and children, stood watching. I was awestruck by the attendance.

I turned to the casket, a basic oak box adorned with long brass rails and handles: simple, elegant, and mine. I swallowed tightly.

As the pastor began speaking, I took the time to tear my focus from the wooden box and notice all the others like me mixing in amongst the living people.

They mingled in and around the officers and civilians standing, stopping every once in a while to lay a gentle hand on someone who was grieving. Tash stood behind my parents, a hand on each of their shoulders, relieving the worst of the pain they must have felt at burying their only child.

A sob stuck in my throat as I witnessed the sadness on their faces, and I walked to them, wanting to reach out and console them, to tell them that I was fine, that I would watch over them and not to worry. Tash was so intent that he either ignored me or didn't realize I was there, until I laid my hands over his.

A wave of emotion roared between us as his deep chocolate eyes opened and met mine. His ability to calm was immense, and it filled me, but I pushed it away from me and back to my parents.

My father emotion roared between us as his , and my mother sniffed.

"I love you both, so very much. Please don't be sad, I'm safe and watching over you. Celebrate my life, and when the day comes, I will see you both again."

My voice was soft, floating on the air between us, yet I knew they heard me. The peace that passed over both their faces told me that.

"They feel your presence, thank you. You have made my job much easier." Tash closed his eyes and went back to concentrating on them.

"I can't believe they can hear her. How is that happening, Montgomery?" David's voice came from behind me, but I ignored it and turned toward the pastor.

To the right of him sat the six officers who had carried my body. Mitch sat silent and still, staring off into space while the rest watched the pastor as he spoke—hell, all of them except Joe, who stared at me.

Was it strange that he gave me the creeps? How did he get picked to carry me? If he was an Os Malos, then he walked with the evil side. How had I never known he was evil? He had always been nice to me, always friendly to everyone. I turned my back on him and walked to stand behind Mitch.

Even though I knew that my parents had felt my presence, I was afraid to reach out to him, so terrified that if I touched him, I would not be able to stop. Instead, I focused intently and sent him every ounce of love that I felt until the service ended, and he stood to gather my casket one more time.

The group walked forward and then turned. Joe focused on me, the corner of his mouth turned up as he fought to hold back a smile. Anger pulsed through my veins that an Os Malos would have the gall to carry my body.

Brock stepped up beside me and then David on my left. We all watched them carry the wooden box away. The sound of the bagpipes made my heart heavy, and the beat of the drum vibrated through my being.

I stood frozen in place until everyone cleared from the stadium. I knew what would come next, and I knew that part would be the hardest for everyone, including me.

With one step forward, David stopped me with his words. "Coralenna, you don't have to do this."

"I have never run from anything before, I'm not going to run away now. I need to be here for them. I need to see it, if only to know that my life really is over." I turned to Brock as I finished.

I took another step and then phased without thought. My heavenly body landed in the middle of a vast cemetery. Marble stones of all shapes and sizes were scattered in the dense green grass area.

I walked to my final resting site, contemplated the open pit, and shuddered.

CHAPTER 26 ~ MITCHELL

Somehow I made it through the service. Maybe God had answered my prayers and given me the strength to do it. Maybe Corey herself had stood beside me and encouraged me to move forward. Whatever had occurred, I was grateful I made it through the first part.

As we walked the short distance from the hearse to the gravesite, my stomach turned, and my knees practically knocked together. I wasn't sure if I would be able to keep my composure much longer.

We set her down carefully and took our places behind the officers of her department. Across from us sat her family and close friends.

The pastor started to speak and the soft breeze carried the sound of his strong voice over the area, lifting his prayers to the heavens. Would she hear them? Would she know we were all here and that we all cared so much for her? I examined the sky as I wondered if she would know just how much I loved her and how sorry I was for what had happened.

I hid my watery eyes behind my lids, listening absently to the words being said, and watched moments of our short time play in my mind.

The sad notes of "Amazing Grace" rose around us, and I was no longer the only one trying to contain the tears. As the guns fired the twenty-one gun salute, my body shook to the core with each of the three rounds of seven shots. I swallowed, fighting the tears as they threatened to spill. A heavy gust of air blew down on us as three choppers flew low overhead. I reached up and held my cover on my head before it could take flight.

The final call started, the officers from the department all had their portable radios on, and the radio was sent over a loud speaker for all to hear with perfect clarity. Very slowly, the dispatcher began the roster check.

"Twenty-nine Paul One," the female voice was strained with emotion, and I briefly wondered how she had been chosen to complete such a hard task.

I watched Mark swallow before he lifted his hand to his microphone clipped to his shoulder and answered solemnly, "Twenty-nine Paul One."

The calls continued, skipping over Corey's number so that it would be the last called. As the dispatcher finished with the last officer present, her voice cracked and she took an audible breath over the air before she called out, "Twenty-nine Paul Six."

Silence echoed through the cemetery, not even the chirp of a bird could be heard. Tears dripped off of my face as I listened to the silence. I no longer even tried to hold them back.

"Twenty-nine Paul Six," said the even more emotional dispatcher.

She was answered by nothing but silence.

Ten seconds ticked off before the dispatcher keyed up one last time and called out a final, "Twenty-nine Paul Six." A ragged sob tore over the speaker as she tried to hold it together.

Soft sounds filled the air around me, officers crying for their fallen sister. Friends cried for their lost friend, and her family released the pain for the loss of such an incredible woman.

Her chief keyed up his microphone and emotionally announced that Twenty-nine Paul Six was no longer in service and her end of watch date and time.

The dispatcher cried openly as she keyed up and acknowledged his transmission.

I swallowed and hung my head. My tears fell to the ground below me. At least the grass would be watered well today, I thought to myself.

Mitch, hold your head up high. Do not grieve my loss, celebrate the love we had and the brief time we shared.

I lifted my face quickly, the words so strong inside of my head, as if she stood right there speaking in my ear. I glanced around but only saw others wiping the moisture from their faces.

I love you, Corey, I'm so sorry, I'm so very sorry. I closed my eyes as I felt the sensation of her hand touch my cheek.

I know, Mitch. The accident wasn't your fault, please believe that. I love you.

Corey, I miss you. I miss you so much.

I miss you too, but don't worry, I'm always here with you, right here in your heart.

I felt a soft pressure over my chest and reached up to grasp it, only to find the stiff material of my shirt under my fingertips.

I stared straight ahead and embraced the words that traveled through my mind. Maybe she did come back to speak with me. Maybe she was here watching it all, knowing how much we all loved her.

Suddenly the feeling of her being there was gone—blown away by a gust of wind.

I shook my head as I realized I was dreaming. There was no way she should have just come back to me. No one would be that understanding. I had caused her death, and there was no way she would ever forgive me.

Joe patted my back, "Come on, man, let's go get a drink."

"I don't think so. I'm going to find Beth and head home."

"Come on, man, the sad part is over, now it's time to celebrate life! Let's go get smashed and see what we can get into."

I snorted at his animation, "Sorry, Joe, another time. Right now, I just want to go home and be with my family."

He watched me for a moment, "You sure about that? You never know what you might run into."

"Seriously, man, I'm not up to going out for a drink. I'll catch you later." I turned and walked away from him, suddenly feeling uncomfortable with him.

After threading my way through the crowd, I finally found Beth and followed her silently out to the car. She tossed me the keys over the hood.

I opened up the back seat and unbuckled my duty belt, taking it off and setting it down. After tossing in my hat, I climbed into the front seat and unclipped my tie.

"That was a nice service," Beth said softly beside me. My non-committal grunt was the only response as I put the key in the ignition. The only nice thing about that whole ceremony was that it was over.

"How are you doing?" she asked me quietly as I started to pull out of the parking spot and get into line with the other cars to leave.

"I'm fine." I reached over and turned on the radio, trying to avoid conversation. When Joe had suggested going out, the only thing I'd wanted was to go home. Now that I was in the car with Beth, the only thing I wanted was to not be with her, especially with my turbulent emotions roiling so close to the surface.

I tried to pull back the small sense of peace I had felt during the final part of the ceremony, tried to remember the words that had filled my head, but I couldn't bring the sound of her voice back.

After arriving home, I went straight up to the bedroom and changed out of my uniform. With shorts and a T-shirt on, I grabbed a beer out of the fridge and walked out to the porch. Sitting down in one of the Adirondack chairs, I guzzled about half my beer before I allowed the scenes of the funeral to fill my mind.

Would Corey really forgive me? Was I really to blame for her death? Maybe I could push the blame over to the driver of the other car.

No, the fault was mine. I knew that a majority of the fault lay with the guy who was fleeing, but I had pursued him. I had forced his hand. If I had called off the pursuit, if I had never seen the car, then she would still be alive.

I took another slug of my beer and picked up my phone from the side table where I had put it. There was a text message from Joe with only the name of a local bar.

Beth walked out on the porch, "What would you like for dinner?"

I tapped my phone on my thigh, thinking. "Nothing, I'm going to go out for a while." I stood up and went to throw on jeans, the thought of being home with Beth while all these emotions roared through me was not something I wanted to deal with. I'd rather be drunk at a bar than sitting at home with her watching me.

I don't know if she responded or not. The sound of the porch door slamming closed drowned out anything she might have said.

A few minutes later, I climbed into my truck and pulled out of the driveway, determined to drink away the pain.

CHAPTER 27 ~ COREY

*S*taring into the dark moist earth was like touching dry ice: cold and painful. I had never been so thankful for the feel of an arm around me than when Montgomery joined me.

The final part of the ceremony was heart-wrenching. I jumped as each shot was fired, as if they were striking me directly. With my head tilted back, I pretended the wind rushed over me from the blades of the helicopters as they flew low overhead.

When they began the last call, I walked from one officer to the next, watching tearfully as he or she answered his radio. When they called my number, I stood in front of Mitch. The moisture that ran down my cheeks matched the ones on his handsome face drop for drop. There was so much emotion displayed on his face.

He hung his head as if the pain was so heavy he could no longer hold it up. I wanted to make it easier for him, wanted him to know that I was here and that I loved him. I reached out for him with my words, not knowing if they would reach him.

Mitch, hold your head up high. Do not grieve my loss. Celebrate the love we had and the brief time we shared. My words were so soft they were barely audible to my own ears, but his face came up. His beautiful blue eyes opened and stared straight into mine for a moment as if he could actually see me standing right before him. He gasped a breath.

I love you, Corey, I'm so sorry, I'm so very sorry. The pain in his words tore at my heart, and I delicately reached out my hand to him. I needed him to know that I loved him and that I would never blame him. My hand caressed the planes of his cheek; I couldn't feel his skin, only a slight pressure under my skin. I choked on a sob, wanting so badly to feel him.

I know, Mitch. The accident wasn't your fault, please believe that. I love you. I sent all the love I had in me towards him, watching him as he tilted his head towards the pressure of my hand. He knew I was there, he could feel me. My vision blurred behind more unshed tears to know that I was able to reach him in this small way.

Corey, I miss you. I miss you so much. Pain echoed around the sound of his strong internal voice.

I miss you, too, but don't worry, I'm always here with you, right here in your heart. I placed my hand gently over his chest, and he reached for it.

How much I wished we could really touch, just one more time, that I could hold him, kiss him, and whisper in his ear that he would be alright and that someday we would be together again.

"Coralenna," a strong hand gripped my arm and pulled me away from Mitch, breaking the thin line that held us together, "It's time to go."

"No! No! I want to stay! I'm not done!" I spun around towards David, but he wasn't the one who answered.

"Oh, yes, you are. You are done. We need to leave, you're being summoned. If you weren't so lost in him," Brock nodded towards Mitch, anger—or was that pain—in his expression, "you would have felt it."

I stopped and thought about what he said. Instantly, a vibration deep within me tore through my entire body. How could I have missed that?

CHAPTER 28 ~ BROCK

"*D*ammit, she's phasing again!"

"Go! I'll get David and follow you." We both left the room as the same moment, not knowing where we would end up.

She stood watching the hundreds of people, no not hundreds, thousands! My jaw hung slack while I tried to comprehend what was in front of me. David and Montgomery landed beside me. I saw her first and phased to her as she walked towards Mitch.

When she focused on me and said maybe this was how she could let go of him, how could I have said no? I didn't know whether she was telling the truth or not, but I had to trust her.

We watched her every step, concerned that she would become emotional, concerned that she would overstep the bounds and somehow cross over to the next level.

What a scene it would cause to have her materialize out of the blue into the middle of her own funeral. An eerie shiver raced down my spine at the thought.

I focused on her feelings, knowing that she felt the pain, but amazed that she instantly knew how to push her love out to others.

We all saw the effect she had on her parents. Montgomery and I shared a quick concerned glance while David vocalized our thoughts. None of us had an answer.

As she stood behind Mitch, I feared she would reach out to him, so afraid that she would connect to him from this side. I ground my teeth tightly.

"Keep it up and you'll be visiting a dentist in the living arena," Montgomery mumbled from my side.

"She was able to connect with her parents, so I have no doubt she will be able to connect with any Earth body that she comes in contact with. I just don't want it to be him. It won't make matters any better."

"Brock, you have to allow her to do this. If this is her assignment, then she is going to need to connect with him to complete it," he whispered softly to me.

"But what if she goes about it wrong? She has had no training. What if she steps over? We can't protect her there."

Montgomery shook his head and watched the officers stand to move back to the casket. Coralenna stood stiffly, staring over the shiny wooden box at Joe. Tension filled her frame, and the expression on his face was mocking. We all phased to her side.

Once they walked past us, her shoulders dropped, and she started to follow them. Her pain was so obvious to all of us, and David gave her another chance to leave.

"I have never run from anything before, I'm not going to run away now. I need to be here for them, I need to see it," she turned her dark blue stormy glare to me, "if only to know that my life really is over."

So much grief rolled through her. She instantly phased, and David gasped beside me.

"How does she do that?" his face was filled with awe, and I shrugged, following her to her new location with David and Montgomery right behind me.

She stood silently beside the hole in the Earth, staring down into the depths. Anguish tore through me as I saw her knees tremble.

"Go to her, Brock," Montgomery said quietly beside me.

"I can't, not here, not now."

"She needs your strength." I saw the stern glare he gave me from the corner of my eye.

"I can't give her that right now," I swallowed the lump in my throat.

"You fool," he muttered and walked to her, resting his arm around her shoulders and pulling her to his chest.

"I can't believe my body goes into that." She didn't need to explain anything else. The grimness of her face explained it all.

He squeezed her gently, "Don't think about that. It is just a body, your soul is what is important and it is right here."

She nodded as the first of the procession pulled into the cemetery. When she moved away from the edge, I walked to stand near her.

Hundreds of cars pulled in and wound around. People walked from all sides of the cemetery. They would sneak glances at the grave, but quickly turn away.

A sea of dark blue filed around three sides of the grave, the fourth side left for the people not in law enforcement. The bagpipes continued to play an eerie tune while everyone lined up and prepared to say the final goodbye.

Mitch and the others carried her slowly over the soft ground. The pounding of the drums vibrated in my ears, every face somber, every face but Joe's. He stared at Coralenna, almost salivating at her presence. David put his hand on my shoulder as a low growl vibrated in my chest.

Coralenna took it all in. She scanned around the vast group of people but always went back to Mitch or her parents.

As the ceremony started, the bagpipes grew quiet, the drums went silent, and only the muted sound of the breeze and the voice of the pastor filled the air.

Coralenna focused on me, and her sorrow struck me like a physical blow. My hands and arms hummed at the need to pull her to me and support her as these final moments moved forward. I crossed my arms over my chest, hands fisted close to my body.

The shots were fired, and I could almost feel the whip of the wind around me as the helicopters flew overhead. As the last words were said, I watched her face, watched the emotion roll over her. Unshed tears filled her eyes as her call number was called and put out of service.

She stood in front of him, and I found myself coiled tighter than a snake ready to strike. David stood beside as if guarding me, and we watched her hand reach out to him. He knew she was there, he could feel her. The love the two of them shared crossed over the boundaries of the two worlds. I didn't have a chance in hell, I thought as I tried to breathe calmly.

We all felt her summons, yet she was so connected to Mitch that she didn't realize it. Once we interrupted her, she was pulled to the Maker. David and Montgomery phased back, and I stood and watched Mitch leave the cemetery.

I followed him home and then rode with him to the bar where he met up with Joe. Joe and I stared at each other over the dark bar where they sat. When Mitch got up to use the bathroom, Joe turned to me.

"Why are you here?"

I spoke to him from where I stood on the other side, "None of your damn business."

"It is my business, especially if it's damned. You might have gotten her, but he's coming to our side."

"Don't be so sure about that, Joe. If you think she's going to allow that, you're very wrong."

He threw his head back and laughed, "She's a young one, and there is nothing she can do to stop it. It will be years before she has the strength to fight my power, by then I will own his willpower."

I smiled, and his face lost some of its humor. "If that's what you think," I mocked. "In my opinion, I think you are about to have a run for your money."

CHAPTER 29 ~ COREY

The vibration was like nothing else I had ever felt and instantaneously I had the urge to follow it. I phased without trying and found myself in a bright area, not a room but more of an open space. Whiteness surrounded me so brightly that I blinked a few times to adjust to the light.

I explored the area visually, but I saw nothing but light. Peace floated around me, and I embraced the feeling after the emotions of the funeral.

A voice neither male nor female filled the area around me: "Welcome, my dear child."

"Thank you," I spoke softly even though I knew I would be heard without words.

"Normally, the Gardaí are not allowed the rein that you have been allowed. I am finding it interesting to see what you are already capable of."

"Why is that? Is that because of what everyone believes I am, special?"

A sound similar to a laugh bounced around me, making me glance over my shoulder. "You could say that. You appear to have abilities that many do not, but you must now focus on them and learn to use them to the best advantage. You will not be allowed to move down to the living arena again until you are ready. Then you will be assigned to your chosen ones."

"I thought I had already been assigned," I said, momentarily confused.

"There will be no more questions. For now, you will stay within the Realm and finish your training."

I nodded, not sure how to respond. Suddenly, anxiety washed through me at not being able to see Mitch. A rushing sensation flowed over me, and I was standing in my quarters alone.

The peace that I had absorbed only moments ago dissipated, and I found myself agitated. My feet paced the room restlessly. I felt like a cornered animal and wrung my hands in front of me.

If I couldn't leave the Realm, how was I going to see Mitch? Was he my charge? Maybe he wasn't the one I would be assigned to guide and protect. What if he wasn't and I never got to see him again?

CHAPTER 30 ~ MITCHELL

I went back to work two days later. I had tied one on after the funeral and spent a major part of the next day sleeping it off.

Back in the car after several days off, I felt like my life might get back to normal. If I could keep any thoughts of her out of my mind, then I might just make it through the day.

Driving around answering calls one after another became habit for me. I stayed to myself and just did my time. I wasn't interested in the normal banter and gossip that the other guys on the squad did on break times or between calls. I forced myself to focus on my job and tried to block everything else out.

Four weeks after the funeral, I found myself driving my motorcycle. I had no destination in mind and was surprised when I rolled up to the gates of the cemetery.

I stared up at the tall black metal doors standing open and welcoming on each side of the road for a long time. With both my feet planted on the ground, I gazed beyond the gates and tried to gather the strength to enter. Many times over the last month I had wanted to visit her grave, but I just couldn't find the willpower to do so.

With a deep cleansing breath, I lifted one foot off the ground to the foot peg and started to move through.

I had no problem finding her plot. The location would forever be ingrained in my head. I slowed and came to a stop at the closest location.

After turning the key off, the silence that met my eardrums was deafening. I sat staring up the hill. My glance fell on her small piece of land. Her gravestone had been delivered.

With a shake in my knees, I made the walk to her final resting place. I focused on the large gray marble marker. An angel statue was carved into the top of the stone, very fitting. The sod was now knitting itself back together.

"I never knew your name was Coralenna," I said softly. "I guess there were a lot of things I didn't know about you."

I gently placed my hand on the cold marble. The chill traveled through my fingertips, up my arm, and right to my heart.

I sank down to the ground, pulling my knees up slightly and resting my arms over them.

"You have a nice view from here." Her plot stood near the top of a hill and looked out over the vast area where marker after marker popped up from the land. Tall trees ran around the area, protecting the souls from the outside world.

"I miss you, Corey. Every day, I miss you so much. I can't seem to move on. I feel like I am frozen inside, like life has no meaning anymore." I turned back to the gravestone.

"No one seems to understand, especially Beth. She pesters me on a daily basis to talk to her, to open up and let out the emotions. She even suggested I go talk to a shrink." A blunt burst of laughter left my lips.

"She has no idea that no matter how much talking I do, I'll never get over you. I don't even know if I can stay with her, not after everything, not after you." I bowed my head.

"Why you, Corey? Why couldn't it have been me?" I whispered.

There was no answer, no feelings of her presence like there had been at her funeral. There was only silence, the soul-jarring echo of my own pain that I now lived with every day.

CHAPTER 31 ~ COREY

*T*ension spread through me so tightly that I felt I would explode. I phased down to the martial arts locker room. Inside my locker, I pulled out my dobok and dressed quickly. I needed something to focus on, some way to let out the frustration that filled me.

Walking into the dojang, I bowed at the flags before I stepped onto the floor and started to stretch. Images from the funeral plagued my mind with painful pictures. The expression on Mitch's face, the pain he felt, the tears he shed, and the words we spoke rattled around in my mind as I bent over and tried to loosen my legs.

I worked through my routines as soon as I felt limber enough and forced all thoughts out of my mind as I concentrated with all my energy on my forms. Over and over again I did them, moving slowly then faster, keeping my movements precise each time, holding the position longer than normal just to feel it deep within—but the memories kept barging through.

I moved on to work with the weight bag. Kick after kick landed on the bag. If I were still on Earth, my feet would have been swollen and red from the abuse they took. I punched hard, spun and landed one kick, then slid back and jumped forward to deliver another combination, one after another into the large black bag until my energy was depleted, and I could barely stand.

With my hands resting on my knees, I gasped for breath and wiped the sweat from my forehead with my sleeve.

"Feel better?"

I wasn't surprised that Brock was here. I had felt his presence a while ago and had ignored him. It had felt good to ignore him.

"Not really." I stood and put my hands on my hips, still trying to get my breathing under control.

"Let's take a walk on the beach," his voice was soft, and I studied him as he leaned back against the muted white wall as if he had no cares in the world.

I shook my head and turned away from him, "Not in the mood." I started toward the locker room.

"I'm not giving you an invitation, Coralenna," his voice deepened. I spun around to face him, immediately phasing to stand in front of him. His eyes enlarged, and his shoulders shifted back in surprise at my movement. His jaw clenched, and I realized he didn't like to be surprised. Score one for me.

"Stop calling me Coralenna. My name is Corey, and I don't want to go for a walk with you." I stared him down, anger blazing on my face. I wanted to take my frustration out on someone, and he had showed up just in time to take the brunt of it, whether he liked it or not.

The chuckle that escaped his chest infuriated me, and I was tempted to push him. With his arms crossed over his chest, he leaned in close to me. My line of sight was automatically drawn to his mouth, and I watched as his soft full lips parted the closer they got to me.

Four inches separated our mouths, the soft grazing of his breath flowed over my face as he spoke, "I don't care what you want right now, Corey." The way he said my name was a caress similar to the way his soft breath washed over my heated skin.

He glanced down at my lips. I felt his body responding to mine like they were talking to one another, and my mind began to war with my body.

I swayed slightly toward him, and he jerked back suddenly, realizing how close we were. He turned and started to walk towards the hallway while my body felt as if it had been denied something. I mentally chastised it for the feeling.

"Take a shower. Meet me at the beach. Your training starts now." He didn't turn as he walked out the door, the sound of his feet echoed on the wood floor as he walked down the hallway.

I wanted to stomp my foot and ignore him, but at the same time, I wanted to start my training. The faster I did that, the sooner I could go down again and see Mitch. With a deep sigh, I phased back to my quarters.

Standing under the hot water, I pictured Brock before me again. His full lips had been so close, it would have taken only the smallest movement to touch them. What would it be like?

I turned around and lowered the temperature of the water when my body grew warm. Cold shower, I needed a cold shower to wash that thought out of my head.

I didn't rush to finish my shower. I might not have a choice in meeting up with him, but I did have a choice in how long it took me to get ready.

After my shower, I took my time drying my long hair completely, then adding extra brush strokes to make it shine even more. I rubbed citrus lotion over my entire body, even getting in between my little toes. The thought of Brock putting the lotion here gave me goosebumps that I tried to rub away.

I pulled open the little closet in the bathroom, searching for nail polish. I smiled to myself as I realized that I now had an excuse for another thirty minutes or so. A girl needed to pamper herself once in a while, right?

After very cautiously painting my dainty toes a vibrant pink, I trimmed my cuticles and filed my fingernails, also adding the warm color to the nails there.

I sat back on the bed, leaning on the pillow to better allow my fingers and toes to dry. Funny, when I was alive, I never took the time to do this. I had never really cared about primping.

I told myself that I was only doing this to annoy Brock, not to make myself look better. After pulling on a pair of soft light blue Capri pants and a sleeveless pink silk blouse, I checked the mirror and decided I couldn't put it off any longer. Forgoing shoes, I left my quarters by way of the door, deciding that a walk would do me good and would kill some more time before I had to meet up with Brock.

I inhaled deeply when I stepped outside, filling my lungs with the sweet scents of the evening flowers. The soft colors of a glorious sunset filled the sky and a part of my essence at the same time. I made my way slowly to the beach, never taking my focus off the horizon and the sun slowly setting there.

I didn't need to search for Brock. I could feel his presence pass over me like a warm blanket on a cold day. I smiled to myself as I realized he was not exactly happy at my delay tactics.

I walked to stand beside him, his shoulders and back rigid. His arms were crossed over his chest, and the fists of his hands peeked out from under the heavy biceps.

As I stopped, I saw his nose flare slightly and he blinked rapidly for a moment. His hands clenched even more tightly, if that were possible.

"So what are we working on?" I stepped in front of him.

He glared at me, hot fire in the depths of his eyes. I fought to keep still as they took in my face and traveled slowly down the length of my body, burning me as they moved.

Did he just shiver? He turned his head back to the sunset after taking in my polished toes. I watched him shake his head.

"Can you feel my presence?" his voice was stilted as he spoke.

"What do you mean?" Did he want to know if I knew where he was or if I could feel the desire flowing from him towards me? I'd be honest with one, but there was no way I would admit the other.

"Did you know I was in the gym watching you?" he scowled at me for a moment before I answered him.

"Yes." I walked past him, nervous as he kept frowning at me. Maybe the desire wasn't him, maybe it came from me. Maybe he was like living guys and just lusted for a pretty face.

"How long was I there?" He stepped beside me and we started to walk in the sand.

I thought about it briefly, "I was working on the spinning back kicks and reverse punches when you arrived."

I saw him nod in my peripheral vision. "Good. You know when I am in the room, now do you think you could follow me?"

I was confused, "What do you mean?"

"I mean when I phase. Do you think you might be able to follow my energy pattern?" he raised his eyebrows as he asked.

I thought about it for a minute, "Maybe. Let's see."

"Concentrate on me." He stopped and turned. I stared into his face. How could I not concentrate on him? The light of the sunset highlighted the dark colors in his hair and made his skin glow a golden brown.

He stepped back, and I realized that I had been staring hard. "What?" I feigned innocence. "I'm concentrating on your energy." Really, I'm not staring at you and seeing just how beautiful you are in the fading light. I'm losing my freaking mind, I thought to myself.

"Coralenna, I'm going to phase someplace, someplace simple for you. A place that you have been to before and I want you to see if you can follow."

"Sounds easy enough," I smiled, ready to get started.

He grunted, "Yeah, maybe for you, but not for most people." With the words just out of his mouth, he disappeared from view. I focused on what I had felt coming from him. My body tingled, and I allowed the tingling to grow and pull me. I opened my eyes to see Brock standing in the large living room where I had visited when I first arrived.

I giggled happily, "I did it!"

He returned my amusement and said, "Good, let's try it again."

He disappeared from view, and I again allowed the tingling inside my body to pull me to him. This time, he was standing in the dojang in the center of the mats.

"Hey, you're not supposed to step on them with shoes on," I said when I found him.

"My bad. Again," and he was gone.

It became a game with him popping in and out of places I had been, my balcony, the garden, the weight room, and the beach. One time he phased to my bedroom, and I found him lying on my bed.

169

"You're lucky that when I follow you, I don't land in the same place that you do," I threw out to him playfully.

He grinned, "Yeah, that would be really bad, wouldn't it?" He chuckled deeply. "You have the hang of this, you know these places. Let's try places that you don't know."

Before I could respond, he was gone. I reached for him internally and found him. His signature was pretty easy to follow now. I allowed it to surge through me, but unlike before, strange colors and sensations tickled my insides this time as I moved to an unknown place.

I blinked to see Montgomery sitting on a couch, reading something. He smiled happily at me.

"Playing hide and seek?" he asked as I grinned back at him.

I hadn't thought about that, but we kind of were. "Yeah, I guess so. It's kind of fun."

I watched Montgomery close his eyes for a moment and his brow crinkled slightly, then he opened them again.

"Sorry, had to check in with a charge. He is having a rough time these days."

"Oh, I remember, you don't have to go down to help people." I sat down on the couch next to him and glanced up to see Brock lean against a doorjamb.

"Right, we don't always have to leave here. Eventually, when you get strong enough, you don't ever have to leave here. You can do it all inside your mind, although it is nice to visit the living arena and see what changes down there, technology moves so fast."

We both laughed and I turned to see that Brock was gone. I had not felt him leave. I spun around to see if he was behind me and reached out for him, but he was no longer in the room with us.

"Where'd he go?" I asked Montgomery.

"Isn't that your job to find out?" He quirked an eyebrow.

I focused and reached out for Brock, quickly finding his energy and allowing myself to follow.

I landed on a dark balcony that faced out over the gardens.

"Whose balcony is this?" I asked as I turned to the railing. Some of the flowers below seemed to glow in the darkness, a soft breeze floated around me, bringing their scent.

"Listen and you will know," he whispered as he stepped up beside me.

I stood still and listened, the night was quiet, but I could hear soft sounds coming from behind me. I turned to face the door, the sound of kisses and soft words reached me. A voice I knew quite well was saying something about doing it again. I felt a blush rise up on my cheeks.

"That's David!" I said in a rushed whisper. "Is he doing what I think he's doing?"

Brock grinned, "What, you think we don't make love in heaven?"

The heat in my face scorched my skin with his words. "Brock phase, please, come on. I don't want to stay here and be accused of being a Peeping Tom."

He chuckled quietly and phased away. I followed just as quickly, and we landed on a boat dock. The water was softly lapping against the wood underneath. Brock sat down, letting his feet hang over the edge. He patted the wood next to him, and I moved to sit.

"You have something against people making love?"

"Of course not, but I don't need to listen to them. People deserve their privacy, especially during intimate times like that."

"In this world, Coralenna, we celebrate. We share in these moments. Making love is a beautiful thing, much different than on Earth where it can be dirty. Here, it's perfect, not dirty, not something that people don't want to talk about or share. People here share it with others. It connects us, helps us be one, and makes us feel good."

"Are you saying people have sex with other people all the time, and there is nothing wrong with it?"

He studied the half moon, the light casting a glow on the side of his face that I could see, enhancing the sharp jut of his chin.

"There is nothing wrong in loving someone."

"In my world, you only love one person at a time." Mitch's face replaced the view of Brock before me, and I turned away from him.

CHAPTER 32 ~ BROCK

I saw Mitch coming back to his seat, and I phased back to the Realm. I immediately searched out Corey and found her fighting her inner demons in the martial arts room.

I watched her; she knew I was there. She was strong, physically and mentally. She would give Joe a run for his money if she could learn what she needed to know.

I didn't want her to be connected to Mitch, but I didn't want to lose him to the other side either. He was a good man, and he deserved better, much better. Maybe my own demons were fighting within me when Corey stopped and tried to catch her breath. Maybe that was why my voice came out so harshly and I all but demanded she do as I told her to do.

I was not surprised by her rebellion, and it gave me the time to calm my warring emotions. When she stepped up beside me on the beach, her citrus scent scorched my nasal passages and burned into my mind.

She had always loved that lotion. I had watched her apply it hundreds of times, but until this moment, I had never smelled it mixed with her perfect heavenly scent. If she never wore it again, I would never forget the incredible smell.

The training was more of a game. She caught on quickly, much more quickly than most, and before I knew it, she was easily following me from one place to another, relaxed and with a smile on her beautiful face.

Maybe that was why I landed on David's balcony. I wanted to see how she would react to the way we cared about people. Would she accept the openness that we shared here?

Thoughts of holding her and loving her grew more intense each time I saw her. The tightly-wound tension between us practically cracked with electricity when we stood inches apart.

Would she one day be able to love me? Or would I lose her before I'd even had her?

"There is nothing wrong with loving someone." The soft sounds of water lapped under the dock we sat on. I felt her almost playful mood shift as I spoke. I knew her thoughts went to him again.

"In my world, you only love one person at a time."

"This is your world now, Coralenna, you must accept that. Do you think it is not possible to love more than one person at a time?"

"Are you talking about emotional love or physical?" I saw her glance towards me, her feet swinging gently off the side of the dock.

"I don't know, both maybe."

"I believe in being faithful, Brock. If I love someone, I love only him. I give myself to only him." She grew quiet after she spoke, and I allowed her to reflect.

"Would it surprise you to know I feel the same way?"

Her feet stopped swinging, and she turned to me. I raised an eyebrow, waiting for her to answer.

She searched my face, and I felt the need to squirm under her scrutiny, but I held still.

Her answer was not what I expected, "No, it would not surprise me." She laughed, "Why such a look of shock?"

I chuckled with her, "I don't know. I guess I just expected you to think I was like everyone else."

The smile stayed on her face as she turned away.

"I'm not though, like everyone else," I grinned playfully.

She turned back to me, "I know, Brock, I can tell."

We both went back to silence and relaxed with the soft breeze and gentle sounds of the water.

"Have you ever loved someone so much that it hurt, Brock?" her calm voice broke the silence.

I couldn't keep from staring at her as I answered, "Yes."

"And did you know right down to the center of your being that she was right for you?" She met my gaze.

I swallowed the lump in my throat, "Yes."

"Were you married to her?" she tilted her head as she asked.

Somewhat relieved that she had not noticed my distress, I turned from her before answering. "No, I've never been married." I stood up, "Let's call it a night. You've had a rough day. Why don't you go rest? I promise to give you peace tonight, if you promise me you'll stay inside the Realm."

"Well, that's an easy promise." She stood up and dusted off her pants. "I've kind of had my wings clipped, so I can't leave even if I wanted to."

We shared a smile, and she turned to walk away. The sight of her hips swaying and her bare feet gently touching the wooden dock entranced me.

She turned a few steps down, "Brock, what happened with the woman you loved?" Her face was in shadows but so familiar to me that I could picture her speaking the words and the questioning look that would be on her face.

"Nothing yet," I cleared my throat, "I'm still waiting to see if she will love me back."

If my feet had not been stuck to the spot by fear, I would have walked to her and taken her then.

"Brock," her voice cracked on the breeze, "who is the woman?"

"Go rest, Coralenna, we have a lot to do tomorrow." I phased from the dock before she could question me any further. Part of me prayed she would follow me; demand to know who I was talking about, while the other part of me feared that she was not ready to hear the truth—that I loved her.

PART 5

The Return

CHAPTER 33 ~ COREY

"*I* don't want to know, I don't want to know, I don't want to know." I spoke the words almost like a chant over and over again as I made my way back to my quarters.

Brock's last words haunted me. I told myself he wasn't speaking of me —or could I be the one he was waiting to find out about?

With a muffled grunt, I punched the button on the inside of the elevator to take me to my floor, my emotions too conflicted to allow me to phase. I stood trying to see through the glass wall of the elevator, but with the darkness behind the glass, only my tense body was reflected back to me.

When the elevator binged, I spun around and slipped out the door just as it started to open, just barely sliding through sideways. The feeling that I was being chased tapped at my heels, and I moved quickly down the hall to my room.

At the front of my door, I stopped and stared at the door knocker. Once upon a time, my life had been equal, balanced, fulfilling. Once upon a time, I'd had the yin and the yang working side by side. Right now, it felt like the yang was seriously out of whack.

I pushed open the door and was afraid that I would find someone waiting for me on the other side. I listened to the quiet, the view to my balcony right in front of me: empty. I released a sigh, finally a chance to be alone.

Almost immediately I felt the weight of everything come to rest on my shoulders. I made my way to my bedroom and pulled out a soft, long T-shirt to wear. Climbing under the covers, I rested my cheek on the soft down pillow.

Silence echoed off the walls around me, not just in the room, but in my mind. There were no voices calling me, no feelings of sadness and pain.

Mitchell—the word filled the void as his face graced the back of my eyelids. My heart ached to see him. Are you dealing with this, Mitch? Are you still blaming yourself? Do you still miss me?

Memories of my last kiss with him settled into my mind, and I started to drift off to sleep.

CHAPTER 34 ~ MITCHELL

*N*inety-eight days…ninety-eight days ago, you left my world. The thought raced through my mind as I revved the throttle on my bike and drove faster on the highway.

When I wasn't working and the weather was at least somewhat decent, riding had become my new daily habit. The memory that I had never taken her for the ride she wanted stood forefront in my mind each time.

I would climb on the seat and rev the engine up, always pretending that she was seated behind me as I drove the curved mountain roads north of where I lived.

I put hundreds of miles on my bike with a memory sitting behind me, soft strong arms wrapped around my stomach, tight thighs pressed to my butt and hips.

She had trusted me. I had promised to keep her safe. I had broken that promise.

I pulled over to the side of the road, shut down my bike, and listened to the endless silence. Since the day of the funeral, I hadn't heard her voice in my mind or felt her presence. I was alone with my memories and my pain.

I stood at the top of an observation point, nothing but forest dotted the landscape in front of me. I pulled out my cell phone; our last text message conversation was still there. I rolled my finger over the message, reading the words one more time—not that I didn't already have them memorized. I'd read them a thousand times, but seeing the words on the screen reminded me that it had once been real.

Before putting the phone away, I glanced at the clock, 1:52. I slipped my phone back in my pocket and climbed onto my bike. My order would be ready when I returned.

I drove the forty miles back, allowing the wind to brush past me and suck at the memories that gushed like a swollen stream over large river rocks.

The small strip mall lay just outside the city I worked in. I parked my bike and made my way inside the florist shop. Since my first visit to her gravesite, I had been coming here every week and picking up a special order.

The bells jingled as I walked in. The tinkling of the metal on the glass had a magical sound, and I felt the grimace on my face loosen for just a moment.

"Officer O'Reilly, I was just thinking about you," the shop owner called out as she popped her head around the corner from the back room.

"Karen, I keep telling you to call me Mitch," I smiled as I walked to the counter. When I had come in here months ago and asked if she carried the spotted toad lily, she had looked at me with evident surprise on her face.

Surprise filled her features when she asked why I wanted this particular flower, and I quickly explained it was my friend's favorite. I had learned that about Corey during our twenty-question games on our in-car computers while we worked.

Tears misted in her eyes, and a small smile had crossed her lips when she'd mentioned there was only one other person who used to ask for those flowers and she had never hoped to have the occasion to order them again.

Since that day, she had made sure to get a small fresh supply each week for me. We never talked about where the flowers went or why, but she knew that I needed them to be gravesite ready without all the tissue paper and ribbons.

"I know, I know, but I have a hard time not respecting an officer of the law." She laughed as she walked to the cooler on the side of the shop. My arrangement lay on the top shelf, as always.

"I appreciate that, but I'm not on duty, so please just call me Mitch."

She nodded and laid the flowers on the counter. This week they were a little more purple with darker spots on the petals than normal. I reached out and gently felt the soft flower.

"I love the color of these Tricyrtis this week! The color is so rich-looking." Karen was always excited about her flowers.

"Yes, they are." I handed her the cash, the same amount each week, and picked up the flowers. "Thanks, Karen."

Her smile was hearty, "No problem, Mitch. I'll see you next week."

"See you next week," I called over my shoulder as I reached for the door handle.

Outside, I opened up one of my hard plastic saddlebags and slipped the delicate flowers into the space. I took care to close the lid so it would not pinch the flowers.

The ride to the cemetery was quick. I no longer stopped at the gate and braced myself. Now I roared right toward the lane that led to her resting place.

On the hill, her memorial stone stood proud in the late afternoon sun. Flowers in hand, I made my way to her plot.

The flowers from the week before had already been removed. The caretakers were now familiar with my schedule, they made sure the sad and wilted ones were gone when I came by with the next batch.

"Hi, Corey, how are you?" I stood in front of her stone, staring at it like I expected an answer. I sighed and set the flowers down gently at the base when I felt no response.

Dropping down to the grass, I sat cross-legged and pulled at some of the dark green blades.

"It's been ninety-eight days now. Ninety-eight days, man, I can't believe that." I shook my head and ripped up a handful of grass. I allowed the pieces to fall through my fingers back to the ground.

"I thought that it might start to get easier now, ya know? You've been gone for three months," I raised my knees up and wrapped my arms gently around them, "three long months."

"I can't seem to let it all go. Every day I remember what happened. I see you lying on the ground, not moving, and it's like it is happening all over again." I lifted my face to the sky. Soft, light, fluffy clouds moved slowly over the blue above me.

"I miss you, Corey. I don't know how to stop thinking about it. It consumes me. I can't even seem to do my job these days." I studied her headstone quietly for a moment.

"And that prick, Joe, do you know that he tried to get me to split some money he found on a dope dealer the other day? What a freaking idiot he is. We arrest this guy with a few baggies of crack on him, and he's got a little over four hundred dollars from his pocket. He wanted to peel off two hundred and split it with me, said no one would ever know." I shook my head.

"I don't understand him these days." I watched a vehicle pull along the lane near my motorcycle and turn the corner down another lane.

"Hell, I don't even understand myself," I mumbled. "I mean, I almost took the money. I'm not like that, you know that. It's just—" I closed my eyes, "it's just that I don't seem to care—about anything." I paused, thinking for a moment. "Maybe if I knew you were alright, maybe I could move forward." I took a deep breath, slowly letting it back out. "I doubt it. I don't think I will ever be able to move forward."

I sat thinking for a few more minutes. I could only feel close to her beside her grave. Sadly, a cold marble stone was the warmest part of my week.

When I stood up, I kissed my fingers and laid them on the stone. "I miss you."

When no feelings or words reached my soul, I lifted my hand, lowered my head, and turned away.

CHAPTER 35 - BROCK

The steam from my coffee cup reached my nose, and I inhaled the strong rich aroma. I took a sip, but it tasted bitter on my tongue. I held my cup out and poured it over my balcony to the ground far below.

I looked up, not to the sky but to the ceiling above me, the one where Corey's balcony blocked the sight of the sky directly above my head.

Of all the stupid things to say. I sighed and was about to go back inside when a figure running along the sand caught my eye: Coralenna.

I leaned my elbows on the railing, watching her as she dashed along the hard-packed sand next to the shore. Her arms were pumping hard, her legs strong and fast.She looked like she was trying to run from something. Was she running from me?

The urge to phase down and run beside her grew strong, but I resisted it. I needed to give her space. She would not want to see me right now. I knew that.

I turned back to my quarters, dropped off my coffee mug on the black granite countertop, and phased to David's quarters.

He was standing at the stove, stirring eggs. "Morning, Brock," he said without turning around.

I grunted and pulled out a stool.

"So how did that work out for you? Bringing Coralenna here, I mean." His left eyebrow quirked up.

"What do you think?" I picked up a paper napkin and began folding it into triangles.

David laughed and dumped his eggs onto a plate. I heard the toaster pop and watched him reach for his toast.

Once he was seated, he blew on his eggs and took a big bite. "I imagine she was rather embarrassed and surprised."

I snorted, "You could say that." I tossed the napkin to the counter and leaned back.

"So did it hurt or help? Did you guys connect?" He slurped some coffee from a mug that was about half full.

"I don't think it helped. Look, I need a favor." I tapped the fingers of my left hand on the counter.

He stopped chewing and raised both eyebrows. "Yeah?"

I avoided his face and turned my attention to my hand, I stopped my fingers from tapping. "I need you to hang with her for a while, help her train."

"That's your job." He started chewing again and scooped up another bite.

"Come on, David. She doesn't want to see me right now. I just need—" I shook my head.

"What? You just need what?"

I watched him take a chunk out of his toast and chew.

"I just need help. It seems like when I get around her, I just say the wrong things."

"The big old Brock needs help!" he laughed around the food in his mouth. "That's one for the books." He wiped his mouth with the napkin I had tossed down.

I climbed off the stool and walked to his kitchen window. I watched someone cutting some fresh flowers out in the garden.

I ignored his comment. "So will you?"

The scrape of his fork on his plate made the hair on my neck stand up for a second.

"Yeah, I'll help, but not for you. I'll do it for her."

I nodded, not sure if he saw it or not. "Thanks," I muttered before I phased down to the world below to busy myself with my charges.

CHAPTER 36 ~ COREY

*T*he sand felt good under my toes. The sun warmed me from the outside, and the energy I burned warmed me from the inside.

While the sleep had been restful, I still woke up feeling agitated. I never imagined that when I died I would feel anything but peace, but I felt more stressed these days than during my life.

I felt his presence as he landed beside me, quickly dropping into my pace. I glanced at him and nodded. My breathing was too heavy and quick for me to speak.

David's smile was fresh. The memory of the sounds I'd heard on his balcony the evening before flushed my face, and I pushed just a little bit harder.

We ran side by side, not saying anything for a good fifteen minutes. Finally, he slowed a bit, "Can we slow down? I'm getting a cramp. I just ate."

We slowed to a walk. The sound of the water rushing up on the shore matched our heavy breathing for a few moments. His hand cradled the side of his waist.

"So what are you running from today?"

I snapped my head to the side, narrowing my gaze at him. "Why do you think I am running from something?"

His smile grew, "You forget I have followed your training for several years. You only run when you are trying to get away from something."

"Yeah, well you're wrong. I woke up with a lot of energy. I just wanted to work some of it out." I wiped a few drops of sweat from the side of my face. "Why are you here?"

"What? You don't like the company?" He acted hurt, placing his hand over his heart.

I chuckled quietly, "No, I don't mind your company. I'm just wondering if Brock sent you to check on me." I glanced his way and saw him direct his attention out over the water.

"He had other things to do. He asked if I would help you train for a while."

I muttered under my breath, "Yeah, I bet."

"Hey, don't shoot the messenger." He contemplated me for a moment, "He thought you might want a break from him."

I stood beside him and shrugged, "Yeah, sure. Sure I need a break from him." Why did those words taste sour in my mouth?

"So what has he been working on with you?" We turned to start the long walk back to our building.

"I was learning to follow him. Hide and seek Montgomery called it."

"How'd you do with that?"

I laughed, "Pretty good. Once I figured out how to find his energy pattern, I found it easy to do."

The laughter that came from him was so full of joy, "I'm not surprised. Everything is easy for you."

The image of tears on Mitch's face came to mind, "Not everything."

David stood beside me and reached out to touch my arm, "Coralenna, I know it's hard. It's hard to leave the living world behind, but it will get easier."

"When?"

"I don't know. Maybe it is just harder for you because you remembered it all so quickly and you were able to go back and see the people you cared about when the pain was fresh." His hand rubbed up my arm, the warm feelings of friendship and caring traveling into my heart and mind.

"Most of us don't remember for a long time, by then we have been in training for a while, and we have come to terms with our death. When we are finally able to leave the Realm, our loved ones have learned how to deal with our loss and have moved on."

I don't want him to move on, I almost cried out.

"You need to let Mitch go, Corey. He has a life, a family. He needs to move on with that."

I scrunched my eyelids tightly closed to fight back the tears that threatened, "I know."

"You'll see him again, and I bet when you do, he will be putting his life back together and thinking positive thoughts about the memories you shared." He cupped my cheek, and I leaned into his hand.

"Thanks, David," I smiled tearfully up at him and he pulled me into a hug.

After a minute, he leaned back, holding onto the top of my arms, "So, you want to see if you can follow me?"

"Try to lose me!"

He flicked my nose with his finger, "Okay, here it goes." He phased away quickly. Taking the feel of his energy inside my body, I searched for it. I found it easily and followed, landing in my bedroom.

David was walking into my bathroom.

"Um, David," I called out to him as I heard him turn the shower on, "what are you doing?"

David grinned as he walked back into the room, "Shower first, and then we will play. You need one after your run." He waved his hand under his nose and scrunched up his face.

"Are you trying to say I stink?" I lifted my arm and sniffed, "Whoa, okay, shower then play."

"I'll meet you on your balcony when you are done. I'm gonna go grab one myself," he turned as he was walking out of my room, "unless you want to conserve water?" He hiked up his eyebrow mischievously.

I laughed, "Yeah, like that would go over well with someone."

David matched my laughter, "Yeah, you're right. Brock would probably have a fit. See you in a little while." Before he reached the door, he was gone.

I walked into the bathroom and stopped in front of the sink thinking about what he had just said. Why would he bring up Brock's name?

"Like I care what Brock thinks," I called out to the mirror as I pulled my T-shirt over my head. I don't care, do I?

CHAPTER 37 ~ MITCHELL

*W*ith dread, I knocked on the door frame of my chief's office.

He lifted his head from the papers he was holding, his gray eyes meeting mine over his reading glasses. "Come in, Officer O'Reilly, I've been expecting you."

I entered, trying not to appear nervous. Normally, it was rare to get summoned to the chief's office. Unfortunately, this was the second time in a month for me.

"Close the door and have a seat," he called out as he shuffled his papers and put them aside.

I closed the door and walked to the beat-up old leather chair in front of his large mahogany desk.

"You wanted to see me, sir," I said as I sat down, my ankles crossed, my back straight and stiff.

His face was tight, his lips pursed as he assessed my face and body. I tried to hold a blank expression on my face, the one we use on the street so people couldn't read our thoughts.

His hands held his reading glasses, and he tossed them to the desk. I watched them bounce once and slide over the desk blotter.

"I didn't expect to have to call you back into my office after our last conversation."

A pregnant pause ensued between us. "I didn't expect to be called back, sir."

He leaned on his desk, resting his elbows on the wood. "Then can you tell me why I just received another complaint on you?"

I tried to keep the embarrassment from warming the skin on my face. I knew what he was talking about, how could I not?

I considered my hands folded in my lap for a second as if they might have the right answer, "I'm sorry, sir. I just got a little frustrated."

"Frustrated? You call slamming a kid up against the wall and calling him a raging asshole, then telling him he should have kept his dick in his pants if he didn't want the responsibility of raising a kid being a little frustrated?" He shook his head and picked up a pen. He leaned back in his chair again and clicked the lid of his pen on and off for a moment. I listened to the tic-tic of the cap, watching his fingers move back and forth slightly.

"What's going on with you, Mitchell?" he asked sternly but quietly.

I glanced up from his pen to his face, looked away and shrugged.

I felt his sigh from across the room, "Is this about Officer Hamilton?"

My stare shot back to his. "No," I answered tersely.

He regarded me with a tight expression. "Somehow I don't believe you. You've been with us for over three years with not a mark on your record, but now your performance has gone down, and we've had two complaints on you this month. Your sergeant is worried about you. Hell, I'm worried about you."

"I'm sorry, sir. I'll do better," I replied, hoping that would be the end of it. My feet shifted apart, ready to stand and leave if he said I could.

"How are you dealing with her death?"

My throat tightened when I tried to respond, my swallow more pronounced. He glanced at my throat, not missing a beat. "I'm dealing."

"I don't think you are." He crossed his left leg over his right at the ankle and leaned back further in his chair. "See, I've heard the rumors. I know that you were involved with her."

"I wasn't sleeping with her, Chief," I blurted out, angry at the turn in the conversation.

"I didn't say you were, Mitch. Whether you were having a physical or emotional relationship has nothing to do with it. You cared about her. You watched her die. I know that it has affected you."

I visually explored his office, unable to meet his stare or deny my feelings.

"Do I need to send you for counseling?"

I shook my head, "No, sir."

The room grew quiet. "It's been five months since the incident. You need to move forward. You still have a long career in front of you, and if you keep going the way you are going, then you are going to lose that. Do you understand?"

We focused on each other, "Yes, sir." My anger was bubbling under the surface, barely leashed. He had called it an incident—an incident!—like it was just another stupid routine call. I locked my jaw down, grinding my teeth.

"Just so I make myself clear, I'm going to allow you to deal with this a little longer on your own. If I get another complaint against you, or your sergeant tells me your performance is not coming back up to par, I will," he paused for effect, "put you on suspension and require you to attend counseling."

He leaned forward for emphasis, "Do you understand me, Officer O'Reilly?"

I relaxed my jaw and cleared my throat so I could speak, "Perfectly, sir."

"Fine. Now get out of my office and don't come back here like this again."

I pushed up on the armrests of the chair, only too happy to be leaving his office, "Yes, sir. Thank you."

As I reached the door, the chief cleared his throat, "And, Mitch."

I was almost free. I blinked twice before I turned to face him.

"You need to let her go. You have a family, here and at home, that needs you."

My voice would not have worked if I had tried, so I merely nodded to him and opened the door, stepping quickly out of his office and walking to the locker room.

Inside, I rested my head on the cold gray metal. Five months—if I can't get past this in five months, can I get past it in five years?

My fist met with the steel door of my locker, the sound echoing through the room to my ears alone.

Corey, damn it, Corey, I miss you so much.

CHAPTER 38 ~ BROCK

I felt the weight of his fist as it met the hard metal. I stood with my arms tightly crossed over my chest, leaning back on the opposite side of the locker room.

I wasn't supposed to be here, but I couldn't stay away from him. He wasn't dealing with this very well, and I dreaded thinking about Corey coming back to find him like this.

It would be only a matter of time before his voice would call out to her and she would once again hear it. None of us knew when, but I knew that her time was coming.

The Maker would send her to help him. Mitch was falling hard in the wrong direction, and I knew that the Maker did not want to lose this man to the other side. I didn't either.

I was so tempted to reach out to him and comfort him, but I knew if I did, the punishment that I had already been dealt would become more severe. I had promised to stay out of it, to allow Coralenna do what she must do, even if it destroyed her in the process.

I winced as Mitch slammed his locker shut and walked towards the door, just as it opened from the other side. I stood straighter, tensing.

"Hey, Mitch, how did it go with the chief?" Joe asked as he walked into the room, unsnapping his gear belt.

"Just freaking lovely," Mitch grunted at Joe's back.

Joe laughed and turned towards me, the evil sneer on his face as our eyes met angered me enough that I wanted to fall the distance to the living arena and punch him in the face.

"You wanna go grab a beer?" Mitch asked as he washed his hands.

"Sure. You look like you can use it."

Mitch's laugh was almost painful, "Yeah, I can." He dropped his paper towel into the trash.

"Anything to help a friend," Joe said as he dropped his duty belt into his locker. "Give me ten to shower and change, and I'll meet you at Harry's."

Mitch was opening the door when he threw out his response over his shoulder, "Fine."

"You going to stand there and watch me change or follow him around for your girlfriend?" Joe said as the door closed behind Mitch. "Hmm, ironic that you both love her. I wonder which one she will choose."

"You know nothing about it."

He pulled off his shirt. "I might know more about it than you think. Obviously, I must be doing my job and making you nervous if you would risk watching over him."

"Whatever, Joe." I phased before he could respond with another snide comment. He was right, I was concerned.

I landed in the common room of our building just moments before Montgomery joined me.

"You've been hiding," he said with amusement as he sank to the couch and leaned back, crossing his legs out in front of him.

"No, I haven't." I sat on the arm of the opposing couch, crossing my arms.

He laced his hands behind his head, "And you were just with him."

I stared down at his relaxed but intense position. "I was just checking on him." I swung my foot slowly back and forth.

"And how is he doing?" he asked, genuinely interested.

"Not good. Joe is moving in on him, and Mitch hasn't let go of her at all. It's making him easy game."

"Is it really that bad?" concern etched his voice.

I nodded, "Yeah, it's that bad." I stood up and dropped full onto the couch, slouching back. "I don't know, maybe I made a mistake by taking Coralenna so soon. Maybe I should have allowed it to take its course."

"What do you mean, 'Taking me too soon'?" Coralenna appeared in the room just as I spoke the words.

Montgomery and I exchanged quick glances. "Nothing, we weren't talking about you."

"Yes, you were, Brock, I heard my name. What did you mean by taking me too soon? When I first got here a few people made reference to that."

She stood defiantly in front of me, arms crossed. I wasn't surprised she didn't forget the remarks someone had made when she'd entered the Realm. "Wasn't it you that told me lying was a sin?" Anger vibrated in her tone.

I turned to Montgomery for help, he shrugged, "Might as well tell her."

I stared at him like he had two heads, my mouth slightly parted. Did he have any idea how bad this was about to turn?

"Yeah, might as well tell me." She straightened her back further.

What the heck was I supposed to tell her? I tried to find words that would make it sound less horrible. Sorry I took you because I wanted you to be here with me. Yeah, that was not going to work, but that wasn't the only reason.

"Speak, Brock, I'm waiting."

I stood up and faced her, her pulse was beating fast in her neck, she was nervous.

"Have a seat, Corey." I stepped away from the couch to allow her my spot.

"No, thank you, I'm fine. Speak." She tapped her toe. "What do you mean about taking me too soon?" She actually air quoted the taking-me-too-soon part with her fingers.

I continued to watch her. She held my gaze, unwavering. My heart sped to match hers.

Montgomery slapped his hands down onto his lap, expelling a loud breath. "Coralenna, dear, Brock only means that he brought you home just a short time before you were actually supposed to come home."

Her head snapped towards him, her eyes moving into slits as she did. "Do you mean I wasn't supposed to die?"

"Yes, well, no. You were supposed to die, just not that day." My anxiety caused the words to rush out of my mouth.

Her neck twisted back to face me, "What do you mean, I wasn't supposed to die that day! You took me away from my life before my time?" Her voice rose as she spoke.

"Corey, look, it's not what you think." I stepped closer, my hands out and palms up to plead with her.

"Not what I think? You took me away from my life, the people I love. You took me away from Mitch! Why?"

I stared at my feet.

"Why, Brock?" she shouted.

"Coralenna, calm down," Montgomery stood up and reached for her, she jumped back from him. "Don't touch me, Montgomery; I'm just as mad at you."

He put his hands up to ward off her anger and stepped back.

"How dare you! Why did you do it, Brock?" She crossed over to me, stopping inches in front of me. "Why, Brock? Did you think if you took me away from Mitch, I might just love you?"

I swallowed, how close but so far away she was from the truth. "Corey, listen," but she didn't. She spun around and stalked away.

She stopped when she reached the door, "If that's what you thought, Brock, well then it will be a cold day in hell before that happens."

I watched her stiff back walk out of the room.

"Well, that went just dandy," Montgomery muttered as he flopped back to the couch.

I sat down, pushing my head into the palms of my hands as my elbows rested on my knees. Swiping my face hard, I said, "What the hell am I going to do now?"

He shook his head, "I have no clue." We were both quiet for a time, "I guess you will just have to give her a chance to calm down and then go speak to her. You are going to have to tell her the truth."

I stared at the oak floor. "I should have done that before."

"I won't disagree with you there. Let me go find David and have him check on her. I doubt she will want to see me either right now."

God only knew if she would ever give me the chance to talk to her again, or even try to explain. I watched him phase and dropped my face back into my hands, a tightness in my chest I had not felt for eight years.

CHAPTER 39 ~ COREY

*T*hat arrogant SOB! I screamed inside my head. How could he do that? How could he take my life away before it was supposed to be over? Who made him God?!

I phased to my quarters, stalking the room like a tiger about to go mad. Minutes later, I phased to the beach, but the sound of the water did not calm me. I kicked at a wave as it came rushing in.

"Why?" I shouted up at the sky.

Tears threatened as I felt David arrive beside me. I spun on him.

"Did you know? Did you know he was going to do it?" I accused him without thought.

He put his hands up defensively, "No, Corey, I didn't know anything about it. I swear. I was surprised when you showed up early, but that's a good thing."

"A good thing?" I shouted again and clapped my hands in front of me in fake joy. "Please tell me how that's a good thing! Please explain to me how taking me away from my life *before* I was supposed to leave was a good thing, David."

Angry tears broke through the walls and streaked down my face. When David pulled me into his arms, I was stiff. As his hand rubbed over my back and his compassion raced through my body, I softened and leaned into him.

"Let it out, Coralenna, go ahead and let it out." He whispered into my ear and, as if his words opened the door to the pain, I grabbed hold of him and sobbed into his chest.

For a long time, he held me, rubbing my back as the pain of what I had learned forged through me. He kissed the top of my head when the tears started to slow, squeezing me more tightly.

"I don't understand why he did it." His strong chest muffled my voice.

He pulled back and searched my face, wiping a tear from my cheek. "I have known Brock for a long time, and he always does things for a reason. They might not seem like good reasons at the time, but they end up being good ones later." He smiled, "He wouldn't be here if they weren't. You have to give him a chance, Coralenna. He does care about you."

I snorted, "Yeah, isn't that why he did it? Because he cares so much for me that he wanted me for himself?"

"Look, it might seem like that, and I can't tell you exactly how he feels, because I have never felt what he does, or knew the pressure of what that feeling would do, but I can tell you that what he did was to protect you and the ones you love," he hesitated, "including Mitch."

I was confused. Why would Brock feel pressure about the way he felt? "What do you mean about feeling pressure? That doesn't make sense." I stepped back from him and wiped my hands down my face, removing the last of the wetness.

David considered the gentle waves for a moment, "Come on, let's get a change of scenery and talk for a few minutes. Maybe it is time someone told you a bit more about what lies ahead for you here."

David took my hand and pulled me through to the gardens. We sat down on a teak bench next to a small fountain. I inhaled the vibrant scent that arose in the air.

A scent I recognized very well had me searching the area. I saw the spotted toad lilies in the dirt bed a few feet away and could not contain the smile they brought to me.

Karen had always kept a fresh supply of them just for me. Once a week I would purchase them, and I would display them on my kitchen table or sometimes in my bedroom. David's voice beside me broke me from my memory.

"Have you heard us mention a connection?" David asked from beside me.

I turned to see him sitting back with his elbows resting up on the back of the bench. "Yes," I replied.

"It is said that there are those few that would find each other and connect in such a way that no forces could tear them apart, and that, together, they could fight through anything and protect all those that fall under their care." He turned his head from where he was scanning the gardens to me, waiting for me to absorb what he said.

"And that has to do with me how?" I asked quietly.

The fountain gurgled as water bubbled up and spilled over into the pond below. He watched it as he mulled over his words.

"It is believed that you and Brock are one of those couples."

His words echoed in my head over and over again, and then I laughed. David watched me, but I couldn't see him through the tears in my eyes and the fact that I had thrown my head back to expel the sound to the sky.

I grabbed my stomach as the laughter continued so strong my stomach muscles were cramping. David said nothing. He just watched me.

When I was finally able to speak coherently, I wiped the moisture from my face, "You're kidding, right?"

His eyebrows rose, "Why is that so funny?"

"What's not funny about it? I mean we are talking about Brock and me here. How could I have a connection to him? We are nothing alike; he doesn't even have any compassion!"

"Oh, you are wrong about that, Coralenna. You just haven't seen it. Since you got here, you two have been walking on eggshells around each other."

"We have not!" I contested.

"Really?" he chuckled. "You two avoid coming in contact constantly. Do you know how many times I have seen him almost reach out to you and you to him, but you both step away from each other. Both of you are afraid of what could be there."

"Or what could not be there," I threw back. "Who knows if that story is even true? I don't have the kind of feelings for Brock that he does for me. Who knows if I ever would?"

"You might not have them now, but you have only known him for a short time. He has known you for years."

I leaned back on the bench, "So what am I supposed to do about it? Am I supposed to pretend that I care about him for this strange connection you talk about?"

"No, there will be no pretending. When it happens, there won't be any pretending about it."

I turned to him, "If it happens."

The side of his mouth tipped up, "Right, if it happens."

"What am I supposed to do in the meantime?" I heard a frog croaking someplace nearby and tried to search out the source but failed to find it.

"Maybe you need to try talking to Brock. Ask him to tell you why he did what he did, and how he really feels."

"What if he won't answer me?"

He reached over and took my hand, gently squeezing it, "He will. He knows it's time to tell you everything."

I squeezed his hand back, and we lapsed into silence. We were just two content friends keeping each other company, each lost in thought.

I didn't know where his thoughts were, but mine toiled with what this connection was that I was supposed to share with Brock and what that would mean for my feelings with Mitch.

CHAPTER 40 ~ MITCHELL

*J*ust like almost every other night I was off, I found myself sitting on a barstool. Sometimes the whole squad came, sometimes just a friend or two. A few times, I sat alone.

Tonight Joe sat beside me and two shots of whiskey had just been slid across the bar to us, our third set of the night. I eyed the caramel-colored liquid. I hated the taste, but it numbed the pain. I reached out and grabbed it, lifted, and threw it back without a second thought.

It burned on the way down, but the burn felt good—like punishment.

"You know what you need?" Joe said from the stool beside me just before he downed his shot.

I watched him wince as the liquor traveled down. "What?"

He lifted up two more fingers to the bartender, ordering another round of shots for us, and then faced me, "You need to get laid."

"Get real, Joe."

He laughed, "I'm serious. When is the last time you had sex? When Corey was alive?"

"We never had sex, Joe, our relationship wasn't like that. I told you that before."

I watched him shrug out of the corner of my eye, "Okay, so if you didn't sleep with Corey, when is the last time you had sex? 'Cause I know you haven't had sex with your wife."

I snapped my attention to him, "How the hell would you know about my sex life?"

"Because, brother, Beth told me. She said you haven't touched her in over a year." He slapped me on the back, "Dude, what are you waiting for, virgin status again?"

"Why would she even talk to you about that stuff?" I picked up the new shot, tossed it back and then chased it with my beer. I motioned for another one.

I should be pissed that she was saying anything to him about our relationship, but lately I just didn't care what she did.

"Man, she's worried about you. She calls me once in a while to ask how things are and to see if I can talk to you, again."

I stared at him, "She does not."

He smiled, "Yes, she does. She's not stupid, man; she knows you cared about Corey."

"I didn't say she was." I took a long drink of my new beer and found another shot sitting next to it. I twisted it around in my fingers. "I don't think I can stay married to her, not after this, not after everything."

"Then maybe your marriage really is over, but Mitch, man, it's been six months since Corey died. You gotta let that shit go."

Six months, one hundred and eighty days since she lost her life at my hands. I lifted the shot and drank it fast. It didn't burn as much now.

"Look, you don't want to go home to your wife, fine. Take a look around you, dude, all these sweet treats! There are a whole lot of badge bunnies just waiting to be frisked," he leered at me.

"You are one dirty son of a bitch," but even as I said the words, I scanned the room.

He was right; there were quite a few women around. I examined them as closely as I could, there were a lot of young women who wanted nothing more than a quick meeting and another notch in their handcuffs.

A blonde leaned back in her seat and winked at me, I stared back, my vision slightly bleary as the whiskey started to take effect. I turned back to the bar.

"That's not me."

He laughed, "Not you? It's every man! Who doesn't want a good piece of ass for one night? You are already thinking about leaving Beth, so why not start off the rest of your life with a quickie?" He clapped me on the back.

I lifted up the new shot glass that had shown up in front of me. I was drinking more than I normally did, but tonight was different. Tonight was the six-month anniversary of her death and maybe the ending of my marriage.

I threw the drink back and almost spit it over the bar when Joe clapped me hard on the back, "She's coming over here."

I swallowed and checked over my shoulder. The blonde was approaching, a long-neck bottle held loosely in one hand, her other slipped into the top pocket of her tight jeans. I watched her approach. For the first time in a long time, I felt something stir inside me.

"Hey, Joe, who's your friend?" Her voice had a sultry quality to it that matched the seductive eye makeup she wore.

"Hello, Rebecca!" Joe said too loudly beside me. "This is my partner, Mitch. Mitch, my man, this here is my sweet tempting friend, Rebecca."

"Hi, Mitch," she held her hand out to me, and I turned to take it. Her grip was soft, a little too soft for my liking, but the pout on her mouth when she said my name had me ignoring that.

"Hello, Rebecca." I pulled my hand away and watched Joe stand up.

"Rebecca, here, save my seat, I just saw someone come in and I want to go say hello." I saw him wink at her. I blinked and found my vision shifted slightly from the amount of alcohol I had consumed.

She slid easily onto the stool, turning her body towards me, her leg rubbed up against mine. I thought about shifting away, but I was becoming hungry for the touch of someone. I knew in the back of my mind that the whiskey was causing my hormones to flare, but I ignored the wavering thoughts.

"So, how do you know Joe?" I asked before lifting my bottle up to my lips. She watched me drink, her focus on the lip of my bottle. She licked her own full lips. The stirring I felt before was becoming an urge inside of me.

"He helped me out with some things. I used to be hardcore into drugs, he showed me the light, helped me get cleaned up. He's been a good friend." She smiled and drank from her bottle. I watched her swallow, visualized my mouth on her throat as she did. I shifted in my seat. "So you're his partner, huh?" She set her bottle on the bar, leaning forward so her legs pressed tighter to mine.

"Yeah." Even as I drank more, my throat felt parched, I finished my beer and set the bottle down with a thud on the hard glossy wood.

"So what's it like working with Joe?" she asked and casually laid her hand on my leg. The muscles bunched on their own under her touch, she squeezed gently.

"It's never boring." I picked up the new bottle the bartender had just delivered and took a swig.

"No, I guess it wouldn't be." Her hand ran up my leg a few inches. The lack of fulfillment in my life took full notice at the movement.

She used her other hand to lift her beer to her lips, a drop ran past her lips and down from the corner of her mouth. Her tongue slipped out to catch it with a little giggle. I took a deep breath.

"You wanna get out of here, Mitch?" she said softly, peering at me under her thick lashes.

I turned away from her and scanned the bar. Joe was standing on the other side talking to some guys from another department. He raised his bottle to me and mouthed, "Go for it" before smiling.

Screw it.

I turned back to Rebecca, "Yeah, let's get out of here." Tipping my beer back, I guzzled about two thirds of the bottle and then set it down on the bar, stood up, and waited for her to get off her stool.

I walked out behind her, not looking at Joe, but feeling like he was watching me and laughing.

When we stepped out the door, the cooler night air wrapped around us and she slid her hand into mine. She pulled me to the side of the building, one of the lights was out in the parking lot, putting us in deep shadows.

She turned suddenly and pushed me up against the building, not hard, but forcefully enough that it startled me.

Her lips connected with mine a brief moment later and her tongue pushed for entry. All at once, the need to feel, feel anything, rushed over me and I wrapped her in a strong embrace, taking from her what I needed, what my body craved.

She threw her arms around my shoulders, pulling me close, deepening the kiss even more. I spun her around, pushing her against the wall. I felt the growl she released inside her chest. I swallowed it, I wanted it, and right that second, I needed it. My hands went to her butt, and I lifted her up. She wrapped her legs around my waist, pushing against my hardness.

She pulled her mouth back and tipped her throat to me, I nipped, bit, and sucked on the soft flesh all while she softly moaned and rubbed harder against me.

Mitchell, no!

I froze like someone had poured a bucket of ice cold water down my back.

Rebecca pushed against me, "Come on, Mitch, baby, come on, don't stop now."

Mitch, don't do this.

How much had I had to drink tonight? I pulled back from Rebecca, almost dropping her to the ground before she could get her feet under herself.

"What's wrong?" Surprise and a little anger were evident in her voice.

I swallowed. What the hell am I doing? I shouted into my own mind.

Go home, Mitch, you need to sleep.

Why was I all of a sudden hearing Corey's voice in my mind? Was it my subconscious trying to protect me? Was I going crazy?

I stepped back from Rebecca, "I'm sorry. I can't do this." I wiped my hand over my face, trying to clear my head. What the hell had I been about to do?

She stepped closer to me, grabbing the front of my shirt, "Come on, Mitch. I know you want me, just let go, take me. I'm here for you."

I grabbed onto her hands and yanked them off. "No, Rebecca, I'm sorry, but I can't do this."

I spun around and made my way to my car, digging into my pocket to grab my truck keys. I climbed into my cab, wiped my mouth with my forearm and put the key into the ignition after several failed attempts with my shaking hands.

CHAPTER 41 ~ BROCK

I sat in the sand, lifting handfuls of it up and letting it sift slowly through my fingers. I had screwed up. I knew it.

I had to find a way to talk to Coralenna and get her to understand. I froze when her legs materialized right before my downcast eyes.

I blinked. The hurt that was visible in her expression sent pain directly to my heart. I had caused that. I was afraid to speak.

"You need to explain to me why you did what you did, Brock."

"I will. I know you deserve the truth," I said solemnly.

She crossed her ankles and sank to the soft white sand in front of me, Indian-style. She watched me.

"I'm sorry, Coralenna. I never meant to hurt you. I was trying to protect you, protect all those that you loved and those that loved you."

"What were you trying to protect everyone from?" she tipped her head sideways, her hair swinging gently away from her face. I wanted so much to caress her cheek and feel her soft skin.

I swallowed, "The day I brought you home, you were supposed to have been hit by that car."

"Okay," she nodded sluggishly.

I inhaled slowly, "Everyone is right, the original plan for your life was for you to continue living, but I made the decision to bring you home."

She appeared to be trying to control her emotions, forcing herself to take a deep breath. When she released the air, she opened her eyes, "Why did you," she cleared her throat, "why did you do it?"

Finally free to tell her the truth, I let the words rush out of my mouth, "Because if I had not, you would not have had a life. Corey, you were supposed to live in a coma for months before you finally succumbed to death."

She blinked and sat up straighter, "A coma? But maybe I would have woken up?"

I shook my head quickly, "No. The plan for your life was for you to live for a short time after your accident, but you would have died before you woke up."

She looked at everything but me. Finally pushing up from the sand, she moved away from me and stared out over the water, her arms crossed tightly over her body. I saw her shiver.

I stood up slowly, dusting the sand from the back of my pants.

"You didn't tell me why you did it," her voice cracked on emotion.

"I did it so you and the ones you loved wouldn't suffer. You would have lain there, conscious enough to know what was happening, but unable to communicate. Your family would have stood by your side and watched you struggle to fight for a life you would never have. Their constant prayers would have gone unheeded, and everyone would have suffered far longer than they did."

She absorbed the words. A tear slipped down her cheek, but she swiped it away before it could reach her chin.

"So you didn't do this for yourself?" she peered over her shoulder at me.

I shook my head forcefully, "No. I did it for you. I knew you would hate lying there knowing the people you cared about were suffering. I did it for you." I stepped up behind her, close enough that the light scent of sunflowers floated over my senses. I wanted to touch her. Would now be a good time?

She stepped away, "Don't touch me, Brock."

Her words sliced me.

"I'm not ready for that. I know about the connection. David explained it to me." She turned to face me, dropping her arms to her sides.

Well, it seemed David had been rather busy. I guess I shouldn't give him a hard time; he did talk her into coming to me to talk.

"Okay, I won't." I slipped my hands into the pockets of my cargo shorts.

"Do you believe in it?" A soft gust of wind carried strands of her hair into the breeze and over her face. I wanted to push them back behind her ear, but clenched my hands instead.

"Yes, I do believe in it," I swallowed around the tightness in my throat.

"Why? How can you believe in it? How can you know that with one touch we could be connected so strongly that nothing could come between us?"

I stepped closer to her, staring down into her beautiful features. "Because that's what we do, we believe. I was told about this connection years ago, just after meeting you. At first I didn't believe it. I didn't want to be connected to anyone. I had been ruthless when I lived, not caring about people or what I did to others, yet, somehow over the years, I started paying more attention to the good things that you did, how hard you worked for others." I turned away.

She walked around me to stand in front of me again, "And?"

"And I saw the good you did. It made me think a lot about things I had done before I'd died. Seeing how good you were, how happy you could be helping others made me want to be more like you." I tossed my hands up in the air, "I have no idea how I got here, how I got to be a Garda, not after my track record, but when I watched you, I had to believe that the reason was because of what we would have one day. I had to believe that."

I watched her face as her gaze traveled over mine. She searched it, hunting for some great clue or maybe just trying to see if I gave her a straightforward answer. I had told her more than I had planned, but I needed to be honest. If Corey was to trust me, then I had to be honest with her.

"How did you die?" she asked almost casually.

I blinked and was confused for a moment, "I had an inoperable brain tumor."

"Did you suffer long?"

"No." I cleared my throat.

"How long would I have lived?" she asked softly.

"Four months, you would have lived for four more months."

We watched each other, the gentle winds tugging at our clothing, pulling her hair out and around her head. My hand slipped from my pocket, slowly moving towards her.

Then we both felt it. Her body vibrated deep within. She blinked rapidly and stepped back from me. "I'm being summoned."

"Corey, wait!" but I was already too late, she had vanished. "I'm sorry, Coralenna." I whispered into the space she had just emptied.

CHAPTER 42 ~ COREY

I listened to David, and then he left to allow me to think. Maybe I was being unfair to Brock. Maybe he did have a good reason for doing what he'd done.

There was only one way to find out, so I reached out for him. I was so attuned to his energy that as I moved to stand before him, I felt his pain internally, like my own.

I sat, afraid to hear what he would tell me, but knowing that I needed to hear the truth.

To learn that I would have been left as a lifeless body while I was able to still process what was happening around me left me chilled. I stood up suddenly, the need to know I was in control strong.

Brock was right. I would have hated knowing my family was praying for me and watching me suffer. I couldn't fault his decision even though I hated it, hated knowing that I had been ripped away from the people I loved earlier than I should have been.

Maybe I could have found a way to say goodbye, though. That thought surged through my mind as Brock stepped up behind me. As he moved, I remembered the connection that David had explained, and I stepped away.

"Don't touch me, Brock." I felt the sting of my words. The only way to make him understand them was to explain that I knew about the connection.

I didn't know if I could believe in such a rare occurrence, especially in one that said I would be connected with someone so strongly, someone that I barely knew.

Could my life have made such a difference to the man who stood before me? Could I have helped him to become a better person?

I observed him closely. He was so very handsome, and I felt I did know him in a way. His features seemed so familiar, but that was probably from staring at him so often recently.

He died from a brain tumor. That seemed like a painful way to die. Would I have been in pain lying in a coma?

"How long would I have lived?"

His voice was husky as he replied, "Four months, you would have lived for four more months."

Four months. I would have had four more months with my family, four more months with Mitch. Four months to watch my family struggle with my pending death.

I decided then as I examined his light green eyes that he had indeed made the right decision. I knew he was about to reach for me, and suddenly I wasn't afraid. He had protected the ones I loved in a way that I had not been able to.

Would it be so bad to be connected with such a strong man, a man who appeared to actually have a great deal of compassion? Obviously, he was good deep inside, or he wouldn't be here.

Just before he lifted his hand, I felt the rumbling deep within my soul. I was being pulled to the Maker against my sudden desire to stay where I was.

I heard his fading words as he called out for me to wait, but I had no choice.

I blinked at the bright light. The sudden stillness of where I was felt almost oppressive to the soft breeze of the shore.

"Welcome, Coralenna."

I cleared my throat, "Thank you."

"You seem upset that I have brought you here," the voice echoed around me.

I shook my head, "No, not upset, just," I bit my lip, "just seemed like bad timing."

A vibration of laughter filled me, "It is not time for you and Brock yet."

I glanced around, "Then what time is it?"

The voice grew serious, "It's time for you to return."

My heart sped up. Return where? Return to Earth? To Mitch? I wet my dry lips.

"Relax, my child. You are needed in the living arena. Your friend is having trouble with your death, and you need to find a way to help him."

I struggled to say his name, "Mitchell?"

"Yes. Do what you must do to help him deal with the situation. The evil ones are barking closely at his heels, and I do not wish to lose him. I have plans for him."

"Not anytime soon I hope?" I whispered, afraid to know that his life was in jeopardy.

"That, dear child, is up to you." A whisper of a breeze floated over me. "Now go, you must only think of what you might need to succeed in your mission, and it will be yours—within goodness that is."

"But what do I have to do?" Suddenly I was afraid. What if I could not save him? I had no idea of what to do once I got there.

"You are one of the strongest we have had here. You have proven that over and over again. I believe in you."

"You believe in me?" tears blinded me momentarily.

"No tears are needed, my dear, go. Your friend is in dire need of your assistance. The path has been opened for you."

A chill raced down my spine and I felt as if I were falling. My stomach dropped as if I was on a roller coaster, and I opened them to a dark parking lot.

I glanced around for something I might recognize. Near the road was a sign for the business, Harry's. I had been to this bar a few times, the cops hung out here after shift.

The sound of two people kissing came from the darkest part of the lot and I moved there, suddenly sensing Mitch's presence.

He had a woman pushed up against the stone wall, her legs wrapped tightly around his body, her arms holding him close. He was kissing her neck so I got a good view of her face. That wasn't his wife.

Mitchell, no! I shouted.

He suddenly stopped moving as if I had flipped the off switch.

The woman gawked over his shoulder and our glares met. She was Os Malos and she saw me. Evil glittered in her shiny globes as she pushed her body against his, begging him to keep going.

Mitch, don't do this.

He shook his head as if to clear it, stepping back from her so fast she almost fell. I would have enjoyed that. Anger was pulsing through my veins as I watched her come at him again.

I watched his unsteady gait, saw him weave slightly. He was drunk.

Go home, Mitch, you need to sleep.

He stepped further back from the woman, swiftly trying to sober up, and apologized.

Don't apologize to her, I thought.

One more time she tried to get him back under her spell, but he had heard my voice, and it had woken him up from whatever drunken stupor he had been in.

I watched as he stumbled to his truck. He should not be driving, but I would make sure that he got home safely.

I turned to the woman as I heard him start the engine. "Stay away from him."

"Yeah, and who is going to make me?" She sauntered over to me.

"I will." I eyed her from the roots of her bleached-blond hair all the way down to her fancy shoes.

She laughed, "Yeah! You can't take this on. We've been working on him for a long time. It's only a matter of time before he sides with us."

"I will do whatever I need to do, but you will not have him."

I spun when I heard Joe answer from behind, "Why? Is he still yours, sweet Corey?"

I stepped to the side so that I could see them both. "He doesn't belong to you," I said snidely.

"Yeah? Well, he sure doesn't belong to you, either." Joe sauntered up closer, "You're looking good, Corey."

His appraisal roved over my body and made me nauseous. I ignored his comment. "Leave him alone, Joe."

He stepped away from me, glancing around the parking lot. "Where's your new boyfriend? Hiding?"

There was no reason to argue his words, it didn't matter what he thought. "Brock is not here. I'm here on my own."

He turned, surprised, "I can't believe that. Why would they let you loose after only a few short months? They normally keep you there a lot longer."

A few short months? I thought it had only been a few days. "I learn fast."

He laughed, "You must. I have never seen them release someone from the Realm in only six months."

Six months! His words spun through me, and I leaned back.

He watched me closely, "Ha! They didn't tell you how long you were there, did they?"

I guarded my expression, careful not to let him know that his words had just taken me on another roller coaster ride.

"Sweet, sweet Coralenna, that is what they call you up there, isn't it?" He didn't wait for a response and kept talking. "You've been dead for six whole months. Mitch has moved on!" His laugh was evil, "His life is all kinds of different now, and I am proud to say that I have helped him to get on with his life."

I watched him, not sure what to say.

"There's no way you are going to get him back to your side, Corey, so you might as well just go on back to the clouds and get it on with your new man. Mitch is mine." He finished his sentence with a sneer.

"Like hell he is," I spat out between clenched teeth.

He stared at me for a moment, "Well, I guess it's game on, then."

"You can bet on it."

He chuckled and started to walk backwards, "I look forward to it, and I've missed you around here, Corey. It will be like old times."

The woman walked up beside him. He threw his arm around her shoulder, and they turned and disappeared around the dark corner.

I let out the tense breath I had been holding and spun slowly, searching the dark parking lot.

Six months! I thought it had been just a few days! I closed my eyes and searched for Mitch, suddenly desperate to see what state he was in.

PART 6

The Truth

CHAPTER 43 ~ MITCHELL

*T*he steering wheel creaked when I slammed my hand on it in frustration. The street in front of me wavered. I was too drunk to be driving.

Where had the thoughts of Corey come from? Was I so messed up that her voice came back to me? I hadn't heard it in six months, not since her funeral. How was I all of a sudden hearing it now?

Focus, Mitch.

Focus, yes I needed to focus and get home. With a deep cleansing breath, I stared out the windshield, watching the road as closely as I could. I was only a few blocks from home now. I couldn't get pulled over; I'd be in a world of trouble with my job if I did.

I can't believe I am driving. I never drive when I'm drinking. I shook my head; my mind was such a mess.

You'll get through it.

Will I? How?

One step at a time.

Mad laughter bubbled out of me, "I'm freaking talking to myself! No, I'm pretending to have a conversation with Corey. I've completely lost it."

I concentrated on the last few blocks and made it home without crashing my car or hurting someone else. My head fell back against the headrest.

What was I thinking tonight? I was going to have sex with some random chick! For what? What was I trying to prove? Was I trying to prove that I could move on? That I could get over her? That my marriage was over? What?

Go get some sleep, Mitch.

I nodded to myself; I needed to sleep this off. I climbed out of the truck, stumbling to the door on shaky legs. With the door unlocked, I stepped inside and kicked something that lay on the floor. It rolled and bounced off the wall, loudly.

"Shit," I muttered as I pushed the door closed behind me. I heard a noise upstairs.

"Mitch? Is that you?" Beth called down from the top step.

"Yeah, it's me. Go back to bed." In the kitchen, I grabbed a glass and filled it with water. She walked into the kitchen behind me.

"You okay?" she asked quietly, and I snapped.

I spun around to face her, everything in me finally coming unglued. "No! No, I'm not alright! I'm screwed up, Beth! Screwed up! Is that what you want to hear?"

She took a step back from my verbal assault and reached for the lapels of her robe, pulling them closer.

"It's going to be alright," her voice quivered, and she stepped closer.

"It's not going to be alright! I'm losing my mind! I can't focus on work! I can't stand to be home. I keep making all these bad decisions, and now I hear her voice in my head! It's not going to be alright!"

She stepped in front of me and tried to pull me into her arms; I fought against them and lost my balance, falling back against the countertop. I bent at the waist, putting my hands on my knees, my head spun.

Her hand rubbed small circles on my back. "You're going to be alright, Mitch. We'll work through it."

"I don't want to work through it with you!" I bellowed at her as I stood back up and tried to distance myself. She blocked my path.

"Whose voice do you hear in your head?" her face wavered even up close like this. I tried to focus on her, my body swayed slightly.

"I need to go to sleep." I attempted to step around her, and she grabbed my arm and halted me again.

"Whose voice do you hear inside your head, Mitch?" she demanded forcefully.

"You really want to know, Beth? Fine, I'll tell you! I hear hers. I'm hearing Corey's voice inside my head!" Pain etched my words as they spewed from my mouth. All of a sudden I wanted to hurt Beth, not physically, but I wanted her to hurt like I hurt.

She swallowed, but didn't move away. "Were you in love with her?"

"Yes," my voice cracked as the liquid courage raced through my veins from the whiskey. "Yes, I was in love with her, Beth. I loved her and I killed her! Jesus, I killed her!" I spun around from her, put my hands onto the counter, and hung my head. Emotions that I had tried to bury rose with a vengeance inside, and the hated tears came.

"I killed her! I killed her!" I fought the tears that threatened while Beth wrapped her arms around my waist pulling me to her.

At this moment I needed to feel her compassion, and I couldn't believe that she was willing to give it to me after what I had just said, but she did.

I tucked my face into her shoulder and fought to hold the agony back as she held me.

She stroked my back softly and held me tightly. "She was a lucky woman to have your love," pain coated her words, "but you didn't kill her, Mitchell."

"I did."

"No, you didn't. The guys you were chasing did. You have to realize that."

I pulled back from her, embarrassed to have almost broken down again and wiped my face with one hand while the other rested on her hip. "I can't. I don't know how."

"Then let me help you," she put her hands on my face, cradling my cheeks soothingly. Her own tears covered her cheeks, and her eyes were bright in the dim nightlight coming from the wall.

I had hurt her. She had hurt me. Were we even now? Once again the alcohol-induced need rushed through me and I leaned in to kiss her. How long had it been since I had done that? I felt her shiver as our lips met, and she wrapped her arms around my neck, holding me close, taking the kiss I offered.

The heat between us escalated, one of my hands ran up and down her back, the other pulled her tight to me. I needed to feel, feel alive, feel loved. She pulled my shirt out of my jeans, never leaving my lips, and I ripped open her robe.

Within a few moments, we were lying together on the kitchen floor, a tangle of clothes. Both of us burned for different things, yet they were the same.

CHAPTER 44 ~ BROCK

*O*nly moments after she was summoned, mine came.

"Brock, my child, you are upset."

I blinked and tried not to bark out a laugh, "You think so?"

"Anger has no place here," the voice roared over me like a huge gust of wind.

"You knew what was happening. Why did you stop it? I thought that was what you wanted," frustration lined my words.

"Do not question me," the voice was low, "but I will answer you because she asked the same question and I supplied her with a response." There was a long pause before the reply came, "It is not your time."

I put my hands on my hips, staring out over the vast whiteness in front of me, "Not my time. What is that supposed to mean?"

"I just told you not to question me. You must do as you say, believe."

I gazed at the ground, it almost appeared not to be there, as if I was floating in midair, "Believe, I'm not sure what to believe in."

"You must believe that it will all happen as it is supposed to happen."

I rolled my eyes as the sarcastic words fell off my tongue, "Yeah, that makes sense." I thought for a moment when nothing else came. "Where is Coralenna? May I ask that?"

"Yes, you may ask that, she is your charge. I have sent her on to do her job."

"But she's not ready yet!" Nervous anger rotated in my gut.

"She is, and as you have already seen, without permission I might add, she is needed."

I hung my head. Was I to be punished for watching over Mitchell?

"I will not punish you. I understand your concerns and they are justified. I am proud of you for not letting it go and for worrying about his future."

Should I say thank you? I thought.

"There is no need to thank me. You are a strong man, a man of good intentions. You have shown that over and over again, despite what your mortal life was like."

"I was wondering when that would come up again."

The sound was soft as it filled the room, "I bring it up again because it will affect the future, the future of all—especially, the future for you and Coralenna. You must be prepared to deal with that."

How was I to prepare?

"When the time comes, you will know what to do. For now, you must keep your distance from her. Allow her to do this on her own and to make her own decisions."

"What if she comes to me for help? Can I assist her?"

"No," reverberated around the white space. "She must make her choice. She knows how you feel, but she must now decide if her future will be with us or not."

Fear replaced the nerves in my stomach, "And what if she doesn't choose us?"

There was no answer.

"Hello? What if she doesn't choose us?" my voice rose of its own accord as fear replaced my anger.

A soft whisper of an answer wafted over me, "There will be no more questions, Brock. Go back to your charges and do what you need to do. Stay clear of her for now, all will be revealed in its own time."

After a fleeting sensation of falling, I found myself standing right back on the beach where I had been, confused and distraught by the uncertainty of the future.

CHAPTER 45 ~ COREY

eside him in his truck I sat, the wheels rolled unsteadily over the roadway. His thoughts bounced inside his mind like a ping pong ball.

Focus, Mitch.

I tried to calm him without reaching out. He obviously didn't know how to deal with everything. My return at this very point had put him on the edge of a high precipice.

What has happened to you Mitchell? I studied his strong profile, wondering what he had been dealing with.

He spoke out loud, and I kept my thoughts to myself. He was not in a state that I could communicate with him properly. He needed to sleep. No, he needed to sober up!

When he walked into his house, he kicked the ball across the floor. He blinked rapidly and he made a beeline towards the kitchen. Beth came down the stairs quietly.

Her long pink robe was pulled tightly, and it made a soft whisper on the floor as she passed me. She shivered as if a chill had gone down her back when she stepped in front of me. I followed.

She was not the only one surprised by the venom of his words; I had never pictured him to be so harsh as to strike out at someone, but I did not know what had been happening to him since I had left.

She tried to comfort him, and I ached to do the same. The kitchen was dark except for one nightlight in the corner. It threw harsh shadows around the room, but I could see their pain just as clearly as I could see their faces.

When he admitted to hearing voices, I knew that I would have to be careful about how I approached him. Maybe there was another way.

I was proud of her for facing him down. I didn't know a whole lot about her, but as I watched her try to get him to open up, I knew that she loved him.

"You really want to know, Beth? Fine, I'll tell you!" His voice grew louder, slightly slurred by his inebriation. "I hear hers. I'm hearing Corey's voice inside my head!"

I groaned. Yeah, I really needed to figure something else out. If I didn't, I would drive him insane.

I waited to see if he would answer her question and was not only shocked by how he responded, but I was amazed at how she reacted.

When they went to their knees, I phased out of the room. My heart was heavy, but knowing that I had no right to intervene on this scene, I left them.

On the balcony of my quarters in the Realm, I hesitated. I needed help. I had no clue what I should do. I reached out to feel for Brock but felt no sense of his presence.

Funny, I had never not been able to feel him. I went in search of Montgomery instead.

He sat at a big glass table, a puzzle spread out in front of him, his shimmering gray head bowed over two small pieces. I saw a smile form on his face as I walked closer to him.

"Hello, dear. Darn thing, I can't find the piece that attaches to this one."

"Hey, Monty." I walked up beside him, glanced down at the piece in his hand and out over the selection that lay on the glass. I bent to pick up a piece, "Here, it attaches to this one."

His eyebrows knit together, but he took the piece I offered and snapped it into the other piece. "How'd you do that?"

"Sometimes you just need another set of eyes," I shrugged and pulled out a chair, sitting down next to him.

He glanced at me then back to the table, moving some more pieces around in front of him. "You have something on your mind."

"Yeah, I need another set of eyes."

He chuckled, "Got a puzzle you're working on, huh?"

"You could say that." I turned to the table and picked through a few pieces, twisting them to see if they fit. I snapped two together and reached for a third piece.

"You keep that up and I'm going to keep you here. This has been one of the harder ones for me to do."

The puzzle was of a stream and a mountain view. There were a lot of darker colors and not too many shapes. "You have to look for the subtle color changes."

I saw him bob his head from the corner of my eye. "So what can I help you with?"

"Have you seen Brock?" I fit another piece together.

"He's a puzzle alright, but no I haven't seen him. I believe he was summoned and then was sent to the arena."

I lifted my face to Montgomery. "He's not the puzzle. Do you know why he was summoned?"

"Not my right to ask," he shook his head. "So if he's not the puzzle, what is?"

I twisted a small cardboard piece around, trying to get it to fit, "I have been released from the Realm. I saw Mitch."

The quick intake of breath told me he had not known. I forced a small smile over my lips and picked up another section to try.

"That was fast," the surprise registered in his voice.

"Well, not that fast. I had no clue it had been six months since I had died."

"Time is different here. You knew that."

I sat back in my chair, "Yeah, but six months! Come on! You guys could have warned me that one of our days here is like a month or two for them."

I let the colorful piece of cardboard twist in my fingers, feeling the different angles of it as it spun around in my hand.

"Would it have made a difference? Most Gardaí are not released for over a year of Earth time. Just imagine the surprise they must feel to see life going on without them."

"Yeah, I guess." I tossed the jagged piece to the table and put my hands in my lap.

"So how is he?" He peeked up at me from where his head was bent over the table.

"Not good. The Os Malos have been hard at work on him. I found him in a rather compromising position, although I did manage to influence him enough to stop what he was doing." The scene flashed through my mind, he had been about to take a stranger up against the wall. I shook my head.

"Well, that's good then." He went back to his puzzle.

"Yeah, I guess," I stood up and moved to his sliding glass door, hugging myself with my arms, "but then he thought he was going crazy because he was hearing my voice in his head."

"Oh." I heard the chair creak and assumed he leaned back. He surprised me when he touched my shoulder.

"Monty, what am I going to do? How can I help him if he is questioning his own sanity when I speak to him?"

His eyebrows were drawn down, "Why are you calling me Monty?"

I shrugged again, "I don't know, I guess Montgomery is just too stuffy for me—but that's beside the point—what am I supposed to do?" I had opened my hands up in front of me in a pleading way.

He reached for a hand and pulled me over to his couch. The soft beige suede sighed when we sat down.

"Well, if you are worried about his sanity, then maybe you need to try another route."

I scooted up to the edge of the couch, "What route is that?"

"Shock therapy," his mouth spread into a wide smile.

"Shock therapy, what are you talking about?" Maybe he wasn't as sane as I thought he was. Maybe I should be more worried about him than Mitch.

He laughed and squeezed my hand. "If hearing your voice is too much, maybe he needs to be shocked and be able to actually see your face."

My heart accelerated, "What?"

"Maybe what he needs is to be able to see you, see that you are alright. Maybe then he will know that you don't blame him and that he wasn't at fault."

I gaped at him, afraid that this might be a joke. "How?"

A smile so pure it radiated heaven crossed his face, "You step down into the living arena." He patted my hand.

"You can do that?" Had I heard them ever talk about doing that? I had never seen Brock in the living arena before.

"Of course you can do that, although we don't do it very often. Most times it is not a good idea for the dead to be magically alive and walking around in the open again."

"But?" I knew there had to be more.

"But if Mitch is having such a hard time, then maybe showing yourself to him and helping him one on one would set him back on the correct path." He let go of my hand and stood up, "I don't know much about Mitch, but I do know there is a plan for him here when his time on Earth is done."

I shuddered to think of Mitch as dead. As much as I wanted to be with him, I didn't want him to die to accomplish it. If I were able to go back, to walk amongst the living again, I could be with him. I could gaze into his face again, kiss his lips.

Brock's face came to mind, and I pushed it aside. Brock had nothing to do with this. This was about me seeing Mitch again, the chance to help him, to say goodbye properly if need be.

I stood up, "Let's do it. Can you show me how?"

He walked up to me and placed his hands on my upper arms, "Of course I can, but remember that what you do down there will affect you. Your decisions will make a difference on your afterlife, good or bad."

The impact of his words was strong and they soaked into my mind, "I understand."

He examined me hard, "Are you sure?"

After a brief hesitation, I nodded, "Yes, I'm sure."

He squeezed my arms one more time, "Then let's go. We need to get you set up before you get started."

CHAPTER 46 ~ MITCHELL

*W*ith a groan, I rolled over in bed. A shaft of sunlight struck my face, and I squeezed my eyelids shut to keep the light out.

My memory was fuzzy from the night before, but I remembered a few things with perfect clarity.

I remembered the woman, Rebecca. I remembered how I almost took her savagely against the outside of Harry's bar. It was just another one of the bad choices I had made recently. The disgust I felt for myself was overwhelming.

Then I came home and told Beth that I was in love with Corey. My head throbbed at the fuzzy recollection. When I had spoken those words last night, I had expected her to get angry, strike out—certainly not comfort me—but I never expected that it would have ended up with us making love on the kitchen floor. I couldn't remember the last time we'd had sex.

If it had not been for hearing Corey's voice last night, things would have ended up quite differently. I would have become someone I did not want to become—but how was having sex with a stranger different than falling in love with another woman when I was married? Of course there was a big difference. Corey wasn't some stranger, and I had never meant to fall in love with her. It had just happened.

The bedroom door creaked open. "Mitch, are you awake?"

"Yeah," I cleared my throat, thick from sleep.

"I have coffee for you," Beth walked closer to the bed, "and some Tylenol."

My arm slowly dropped, and I tried to open my eyes by blinking rapidly a few times. "Thanks." I pushed up from my back and leaned against a pillow, and then took the mug and two white pills she handed me, all while avoiding her targeted gaze.

She sat down on the side of the mattress. I viewed her profile, her nose turned up slightly at the end, her chin softly rounded. She chewed on her lip. She wanted to say something, but she was afraid.

I took a sip of the hot coffee, still holding the pills in my hand. "Go ahead, Beth, I know you have something to say. I deserve whatever it is."

She looked down to the bedroom rug. "I love you."

I watched her closely; once again surprised she was not venting her anger or throwing hurtful words. Her confession threw me off balance.

Not knowing how to respond, I cleared my throat.

"I know that I hurt you. I cheated on you, and I lied to you, but I never stopped loving you." Her soft green eyes peeked over her shoulder at me, almost pleading with me to believe her.

I rolled the pills around in my hand, "I know."

"How long were you involved with her?" her voice was barely audible.

I didn't want to talk about Corey, but maybe this was my chance to admit my sins.

"We weren't together very long." I threw the two pills from my hand into my mouth and swallowed them with a gulp of hot coffee.

"But you loved her." That was not a question, I knew that, but I felt it deserved a response.

"Yes, I loved her." I set my coffee mug down on the nightstand. "Beth, look at me."

She hesitated, and then lifted her chin, shook back her hair, and turned to face me. Unshed tears brightened the color of her irises, and I fought to keep mine from reflecting the same thing.

"Yes, I loved her and she loved me, but you need to know that I never slept with her. Our relationship wasn't like that; it was more emotional, not physical." There, I had admitted it.

"Were you going to leave me?" The honesty of the question was so intense I wasn't sure how to answer, but after staring into her face for a few moments, I knew I needed to continue being honest.

"I had thought about it."

She blinked quickly a few times and turned away.

"Just because I thought about it, doesn't mean that I would have done it. Like I said, we weren't together very long, and then she died."

"I guess I deserved that," she mumbled.

I sat up and reached for her hand, "No, you didn't deserve it. Beth, you are a good woman, and I do love you. I was going through a lot, I still am."

She squeezed my hand, "Are we going to get through this?"

Our eyes met, and again I had to be honest with her, "I don't know. I really don't know." I released her hand and leaned back against the wall.

CHAPTER 47 ~ BROCK

When I phased into Mitch's room, I knew that Corey was not here. There was a brief lingering of her energy, so I knew she had been recently.

She was released from the Realm and she had gone straight to him. Beth and Mitch spoke softly in the bedroom. Was there a way to help them put things back together, without getting myself in trouble?

Beth walked out the door after saying she hoped they could work things out. Mitch watched her leave the room and his view came to rest right where I was standing. What if I spoke to him?

Mitch closed his eyes and the urge to step over the line was strong, but the consequences of my actions would be too much. I didn't want to lose my chance with Corey.

I phased down to where Beth now stood in the kitchen. Her hands were still under the running water of the faucet as she stared out the window with unfocused vision. She was a beautiful woman. She had a strength inside of her that reminded me of Corey. It was no wonder that Mitch loved them both.

With a loud sigh, she picked up a sponge and started washing some dishes that lay in the bottom of the stainless steel sink. If only I could make it easier for her, but she wasn't my charge.

Turning from her, I felt her pain as if it were my own, and knew some was my fault. I left her kitchen and ended up beside a guy in his car. The feeling of anger quickly communicated to me from the driver.

His driving was aggressive today; he drove less than eight feet behind another car going seventy miles per hour.

Slow down, Gary, relax. Work will still be there when you get there, my voice reflected into his mind.

He glanced down at the speedometer and sighed. The distance between his car and the one in front of him grew as he took his foot off the accelerator for a moment.

Why couldn't all my charges be this simple? I phased to the next one.

CHAPTER 48 ~ COREY

$\mathcal{M}$onty and I phased to the living arena, landing inside the secure gates of a storage facility. We stood between two buildings; the bright orange siding on the walls caught my attention right away, stark white rolling garage doors lined both sides.

"Why are we here?" I asked Montgomery as I inspected the area.

"I told you we needed some things before you stepped down," he grinned, "but first, I need to show you how to step down to the living arena."

Was it anxiety or excitement that pulsed through my body as I thought about coming face to face with Mitch again?

"Okay, what do I do?"

"It's pretty easy once you do it, but you have to remember a few things. You will be a little bit disoriented the first time or two."

"Why is that?" I listened intently.

"When you are on this level here, you can see and hear things, but you can't feel them. Your senses are very strong, Coralenna, and when you step over, it will be a bit overwhelming."

"I don't understand why it would be so different?"

He thought about it for a second, "Right now, you can hear things from the living arena, but they are more of a hushed background noise unless you are targeting something specific, like a conversation. When you step over, you will hear everything, not just those things you target, but everything. The sounds of life and the thoughts of others that are around you can be daunting."

I still didn't get what he meant, but wanted to move forward. "Alright, if you say so. Anything else I need to know?"

Montgomery got a serious gleam in his eye, "Yes, you need to be very careful here. You are not protected down here like you are above. You can be injured."

"I can take care of myself," I brushed his comment aside, eager to get moving. "So what do I do?"

He snickered and shook his head, "Picture a line in front of you that has an invisible wall. You have to step through the wall. Once you start to move through, it will pull you."

"Pull me, right." I nodded and pushed my hands down into the back pockets of my jeans.

"Watch me," I turned and observed him as he seemed to concentrate for a moment before taking a step forward. A small ripple appeared to travel along his body.

"See?" he smiled at me.

He didn't appear any different to me. Was he now at a different level? He didn't appear to be.

"You try it now." He crossed his arms over his chest and waited. I shrugged, didn't look too difficult.

I imagined a clear glass wall in front of me; the bright orange metal wall stood on the other side, and I took a tentative step forward. A thickness started to suck me in, as if I was stepping into a vat of pudding, and suddenly I felt like I was being pulled into a vortex. With a snap, I landed on the other side.

I blinked rapidly at the same time the world struck me. The sounds around me were like standing in the middle of Times Square. The noise of cars driving past, a lawnmower, a dog barking, and voices, so many voices filled my head at once.

I staggered back a step and wanted to slam my hands over my ears.

"Block it out, Coralenna; just try to block it out."

"Block it out? I can't even think straight, much less try to concentrate to block something out!" The sound of my own voice appeared louder than it should have, and I finally put my hands over my ears.

As I stood with my hands tightly on the sides of my head, I felt something that I had not even realized I had been missing. A slight breeze floated over my skin. I inhaled the air swirling around me and picked up the scents of flowers, grass, animals, cars, and people.

I focused on the breeze, allowed it to fill me, and absorbed the soft feeling. The buzz in my ears slowed down. The scents flowing into my nose calmed. I slowly released the tension on my ears and moved my hands away.

The sounds were all there, but by focusing on something else, I was able to push them back to manageable amounts. I turned to consider my surroundings, taking in the colors and the sounds as I viewed the area.

"Better?" Montgomery asked from behind me. I gave him a thumbs up, afraid my voice would be too loud again.

"You did that rather well, Coralenna, but I am not surprised." He laughed at himself. "You just need to remember to focus on something and stay calm. Then the sounds, smells, and feelings won't be so overwhelming."

He walked over to a garage door, pulled a key out of his pocket, then bent down and unlocked the padlock that secured the door. When he stood, he handed me the key.

I studied the small gold key; the metal was warm from being in his pocket. "What do I need that would be stored in the garage?"

He stood back up and grinned. "You can't just go popping in and out of places. People might see that, but if you had transportation, then you would be just like any other person."

He reached down and grabbed the handle to the garage door, pulling it up halfway before putting both hands under it and lifting it over his head.

When the door cleared his hips, I knew what was hidden inside. "Is that mine?" I whispered while my gaze caressed the black hood.

"It's not the one you had, if that's what you are asking, but it's just like it." He turned, sliding his hands back and forth together to get the dust off his palms.

There wasn't anything on Earth that could take the smile off my face as I regarded the sleek black car.

"The keys are inside. I would suggest that you wait until nightfall before you take it out. Remember that people here will recognize you, so you have to be careful about that. It's only Mitch that we want to shock."

At the mention of his name, my heart skipped a beat. I was going to see him, face to face. I had no clue what I would say or how he would react to seeing me, but right now all I could think of was that he would see me.

"Oh," Monty got quiet for a moment, irritation written on his features. "I must go, Coralenna, one of my charges has gotten himself in a predicament." He gave me a lopsided smile, "I wish you the best. Remember that your choices here will affect a lot of things, so be wise in your decisions."

I nodded at him, "I will, Monty, and thank you."

He pulled me into a hug, his strong arms holding me tight and close. The love and friendship that wove through us was strong, and I absorbed it. He pulled away, searching my face as a parent might examine his own child's.

"Be careful, my child." He kissed me on the forehead gently and stepped back.

"I will." We shared a moment of quiet and then he nodded once and was gone.

I inhaled a deep soul-cleansing breath, trying to relax my body as if I were to practice my forms. Releasing the air I held deep inside me, I examined the area around me again.

An old half-crushed soda bottle lay against one wall near another door, a few cigarette butts were strewn about. My line of vision settled on my car again as I heard a horn honk and a dog bark in the distance. I grinned. I was back!

CHAPTER 49 ~ MITCHELL

*T*hings at home the last two days were for the most part better. While Beth and I had not spoken about my involvement with Corey or her involvement with my brother, we seemed to have come to a truce.

I wasn't sure what my feelings toward the whole thing were, but at least there were no more skeletons in the closet.

As I pulled up to the twenty-four-hour convenience store where all the guys on duty were meeting for coffee, I backed into a parking spot. Two other patrol cars were already parked, and I watched the last one pull in while I climbed out of the car.

I waited for Tom to get out of the car. Joe was off tonight, so Tom and I were partnered up for the shift. I liked working with Tom. I didn't seem to make the bad judgment calls I did when Joe was my partner. Tom and I had just cleared a domestic call together. He prattled on about the baby mama drama that we had just dealt with as we entered the store.

The coffee island stood to our right, and we grabbed brown paper cups as we reached it. Tom poured French vanilla creamer into his cup before walking to the canisters to fill his. I made my way straight to the Kona coffee canister and filled my twenty-four-ounce cup to the rim. I liked mine hot and black.

We stood around the island idly chatting over the night's calls, random people came in and grabbed what they needed and left. A few would stop to say hello, but most avoided us. At this time of night, the drunks were coming home from the bars and the seedier people were out and about.

With my hands resting on the green Formica counter, I glanced towards the door when headlights flashed into the store. The lights turned off, and I brought my attention back to the guys around me.

As if an ice cube had been slipped down the back of the shirt under my vest, a spear of anxiety raced down my back as I heard a gentle voice inside my mind.

Outside, Mitch.

I straightened and stared toward the glass doors, out in the parking lot beside the car that had just pulled in stood a dark figure. I tensed as a car turned the corner and the headlights hit the lone person.

Corey? My heart sped and my hands grew damp. The headlights had only flickered over the person, but in that single moment, I saw her. I stepped towards the doors, drawn to her.

The person turned back to her car and opened the door. No lights came on inside as I pushed open the first set of glass doors. I watched the person slip inside the vehicle.

"Hey, Mitch, where are you going?" Tom yelled from behind me.

I barely turned my head, keeping my line of sight trained on the car, "I'll be right back. I need to check on something." I stepped into the vestibule, stopping as the headlights came back on and struck me. I shielded my eyes.

It couldn't be Corey. Corey was dead. Yet, I had just seen her. She was focused right at me. That had been her voice I had heard.

The car started to pull out. As it turned from the space in front of me, I saw the sleek lines of a black Camaro. My heart thumped wildly, and I pushed the second set of glass doors as the car continued to drive away.

Once outside, I watched the car pull to the roadway, stopping briefly before it turned right. I ran to my car, I had to find out who was driving that Camaro. This had to be a bad joke. I reached my car and pulled out my keys to unlock the door when I noticed something on my windshield and hesitated.

A small piece of paper was tucked under the windshield wiper. I grabbed it after unlocking the door. I lifted the single fold and gasped as I read the ink on the paper: *Meet me, C.*

I lifted my face from the paper toward the road. The car was just fading out of sight. Meet you where? Oh God, was that really Corey? The taillights disappeared, and I jumped into my car, pulled out of the parking space quickly, and moved towards the road.

The electronics building was in that direction, the place where we used to meet. I stepped on the gas. In the distance, I saw the back end of the car. The blinker flashed on and the Camaro turned off the road into a parking lot: the electronics place.

My hands were damp, my heart hammered wildly, and my mind reeled. How could it be Corey? I had watched her die. I had watched her get buried. I had carried her damn body for God's sake!

Anger sparked from somewhere deep inside as I stepped on the gas harder. What kind of joke was this?

I slammed on the brake, almost locking them up, and turned without using my turn signal. The sudden fear that darted through my stomach made me feel ill.

I stopped my car before I turned around the backside, squeezing my eyelids closed as my hands choked the steering wheel. It can't be Corey! But I saw her! I shouted inside my own mind.

I forced myself to breathe slowly and put my foot gently back on the gas pedal.

As I made the left turn to drive past the loading docks, my headlights landed on the black Camaro parked on the far side. The lights were out and the door was closed. My foot shook on the pedal as I softly pressed it down to move closer.

Twenty feet away, I stopped. My right hand put the car in park. I wiped my wet palms on my pants before turning my headlights off. There was no movement in the car in front of me. The overhead light on the corner of the building cast a harsh yellow fluorescent light.

Why wasn't anyone getting out? Fear froze me to my seat, not the kind of fear that we get on the job responding to a dangerous call, but the kind that mentally locks you down on the inside. I was afraid—afraid that this was a joke, or maybe I was afraid that this was real. I wasn't exactly sure, but the apprehension choked me even as I lifted my hand to the door handle.

A minute passed before I gathered the strength to pull the handle. I pushed the door open and stepped out gingerly, never taking my focus from the driver's door. I held onto the door frame for a moment for support. The dark-tinted windows revealed nothing as I stood straighter and then stepped back to close the door with a soft click. My heart pounded in my chest in triple time, blocking out all other sounds except the blood rushing through my ears.

I stood staring, waiting for the car door to open, waiting for whoever was doing this to me to step out and face me. I took a step forward but spun around when a soft feminine voice came from behind me.

"Mitch, I'm glad you came."

I sucked in the air as the sound of her voice reached me—Corey's voice. I swallowed as I searched the shadows near the wall of the building. A figure slowly stepped out from the edge.

Her lower legs and shoes broke from the darkness first, and I followed the line of her legs as she emerged further. Black boots covered her feet and disappeared under dark blue jeans. She took another step, and the light revealed the bottom of a black leather jacket open at her waist. My mouth was dry as I tried to swallow again.

Another step forward brought her totally into the light, and my head swam as I gawked from her dark purple shirt into her angelic face. Her soft hair framed her face, her beautiful eyes bright and focused. A small elegant smile adorned her lips and the buzzing grew louder in my ears.

"Breathe, Mitch, you have to breathe before you pass out."

Absently, I did as she said, pulling air in and out of my lungs as I stared at her. My mind was trying to process this, but it just couldn't understand, and the quaking in my limbs grew.

"How?" the strangled word left my mouth.

She walked closer, stopping a few feet away, and I watched as she examined my entire face, a yearning filled her expression.

Could I be dreaming? Had I fallen asleep in my car, and this was all a dream?

I swallowed hard, "You're dead. How are you here?"

Her shoulders rose as she took her own deep breath. "You're right, I am dead, but I'm here."

"Am I dreaming all this?"

She stepped close enough that I could smell her sweet citrus scent. "No, you are not dreaming, Mitch. I'm here, right in front of you." She smiled softly, and my heart threatened to jump out of my chest.

"I don't understand," my voice quivered as much as my body. If I was dreaming, I didn't want to wake up.

CHAPTER 50 ~ BROCK

I moved from one charge to another, making sure they were all going in the right direction. Some were harder than others, but eventually I had checked in on all I needed to and phased back to the Realm.

Once in my quarters, I found myself pacing. While in the living arena, I had been able to keep Corey somewhat off my mind for the most part. Here, she was all I could think of. I reached out to see if she was here, but she wasn't.

What was she doing? Was she with him? I shook the thought from my head.

I changed into workout gear, needing someplace to channel my tension, and phased to the bottom floor to hit the weight room. Maybe if I could wear myself out, I could get her out of my mind.

There were a few people in the gym when I arrived. Most nodded as I walked in and scanned the room. I acknowledged them with my own brief head tip and made my way to the squat rack.

As I lifted a forty-five-pound plate to slip it on the bar, Montgomery spoke from behind me. "I'm surprised to find you here, Brock."

I twisted my face over my shoulder and watched him wipe sweat from his face with a light blue towel. "Why's that?" I asked briskly.

He tossed his towel to the floor and picked up a plate, putting it on the other side of the bar.

"Figured you would stay in the living arena," his glare met mine briefly before he turned to pick up a weight plate.

"Everyone is behaving; I came back for a break."

He slipped the plate on, pushing it all the way in where it clanked against the other plate and met my gaze, "Oh, really? You didn't come back to see if she was here?"

I huffed and turned for another plate. "What difference does it make? I was told to stay away from her." I pushed the plate on until it met the other one. I bent down and picked up the collar that would lock the weights in place, pinching it between my palms; I compressed the clamp and slid it on the bar to rest against the plates.

Montgomery did the same, and I waited until he was done before I stepped into the rack and got ready to pick it up.

"Since when have you ever done what you are supposed to do?" he taunted.

I stepped back into the bar and shrugged. I lifted the bar with my hands on the sides of my shoulders, the bar rested on the back of my neck and the top of my shoulder blades. I took a small step forward to clear the rack. Taking a deep breath, I bent at the knees, went down to a squatting position, then slowly rose back up. After ten squats, I stepped back until I felt the rack behind me. Montgomery helped guide the bar back in place and let go as it dropped a half inch into position.

With each bend that I had made, I saw her face. Her smile, the sound of her voice filled my mind until I felt I would drop the weight.

"Where is she?" I wiped my hands on my sweatpants, drying the perspiration on my palms from holding the heavy metal bar.

"She's down below." He stepped around to the side of the bar, pulling the locking clip off to add more weight for my next set.

I knew she was down below, but hearing the words was like a knife to the back.

"How are things going?" I picked up a twenty-pound plate and put it on the bar next to the forty-fives.

He shrugged and picked up the locking clip, putting it back in place after he added weight to his side. "Don't know just yet, haven't heard from her since I showed her how to cross over." He watched my face as he spoke.

My jaw dropped open as we stared at each other. Like a volcano about to erupt, anger built inside of me.

"You showed her how to cross over?" the terse words spilled from my locked jaw.

"Yep." He stepped back from the bar and crossed his arms over his chest.

"Why the hell would you do that?" I shouted at him.

A smile tipped his lips, "Because she needed to see him face to face."

"Are you kidding? Do you have any idea what is going to happen now? She's going to cross the line, and I'm going to lose her!" Panic and anger warred in me.

Montgomery's smile grew bigger, "About time you admitted that was what you were worried about."

I spun around, not sure what to do. I stared down at the black rubber mats on the floor. What was I going to do? What could I do?

"Brock," Montgomery paused, waiting for me to turn to him. I glared at him over my shoulder, ready to bolt out of the room. "You have to let her do this on her own." He stepped forward and rested an elbow on the weight bar. "You can't get involved, and you know that."

I stared at him, the air burning in my lungs as I gulped deeply. "Like hell I won't!" I spun from him and phased immediately to the living arena. I had to find her before it was too late.

CHAPTER 51 ~ COREY

"*I*'m sorry for surprising you the way I did, but I needed to get you alone." I could no longer keep my distance and I moved closer.

It had been a risk to show myself to him tonight. If one of his coworkers had looked outside as I stood in the parking lot, it would not have gone over well, especially if that someone had been Joe.

I had waited just long enough for him to see which way I went and prayed that he would follow. There was no way I would speak to him again until I could do it face to face.

As I sat in my car, he pulled up. My mind and heart were frantic with the knowledge that I was just moments from being face to face with him again.

Not sure if I could phase while being in the living arena, I tried and found myself standing beside the large warehouse deep in the shadows. I waited till he stepped out and then approached him.

As he turned to the sound of my voice, my knees turned to jelly, but I grasped at the strength from above and moved forward. The wild beating of his heart and the buzzing in his head reached my sensitive ears.

Was there a way I could have shown myself to him that would not have caused such turmoil? I didn't think so.

The closer I got, the easier I found it to get lost in his handsomeness. This close, I could smell his musky cologne and I inhaled it deeply, filling my lungs. I reached my hand out; the feel of his warm skin was like nothing I had ever felt before. He pushed his head into my hand, and I reached with my other one to touch the soft short hair on the other side of his head.

Mere inches separated us. His eyes shone brightly as he pulled me into his strong arms. I welcomed the feel, welcomed the muscular arms that wrapped around me tightly. I pulled his head closer as my arms wrapped around his neck, his breath hot against my sensitive skin.

He leaned back just enough to see my face and ran his hand along the side of my head over my hair. He searched my face and stopped on my lips. He moved closer, and I stopped breathing as he slowly descended.

I had dreamed of this, of the feel of his lips on mine again, so tender and loving.

There was no holding back when our lips met. The feelings we had for one another exploded. Here in the dark, dirty parking lot, we could not get enough of each other as I slid my hands down his back, wishing that he wasn't in uniform so I could feel the muscles on his back instead of the hard Kevlar of his vest.

His duty belt pushed into my stomach, but I didn't care as I pulled myself to stand as close to him as I could. Our lips engaged in a kiss of reunion, our hearts once again entwined as one.

He pulled back. "How?" he whispered to me as we stood almost nose to nose, his palms cupping my face.

"Remember how you said I was an angel?" He nodded once. "Well, you were kind of right. I'm a guardian angel," I smiled shyly at him.

His Adam's apple bobbed as he swallowed, his expression intense as he spoke, "Seriously?"

"Yes." I slipped my hand around to his cheek, tenderly caressing the skin that I had never thought I would be able to touch again.

"Do all angels come back to life?"

"Well, I'm not really alive, I don't think; however, we watch over those who need us, we listen and guide them, and sometimes we come back to those who need us most."

"So I need my own guardian angel, huh?" his husky voice held a hint of teasing in it.

I took a small step back, not out of his arms, but just so I could observe him more easily. "Yes, you do," my voice serious as I responded.

I removed my hand from his cheek and placed it on his chest.

"Why is that?" he asked quietly.

How should I answer? I thought about that for a moment before speaking, "There are people that are close to you, Mitch, that you should not trust. You know what's right and what's not. You need to listen to your mind and your heart and not let others make your decisions for you."

He absorbed my words. I could hear them in his mind as he pictured moments in his memories that had been bad choices. Color rose in his cheeks as he recalled the incident outside Harry's bar.

"Have you been watching me long?" he swallowed, and I knew he wanted to know if I had really been there. The memory of my voice in his mind rattled him slightly.

"Yes, I know about what happened. I was there, and you listened to me guide you."

He stepped back and dropped his arms from around me. I missed the feel as soon as they left me, but I understood the anxiety he felt.

He turned away from me, embarrassed at his past actions. I allowed him to deal with his own demons.

"It's okay, Mitch, you're only human and you have been dealing with a lot, I understand that."

He leaned back against the car, hanging his head low. "What else have you seen me do?"

I put my hand under his chin, lifting his face to mine. "Look at me."

He did. The pain and embarrassment in his facial features were a dagger to my heart.

"I haven't been back very long. I had training to do. Believe it or not, there is a lot for a Garda to learn before he or she can come back to help."

He visibly relaxed as I spoke. I felt the relief that I had not witnessed all the things that he had done, but as they ticked through his mind, I saw them. I fought hard not to say anything; I bit my lip to keep any expression off my face.

259

"So you're here now to put me back on track?" his left eyebrow rose with his lip.

"Yeah, something like that."

He put his hands on my waist and pulled me closer to him as he spread his feet part. I slipped in between his legs and rested my chest to his.

"I'll take every second I can get with you, Corey," he whispered to me as he pulled me in for another kiss.

Lost in the feel of his lips, I never felt the presence enter behind me.

Coralenna, stop! The words shouted in my mind, and I pulled back from Mitch quickly. The abrupt stop startled him and he watched me with a question in his eyes. I put my finger over his lips to stop him from speaking as I answered the voice.

Go away. I didn't need to turn to see the anger on Brock's face. I could feel it in the small connection we had.

No, I'm not going away, and you need to stop this. You can't do this! he seethed.

"I can and I will, Brock!" I spun out of Mitch's arms to face him. He stood about three feet behind me, on the next level. I noticed the pain on his face, the clench of his jaw, and the tightness in his shoulders. For just a moment, I wanted to take them away from him.

"Brock?" Mitch's voice cracked. "Did you just say Brock?" Mitch's strained voice broke the silence while Brock and I had a visual stand down.

With my frustration at Brock showing up, I hadn't realized that I had spoken out loud. I must have lapsed into vocal words absently.

I turned back to Mitch. His body was coiled, anger bubbled in his eyes, while a muscle ticked in his cheek and his hands clenched at his side. I didn't understand the sudden anger.

"Yes, I did. Brock is my Garda," I answered honestly, wondering why Mitch was so upset.

"Where is he? Is he here?" He pushed off the car and stood beside me, glaring in the direction that I had been facing.

I put my hand on his arm, "Mitch, what's wrong?"

"Where is he? Tell him to show himself!" his voice rose as he turned his head left and right, searching the area.

"Why? Mitch, what's going on?" I tried to step in front of him, tried to listen to what was going through his mind, but my focus was scattered, and noises surrounding me made it hard to hear just Mitch.

"Hello, Mitchell," Brock's deep voice rumbled out as he appeared in front of us. Mitch's face turned white as he stared Brock down.

Mitch's jaw clamped hard, and he used his left arm to push me out of the way as he stepped forward. So shocked was I by his movement, that I fell up against the car and spun around in time to see his right fist make contact with Brock's jaw.

Brock was knocked back, and I paused to see if he would throw a punch back. Instead, he put one hand to his jaw and rubbed it. I stepped in between them, putting one hand on Mitch's chest to hold him back, his heart crashed against his chest wall. His entire body was tense and his breathing heavy. The anger in his expression was directed past me toward Brock, and I turned to focus on Brock as he spoke.

"I guess I deserved that." As I watched him speak, I finally realized why he had seemed so familiar to me. I turned my head back to Mitch, scanning his face, and then back to Brock.

"You're his brother," my voice was barely a whisper. The hair color and eyes were different, but the features on his face, the chin, the cheekbones, the set of his eye sockets were the same. How could I not have seen it before?

Brock snuck a quick glance at me while he moved his jaw around and dropped his hand to his side.

"How do you know him, Corey?" Mitch's tense voice reached my ears, and I turned to him to respond.

"He's my Garda." I turned back to Brock. I waited for him to speak; he didn't.

CHAPTER 52 ~ MITCH

"You couldn't have Beth, so you go after Corey?" I had never wanted to hurt anyone as much as I wanted to hurt him at this very moment.

The sight of my brother, standing in front of me after all that I had gone through this last year and a half, unleashed an unholy fury.

"Calm down, Mitch, it's not what you think," Brock's voice was the same as I remembered, slightly deeper than mine.

"Not what I think! You son of a bitch! You slept with my fiancée! You got her pregnant! You both lied to me about it, and then years later I find out that Chase isn't mine! Now you're here after Corey! What the hell am I supposed to think?"

I couldn't stop the words once they started tumbling from my mouth. Corey put her hand on my arm. I shook it off.

"Mitch, stop. Let's talk about this," Corey whispered.

I spun on her, "I don't want to talk about this!" Her expression was startled and her eyebrows rose as she rocked back on her feet from the venom in my tone.

Before I could say anything else, she turned to Brock, "You should go."

"No! I'm not done with him!" I took a step towards my brother, and his shoulders straightened.

"I'm not going to fight you, Mitch. Listen to Coralenna."

I glanced at Corey quickly then back to him, "You call her Coralenna?"

"Brock, just go, please." Corey turned her back to me so I couldn't see her face.

"We need to talk, Coralenna." I couldn't see her face, but I figured she was communicating with him somehow and got the urge to punch him again.

Brock disappeared right before my eyes, and I spun around, searching for him.

"Where did he go?" my voice was deeper than usual, even to my ears.

"He went back to the Realm, Mitch. Relax, he's gone."

"The Realm? Where the hell is that?" I started pacing, trying to release the stress. Why was my brother with Corey? Better yet, why were dead people appearing before me?

"It's a place between heaven and Earth. It's where the Gardaí live and train."

I stopped and stared at her. "And he's your Garda? Is that what you're called?"

I didn't mean to take my anger out on her, but I just couldn't control it. "Yes," she said slowly.

"And he's trained you?" I stepped in front of her.

"Yes."

"What else has he done with you?" My anger simmered right below the surface, fear made my blood feel thick in my veins as I waited for her response.

She watched me carefully for a moment, "Nothing."

"I don't believe that. He wants something from you; I could tell that by the way he gaped at you." The memory of Brock staring into her face, the way I was meant to, shot a pain right to my heart. I spun around and resumed my pacing.

I ran my hands over my head, trying to get the blood to circulate, and covered my face for a moment. I needed to get back in control.

When I removed my hands, Corey stood directly in front of me. I hadn't heard her move, and her appearance startled me.

"You need to let the anger go," she said softly.

"Why? Why should I? He totally screwed up my life! Don't tell me that you're not angry at him either, because obviously that surprised you to find out who he was. How could you not have known?" My voice rose again as I spoke.

She shook her head and put her hands on my chest. The heavy work shirt and thick vest kept me from feeling it completely. I stared deeply into her eyes, wanting to lose myself in them.

"I am angry with him, but I will deal with him later." She put one hand on my cheek. "Right now, I'm worried about you."

"I'm fine." I heaved a heavy sigh, "I'm fine."

Just as she was about to speak again, the lapel mic on my shirt called out my number. I reached mindlessly for it and answered as our stares stayed locked together.

The dispatcher was sending me to a domestic. I wanted to tell them, No, I wasn't going, but I couldn't do that. I responded back and moaned.

Suddenly a thought entered my mind and made my knees weak, "You're not going to leave me again, are you?"

She leaned in and kissed my lips gently, "No, I'm not leaving you. I do have to leave, but I'll be back."

"When?" anxiety laced my words.

"Soon, go do what you have to do, I'll be back soon. Not tonight, but soon, I promise."

I grabbed her by her forearms and pulled her to me in a quick deep kiss. When the dispatcher came back over the radio with more information about my call, I reluctantly pulled away and answered her. Corey stepped back so I could get in the car, and fear coiled in my gut that I would never see her again.

"Relax, Mitch, I'll be back soon."

I jerked a quick acknowledgement and climbed in the driver's seat. I took one last, long view of her through the window, and I put the car in drive and flipped on the headlights, taking off from behind the warehouse before I changed my mind.

Corey was back. Somehow, someway, she had come back to me. Being able to touch her and kiss her again, healed a piece of my heart that had been fractured from the moment I had seen her lying on the pavement.

I gulped as I turned onto the road leading to the residence where the domestic was. She was back, but would she stay? She's an angel? How could she stay? What did that really mean for us?

I pulled up behind my partner's car and pushed the thoughts aside so I could deal with the situation. There would be time enough to dwell on it later.

PART 7

The Accident

CHAPTER 53 ~ BROCK

*I*t wasn't hard to find her when I phased down. She was right where I knew she would be, right in Mitch's arms. Before I could even think, I called out to her to stop.

When she said my name out loud, I internally groaned as I watched Mitch. Surprise and then sheer anger covered his facial features.

The entrance so close to them was not a smart idea, but if getting struck by Mitch helped him deal with his issues, then I would have taken many more from him.

His anger was not the only thing I would have to deal with, her anger would probably be worse. The moment she realized that I was his brother; her dark blue eyes started throwing out stormy sparks. She would want to know why I had never told her. It would be just another thing that she would feel I had held back and lied to her about—and hadn't I done just that?

I didn't want to leave her there with him, but I knew I needed to allow him time to calm down. I would have to find a way to get him to understand, to explain what had happened, but first I would deal with Coralenna's wrath.

Back in the Realm, I stalked into my bathroom, tearing off my clothes and throwing them on the floor. A long hot shower was what I needed.

How could I justify to her that my reasons for holding back this information were worthwhile? I thought that maybe she would have seen the similarities between us, but she never put two and two together.

The steam rose around me as I stepped into the hot spray. Hanging my head, I allowed the water to run over my neck and down my back. I wiggled my jaw slowly; it still hurt from the punch.

I picked up the liquid soap and poured some in my hand. Without conscious thought, I rubbed it over my body as I replayed the scene with Mitch and Corey. The unbridled passion that had consumed them as they kissed had put my stomach in a knot.

After I finished washing, I stood with the water pouring over my face when I felt something unexpected—well, not that unexpected—in the room.

"We need to talk, Mr. O'Reilly," Corey's angry voice bounced off the tile walls. I reached over and slid the door back with one hand while I turned the faucet off with the other.

Our glares met briefly before hers followed the water rivulets down my chest. She blinked when her sight hit below my waist and flicked back to my face, a light blush rising to her cheeks.

She grabbed the thick navy blue towel beside her and threw it at me. "I'll wait on the balcony." She spun around after examining the length of my body.

Like she had once before, I took my time getting dressed. Although I wasn't going to paint my nails, I did dry my hair and shave before finally throwing on jeans and a T-shirt.

With bare feet, I padded out over the hardwood floor of the hallway and into the living room. She stood on the balcony beholding the beauty of the Realm.

I walked out to face the music.

CHAPTER 54 ~ COREY

*D*id the punch that landed on Brock's jaw hurt any worse than knowing that he had once again not told me the truth?

Trying to calm Mitch down and not allowing my own anger to flare was difficult to say the least, but I managed to do it, until now.

Of course being that close to Mitch had helped me to stay calm. The kiss he gave me before he left for his call seared my psyche.

As his car drove away, I put the tip of my finger to my tingling lips. I walked back to my car and climbed in. The car brought back memories of my time with Mitch, and I grinned as I remembered that he never did take me for a ride on his bike. Maybe I would suggest that when I saw him next.

After backing the Camaro into the storage garage, I left the keys on the seat and exited. I tugged the big garage door down and snapped the padlock back into place.

With one quick scan to make sure that I was alone, I stepped forward to cross the level. The feeling of being sucked into a vortex wasn't as strong, and I relaxed once I entered. I found it so much more peaceful on this side.

For a moment, I thought about how my peace was about to end. I phased straight to Brock, reaching for his energy and landing smack dab in his bathroom.

The steam hung heavily in the room, almost as thick as my anger.

"We need to talk, Mr. O'Reilly," my voice was strong and loud, so it could be heard over the water.

The water stopped just as he pulled the shower door open. His expression was hungry as it met mine through the thick mist in the room.

Oh crap, I thought as I took in his wet body from head to waist and stopped myself from going any further. The water beaded on his skin, catching on the dark hair lightly dusted over his chest. Why couldn't I have waited till he was done?

How tempting I found it to stare at him, but I wasn't here to drool over his body. We needed to talk. I threw him a towel and walked out of the room.

The breeze was different on the balcony than it had been in the living arena, softer in a way. I contemplated the majesty of the land before me. How could a place so incredible have so much turmoil? Wasn't this little slice of heaven supposed to be joyous?

What would I say to him when he came out? Each time I started to think about him, I remembered the man who stood in the shower. I blinked away the vision and sighed, trying to bring back the memory of kissing Mitch.

Would his lips feel the same as Mitch's? I groaned as I lowered my head to the railing and hit my forehead twice on the wood.

"I thought you would be trying to knock sense into me, not yourself," his deep voice filled the silence, and I forced myself not to turn towards it.

"Funny," I spat out sarcastically.

He walked up beside me and gripped the railing with both hands. His hands weren't overly big. They were larger than mine, with thicker fingers, but they were not by any means large hands. Would they feel the same?

I shut that thought down and clamped my eyelids tightly, trying to remind myself of why I was here.

"Why didn't you tell me?" my voice came out calmer than I had expected.

I saw the shrug out of the peripheral of my vision. He bent over and rested his elbows on the railing, hanging his head.

"Would it have made a difference?" he asked.

Would it have? No, I loved Mitch. "Why did you do that to him? He's your brother, how could you?"

He sighed heavily, "It's a long story, Coralenna."

I turned to him, "Well, we do have eternity, so spill it."

He turned to face away from the awe-inspiring beauty of the Realm, crossing his arms over his chest, and his right foot over his left. "That was a long time ago, it doesn't matter."

"Doesn't matter?" The anger bubbled up in me, "Who are you trying to convince, Brock?"

His eyes snapped to mine, "I don't need to convince anyone. It's the past, Corey, leave it there."

"I will not! Brock, you should have told me that Mitch was your brother!" I stepped in front of him, the urge to smack him grew, but the side of his face was already slightly swollen from the hit his brother had given him.

He stood to his full height, two inches taller than Mitch, his lips tight. "What difference would it have made? Huh? You would have only thought that I was trying to steal you away from him."

I bit my lip, "Were you?"

"No." He opened his mouth to say more, but closed it.

"No, what? What were you about to say?" I shifted closer to him.

"It doesn't matter, Coralenna." He stood up straight and walked around me.

I spun around, "What do you mean, it doesn't matter? It does matter, Brock!"

He turned on his heel and took two quick steps to stand directly in front of me. My pulse increased its tempo. "Why? Why does it matter to you?"

My voice trembled, "Because I need to know. I need to know why you didn't tell me, why you kept that from me when you knew how much I cared about him."

He looked me straight in the face, his scrutiny traveling down to my lips and back up, "I wasn't allowed to tell you, and I wasn't trying to steal you away from him. You were never supposed to be his, Coralenna, you were only supposed to be mine." His hand started to reach out to me, but I quickly stepped back, drawing in a ragged breath as I did.

"Yours? I was supposed to be yours? Like some kind of toy or something?" I crossed my arms over my chest, clenching my fists together.

"Give me a break, Coralenna, not like a toy," he threw back at me.

"I'm not yours, Brock," I said through clenched teeth, "and the way things are going, I never will be."

I spun around and started to walk away.

"Coralenna, wait!" he called as I started to step into his living room.

I half turned to him. The sun was setting behind him, the blues and purples highlighted his body, and I stifled a sob. "Stay away from me, Brock. Don't come near me again unless you are ready to tell me the truth, all of it—and stay away from Mitch, too." I started to turn but spun back at him, "You got that?"

Pain ravaged the features of his face, but I told myself I didn't care. "Yeah, I got it," he whispered just before I spun and walked out.

CHAPTER 55 ~ MITCH

A week had passed since I had seen Corey—or had I only seen her in a dream? Part of me believed it to be real, but the other part felt like it had been a mental tease to my heart.

Everywhere I went, I searched for her. One day, I actually followed a black Camaro over nine miles before the driver pulled over. The driver wasn't Corey.

Could it have only been a dream? Could my subconscious mind pull up Brock and Corey together? I didn't think so, and the knuckles on my right hand still ached from where I had punched Brock. It had to have been real.

Not only had I been thinking over what had happened that night, but I had thought about something Corey had said, something about people trying to influence my decisions. As the week went by, I started to think that maybe Joe was the one she was talking about.

It seemed that recently, he had been around more and when he was, that was when I made the decisions that were not of the best intentions, kind of like the incident with Rebecca.

"You seem to be in a good mood these days, Mitch, what gives?" Joe said from his car as we sat side by side in a parking lot drinking coffee.

I shrugged; I had no intention of telling him I had seen Corey. He'd think I was nuts.

"You and Beth working things out?" Joe glanced up from the report he was writing.

"I guess." I took a sip of my coffee.

"You've seen her, haven't you?" He put his arm out the window, pointing his pen at me, "She came back to see you?"

Frozen, I stared at him. How could he know she came back? Did she come back to see him, too? "What are you talking about?" The words barely got out of my mouth.

He threw his head back and laughed, "She did! Man, I gotta hand it to her, she's persistent when it comes to you."

My heart raced, "What are you talking about, Joe?"

"Corey, Corey came back to save you," he laughed again.

I didn't understand why he would think that, and suddenly I felt the need to protect her. "Corey's dead."

"Come on, Mitch, I know what she is. You think you're the only—" three tones on the radio cut off his next words, and he lifted the microphone to his lips to answer the call.

An armed robbery was in progress right around the corner. "Time to go play, Mitch!" He tossed his clipboard to the passenger seat and threw his car in gear before racing away. An eerie feeling pulsed through my veins as I thought about our conversation. I no longer trusted him at all.

When we arrived, we both got into a foot pursuit with the suspect. He turned down an alley, and I was right behind Joe as we slowed and made the turn, our handguns drawn as we listened to his footsteps pounding down the filthy alleyway.

Memories of another foot pursuit crossed my mind, and Corey's face flashed inside it.

Be careful, Mitch. Her voice sang through my mind. She was here, I could feel her.

Joe surged ahead and got to the corner of the alley before me, his gun out in front as he made the turn. I saw him stop abruptly and, as if in slow motion, I saw him pull the trigger back, and a flash of flame appeared at the front of the muzzle.

Somehow, a scream and a thud reached my ears over the thunderous echo of the gun against the brick walls. I slid to a stop, staring down the alley at the suspect as he lay on his back, his gun pointed at us.

I raised my gun. "Shoot him, Mitch!" Joe urged beside me.

The urge to do just that raged through my body as I stared at the gun pointed at us.

Don't, Mitch. He won't shoot you; he's just scared.

I ignored Joe and listened to the voice inside my head. "Put your gun down!" I yelled at the suspect who was in obvious pain, his gun hand shook violently in the air.

"Shoot him, Mitch, before he shoots us!" Joe sneered.

I stepped forward, ignoring Joe again and walked towards the suspect, "Put the gun down. You don't have to do this. Just put the gun down so we can get you some help."

The young male shook from either pain or fear, probably a mixture of both.

"Put the gun down, slowly. Let me get you some help." I stepped closer.

The barrel of the gun started to lower, and I thought I had him convinced to give up. When I got to within five feet of him, his head turned quickly and he lifted his gun and pointed it behind me. A shot rang out, and I watched the kid fall back, blood seeping from his head. The gun fell from his hand, clattering to the ground beside him.

"What the hell did you just do?" I screamed at Joe. "I had him putting it down!"

Joe shrugged and walked up beside me. "He was going to shoot me, you saw it."

"He was going to put the gun down!" I watched Joe holster his gun, and I absently did the same, then stepped away and felt the boy's neck for a pulse.

I glared at Joe and shook my head. Anger suddenly blinded me, and I surged up and slammed Joe back against the brick wall.

He threw a punch to my stomach and twisted me around so that I was now against the damp stone. My head smashed back, and the tiny points of the brick dug into the back of my skull. His hand went to my throat, and he squeezed. I grabbed his arm and tried to pull it off my neck, but his grip was too tight.

My eyes closed as the lack of oxygen started to darken my vision, and I gasped as I was suddenly released. I dropped to the ground, sucking in air and touching my throat with one hand to make sure I was still in one piece.

A grunt beside me grabbed my attention. Corey and Joe were locked in a heated visual battle.

CHAPTER 56 ~ BROCK

"We need to do something."

Montgomery put his hand on my arm as he answered, "No, we wait to see if she needs help."

"She needs our help." Corey had unwittingly called out to me when the fight with Joe and Mitch had started, and I had immediately come to her aide with Montgomery right behind me.

"She has it under control. Just wait, Brock."

Corey moved in a slow circle with Joe. David appeared beside me.

"There's the warrior," he said quietly, his smile could be heard in his voice.

"I knew you'd come back for him," Joe stated to her as their dance continued. "He's your weakness."

"He is not my weakness, and you need to stay away from him," she tossed the reply back at him. Joe rushed forward to grab her, but she spun and kicked him in the stomach. A loud grunt filled the alley.

"It's him or you, Corey. What's it gonna be?"

"You will get neither of us, Joe."

He pitched forward again, and she stepped out of the arena just as he was about to reach her.

"You bitch! I'll get you, Corey! This is not over!" He turned to focus on

Mitch. Mitch stood up slowly and pulled his shoulders back. He fisted his hands. Joe advanced on him, but before he got to him, two other officers turned the corner into the alley.

"Thanks for coming," Coralenna said as she watched the scene.

David slapped her on the back, "Love watching you work!"

Corey peeked at me briefly, then she turned away nervously.

We all watched as the other officers took in the situation and heard Joe say that the suspect had been fighting with Mitch. He had shot the suspect to save Mitch's life. Mitch stayed quiet, watching him carefully.

"Come on, Mitch, tell them the truth," Corey whispered.

Mitch looked to the ground when one of the officers walked up to him. They spoke quietly, and then he led Mitch away.

Coralenna and I glanced at each other. Both of us were wondering if he would explain what really happened, knowing that it would be hard to explain.

"Thanks for coming," her look encompassed all of us. "I wasn't sure what was going to happen."

"You did well, Coralenna," Montgomery said to her and hugged her.

David patted her on her shoulder, "You done good, girl!" She chuckled and looked at him.

Montgomery and David left shortly after, and I stood watching her as she studied the scene. Joe was no longer there, and medical staff was attending to the young man who had been killed.

"Do you think he will tell the truth?" she asked quietly from beside me.

I turned to her, "I hope he does." I hesitated before continuing, "Maybe you can talk to him and encourage him to do what's right."

Confusion flitted over her face briefly, "Yeah, okay."

I watched her for another moment, wanting to say more, but not sure how. I knew that if I pushed the situation, with her feelings towards Mitch, it would only push her further away. We had not spoken since the argument on the balcony.

"Is there anything else you need?" I asked her as I started to turn away.

She didn't look at me, "No, thanks."

I nodded in response, but I doubt she saw it, she had already started to phase away.

CHAPTER 57 ~ COREY

I watched Mitch on and off during the week, well, more on than off; however, I did stay out of his house for the most part.

Mitch spent a lot of time thinking about my visit and taking what I had said to heart about his decisions. I knew that he was realizing that Joe was the problem.

I stood beside him as he raced down the alley, calmed him when he might have shot the suspect, and then stepped in to protect him when Joe decided to cross the line.

When Joe had slammed him up against the wall, I had no doubt that he would have killed him just like he had murdered the kid he had just shot.

With barely a thought, I stepped into the living arena and landed a strong side kick to Joe that knocked him away from Mitch. A quick glance reassured me that Mitch was alright as he tried to catch his breath on his hands and knees.

"I knew you'd come back for him," Joe sneered at me. "He's your weakness."

There is no way I would admit that he was right, "He is not my weakness, and you need to stay away from him."

He took the moment I spoke to charge me, but I moved fast and spun, landing a strong strike to his stomach.

"It's him or you, Corey. Who's it gonna be?" The smile he pasted on his lips was evil.

"You will get neither of us, Joe."

I heard feet pounding in the alleyway and stepped back over to hide from the living. Joe was none too happy with my exit.

Mitch stood up hesitantly. Come on, Mitch, don't give in to him, I thought to myself.

Once I knew Mitch was safe, I turned to thank everyone for coming. When I had seen Joe going after Mitch, I had no idea what would happen. I had wished that others were here just in case I needed help. I guess that had been enough to call them.

This was the first time I had seen Brock since I'd told him to leave me alone. Something fluttered in my stomach as I snuck a sidelong glance at him.

We needed to talk. I had to understand why he had done what he had with Beth. Not that this was my business, but I felt that I deserved to know the truth.

Since we had last spoken, I had hoped he would come to me and finally tell me truth, but he hadn't. Should I push it? Or would that just lead to us both being aggravated at each other again?

Standing in the station, I watched Mitch sit nervously outside the chief's office. As was customary in an officer-involved shooting, his firearm had been removed from his holster. They would check it carefully to see if it had been fired and compare bullets from the deceased person to confirm stories.

The door opened, and Mitch was called in.

Take a deep breath, Mitch, relax, and tell the truth.

The truth? Does that mean I'm supposed to tell him about you? I think if I did he'd be putting me on psych leave, he answered me mentally.

I laughed, *No, not about me, but about what Joe did.*

Mitch nodded and stood up. *Stay with me, please, I need your support.*

I smiled even though he could not see me, *I'm not going anywhere.*

"Sit down, Mitch," the chief did not sound happy.

I watched Mitch sit stiffly in the leather chair in front of the large wooden desk.

"What happened out there?" he asked as he sat back in his large executive chair.

"With all due respect, sir, and as much as I would like to tell you, I have to wait until I have spoken to one of our union attorneys."

I raised my eyebrows. The chief stared Mitch down, and I was glad to see that Mitch locked onto the gaze and gave it back.

The chief sighed loudly. "Alright, I understand that." He stood up from his chair and walked to the window, his hands behind him in the small of his back.

"Let me just ask you something, Mitch."

Mitch nodded assent, but the chief had his attention still out the window.

"What do you think of your partner?" the chief turned to him, and I saw Mitch grind his teeth.

What do I tell him, Corey? I felt his mind spin.

Tell him the truth, I whispered into his head.

"Honestly, sir, I think Joe has some major issues." The chief nodded slowly and turned back to the window.

"Alright, thank you. You may be excused, but I want to speak with you as soon as you have had a chance to speak with the attorney."

"Yes, sir," he stood up. "Thank you, sir." He turned to leave the room without the chief saying anything else.

As he reached the door, I felt the pull. The vibration that radiated through my entire being that told me I was being summoned.

Mitch, I need to go. I'll be back when I can. Without waiting for his reply, I phased back to the Realm and into the area where the Master would speak.

As usual, the brightness took me off guard and I blinked as my eyes adjusted.

"You are doing well, Coralenna, I'm proud of you." As usual, the voice instilled a sense of peace.

"Thank you," I replied quietly.

It grew very quiet, and I wondered if I was already dismissed or if there was more to be said. I fidgeted for a moment.

"It is time that you speak with Brock again. The two of you need to move forward, get over the walls between you."

"If he would tell me the truth for once, we might be able to." Tension filled me even though I wished to remain calm.

"Try to keep your anger from pushing the wrong buttons, and maybe he will explain. It is time, and he knows it is."

"Alright, I will." I glanced around, although there was nothing to see but whiteness.

"Keep doing what you are doing with Mitchell. It would be good to remove Joe from his life. It would put him on a better path." The softness of the voice relieved the tension from a moment ago.

"I will."

"Just be careful, my child, you are very close to him." The voice hesitated, "It could cause you problems."

Before I could acknowledge him, I landed in my quarters.

What problems? I wanted to ask, although I knew I would not get a response to such a question.

In my kitchen, I pulled out a wine bottle and set it on the counter. In one of my drawers, I pulled out the corkscrew and opened the bottle, then poured wine into two crystal glasses.

With the drinks in hand, I walked to the balcony. The sun was setting. I loved the sky in the Realm at dusk.

I reached out for Brock mentally. He was in the Realm, so I called him to me. Moments later, he appeared before me. His face confused and slightly guarded as he arrived.

"Is everything alright?" He glanced at the wineglasses.

I held one out for him, "Peace offering?"

He reached for the glass. I moved away from him and sat down in a glider. He took a seat beside me after sipping from his glass.

"Someday, I want to taste this while we are in the living arena. I'd like to see if the taste is different." He passed me a lazy grin, and I returned it before turning my attention to my wineglass.

"What's on your mind, Coralenna? I can feel the weight of your thoughts."

After resting my head back against the glider, I turned to him. He was so handsome. The features of his face were strong, solid, and his eyes, well, his eyes were altogether incredible.

"I need you to tell me the truth, Brock, all of it. I need to understand what you did and why you did it."

He cleared his throat but didn't speak.

"You told me you had a brain tumor; Mitch says you died in an accident. Which is it?"

"Both."

CHAPTER 58 ~ MITCHELL

Thank God Corey was with me when I spoke with the chief, but it would have helped if she hadn't taken off when I had to go talk to the attorney. I was confused that she would leave just then after she had stayed for the first part.

When the chief had asked about Joe, I wasn't sure where he was going, but my answer seemed to satisfy something in him.

After speaking with the lawyer, I left the station. The chief had left word that I was to report to his office the next morning.

I felt better about what had happened once I had the time to speak with my union representative. I had told him as much as I could, leaving the fight between Corey and Joe out of it. I had no clue what Joe would tell him, but I knew that I had to be honest with what I said, well, with as much as I could talk about anyway.

Beth was in the kitchen when I got home. Since our conversations about Corey, things had continued to go well. It was hard to pretend with her about Corey being back, but there were many reasons I couldn't tell her about that.

For one, she would think I was crazy. Another, I had no idea what was going on with Corey and me now. It's not like I could have a relationship with an angel, could I?

When I walked in the house, Beth smiled and pulled a plate out of the toaster oven. "I kept your dinner warm."

"Thanks, I'm starved." I washed my hands and sat down at the table.

"I got your message about being late. What happened at work? I heard on the news that there was a shooting." She sat down across the square table.

What would she say if I told her that Joe had killed a kid, then tried to kill me, then got into a knockdown, drag-out fight with an angel? I almost laughed and shoved a piece of chicken into my mouth to stifle it.

After chewing, I glanced up and spoke, "Yeah, Joe shot a guy today." I cut another piece of meat. "Beth, do me a favor."

She raised her eyebrows and rested her hands on the table, "Sure."

"Stay away from Joe. Don't trust him, alright?" I stared at her hard.

"Why?" she asked, confused. "He's your friend."

With a quick shake of my head, I said, "He's not my friend, and he's not yours either. He's a dangerous man, and you need to stay away from him, alright?"

She laughed, "Oh, come on, Mitch, how could he possibly be dangerous? He's your best friend."

I set my fork and knife down and laid my hands beside my plate, focusing on her face. "Because he tried to kill me tonight, Beth. He's not my friend, and he's not your friend. Please, stay away from him."

Her face paled and her mouth dropped open. "What?"

I picked up my fork again, spearing a piece of broccoli, "I can't say anymore about it right now. It's under investigation, but he's a dangerous man, and you can't trust him."

She still had no color in her face, but acknowledged my request with a quick nod of her head. The rest of my meal continued in silence.

CHAPTER 59 ~ BROCK

"Both," the word felt thick and heavy on my tongue. "What do you mean both?"

I glanced over at her. She waited patiently but intently for me to respond. Her honey-blond hair hung over her shoulder, and a few strands danced in the breeze.

I observed the sunset momentarily, bright orange and pink burst forth, a warm and seductive sky.

"For a few years before I died, I started having symptoms. I would get headaches, forget things, and people made comments about my personality changing." I paused to take a sip of my wine. I then set it down on the arm of my glider.

"At first, I didn't think much about all of it, but then I started to see the personality changes myself." I slid a quick glance to the side to see the expression on her face. She appeared calm.

"I started getting really negative about people and life; I took advantage of people that I shouldn't have." A heavy pause filled the air as I thought about my next words. My hands grew damp, and I rubbed my left hand on my jeans to dry it. "I became someone I didn't like. I did things I would have never done, but the tumor in my head was growing, and I didn't recognize the signs. It put a lot of pressure on my brain tissue."

I traded the wineglass to my other hand and wiped my right palm over my pants. "I came up to visit Mitch and Beth before the wedding. I took advantage of my time there to hang out with some of my old friends, and one night I ran into Beth while she was out with some of her girlfriends."

The sky darkened. Just like my story, I thought.

"She had been drinking—a lot. Anyway, I sat down with her and her friends and drank with them for a little while. I was really just making sure she was going to make it home safe."

"When she was ready to go home, I told her friends I would make sure she got there." I closed my eyes trying to block out what had happened then, but I had to tell Corey this part.

"What happened next, Brock?" Corey's soft voice prodded me.

"In the car, she came on to me. She was drunk, and I kept telling myself that she thought I was Mitch. She snuggled up to me in the car and put her hand between my legs. She started kissing my neck. I made a really bad judgment call."

I heard Corey sigh beside me, "Yes, you did."

"Anyway, what happened then just happened, and the next day we were both mortified that it had occurred. At that time, I still didn't know about the tumor growing in my head. I could barely face Mitch, but neither one of us wanted him to know. We didn't want to hurt him."

"That's understandable."

I glanced at her and she was watching the sky, the pinks were turning a darker purple.

"What happened next?" she asked.

"Six weeks after the wedding, Mitch and Beth announced they were having a baby. I was excited for them. Mitch had always wanted a few kids, although he had said this one was unexpected." The glider started moving back and forth with help from my feet. "A few months after the wedding, I got such a migraine that I couldn't stand. I was at work, and they called an ambulance. That's when they told me about the tumor." I paused for a moment. "They said that the tumor was so large that there was probably nothing that could be done. It was only a matter of time before it killed me."

Corey's chair stopped moving, and I saw her hand move towards me, but she set it back down on the wooden arm of the glider.

"Beth got in touch me with after her twenty-week appointment; just after I had learned what was causing all my problems. She had gone in for her routine ultrasound, and Mitch had had a court hearing, so he wasn't there." My throat felt thick as I continued. "She told me that during the appointment, they found that the baby was bigger than they thought it should be and they started recalculating the delivery date."

Corey started to push her glider back and forth again slowly next to me.

"She told me the child was mine." I swallowed, choking on the words, "All I could think about was how hurt Mitch would be about all of this. I told her not to tell him. I basically begged her to keep it to herself."

I stood up and set my glass down on the table; I moved to the balcony railing. I hung my head, ashamed even now.

"Why did you tell her to keep the secret?" Corey had gotten up also and stood beside me.

"I was dying," I lifted my head. "What good would it do for her to tell Mitch when I wouldn't even be around to get to know the kid?"

I pushed up and locked my elbows, straining my arms on the wood railing. "I begged her to keep it to herself. I told her I wanted nothing to do with it, and that I would sign off any rights I had as long as she didn't tell Mitch."

"What did she say?" Corey leaned against the balcony, her mid-back against the rail, her arms crossed over her chest.

"She finally agreed it would be best. She didn't know I was dying, no one did. I never told my family."

"Why not?"

I shrugged, "I don't know. I guess I didn't want to put a damper on the baby coming. Right after Chase was born, I came to see him. The guilt I felt made it too hard to stay around, so I went back home. A few months later, I was driving home from a chemo treatment, and the tumor put pressure on a section of my brain that controlled my eyesight. I crashed my car, died instantly."

The quick intake of breath from Corey told me I had surprised her.

"I guess when the police contacted Mitch, they only told him I had died in a car accident. At the time, they didn't know about the tumor. The police never gave it a second thought since no one else was injured."

Corey's head fell forward, her chin almost to her chest, "Oh, Brock." She lifted her head and I watched from the corner of my eye as studied me, "Why didn't you want to tell me the truth?"

"I'm not proud of what I did."

"But you could have told me the truth. You've been hurting for a long time, and Mitch and Beth have no idea why you did what you did. You need to tell them."

I pushed off the railing, "Are you kidding me? Mitch doesn't want to hear it, and Beth was so hurt, I'm not sure what I could even say to make it better."

She turned to face me head on, "You need to tell them the truth. While what you did was wrong, there were reasons why you did it. I think they would understand it and eventually accept it."

Was Corey right? Could Mitch forgive me? Would Beth be able to understand why I had chosen to distance myself?

CHAPTER 60 ~ COREY

Finally, Brock was opening up and telling me the truth. While it was horrible to know what he had done, I was able to understand it and forgive him. I knew that I wasn't the one who needed to forgive him, though. He needed for Mitch and Beth to forgive him, and, most of all, he needed to forgive himself.

"I don't know, Corey, I don't think they would forgive me." He turned and walked back to the glider. The muscles in his back were pulled tight with tension. If I wasn't so afraid of touching him, I would have gone to him and tried to ease the suffering he was feeling.

After he sat back down I walked over to him, "What if I try to talk to Mitch about it?"

He shook his head, "I can't ask you to do that. I know I need to try and talk to him, try to get him to understand, but I don't know how."

I sat down beside him, "Don't worry, Brock, we'll figure something out."

The two of us sat in a somewhat comfortable silence for a while. I wasn't angry with him anymore, and I wanted to somehow help him. My thoughts rolled over and over in my mind as to what I could do without any concrete plan coming to mind.

Brock left not long after, one of his charges needed some assistance, and one that he would have to deal with more directly. I smiled as he left. For once we parted without anger or frustration.

Still thinking over what he had told me, I phased down below and watched Mitch for a while. He was standing at an overlook high up on a mountain road. His face appeared to be relaxed, but his body posture told a different story.

His motorcycle sat quiet behind him. I smiled. Maybe this was my chance to go for a ride. I stepped over into the living arena.

"You're in deep thought there, mister," I said softly from behind him.

He spun around, his heart racing.

"Sorry, I forgot how startling my popping in can be."

He laughed and his body visibly relaxed. "Hi, Corey. Yeah, it is a bit frightening to be standing alone on the side of a mountain and then not."

I noticed that the lines around his eyes seemed harsher than the last time I had seen him. I got closer and touched his face gently.

"Are you alright? You seem tired." My thumb grazed over the soft skin of his lips and he grinned.

He slid his arms around my waist and pulled me closer to him, "I'm much better now."

His lips met mine in a soft seductive kiss. My body melted towards him. No matter how many times he kissed me, my body always wanted to respond to it. My hands wound around his neck, and I deepened the kiss.

He pulled back after a few moments. "Let's go someplace a bit more private."

I gazed into his handsome face and smiled. "Sure, as long as I get to ride on the back of your bike."

"I do owe you one, don't I?" he laughed as he spoke.

"Yes, you do, and I now plan to collect on that promise you made me." As I finished speaking, I watched the smile fade from his expression. "What's wrong?"

"I made you other promises and didn't keep them," his voice was hoarse as he replied.

"What are you talking about?" I pulled back so I could see him better.

"I promised to keep you safe, instead I caused your accident." Pain washed over his face.

"Oh, Mitchell," I put my hand on his cheek, "you didn't cause my death. I made the choice to do what I did. This wasn't your fault."

He shook his head, "No, it was my fault."

My left hand reached down for his, and I pulled him toward his bike, "Look, let's go someplace else, and we'll talk."

He climbed on and started the engine. I waited until he nodded at me and I stepped up on the foot peg he pointed to. The vibration of the bike filled me, and I took a seat behind him.

The bike had a backrest, but I wanted to hold onto him, so I leaned forward and wrapped my arms around his waist. He pulled out on the road, and we started heading down the mountain.

The wind whipped my hair, and I reached back with one hand to gather it tightly and tuck it into the collar of my shirt. I held on to Mitch, inhaled his musky scent, and felt his back move as he drove. The sun shone down on us, lighting our way.

We drove for an hour before he slowed down and pulled into a lot. I sat up and recognized the stone lot near the creek we had once visited. When he stopped, I climbed off the back and waited while he dismounted.

"So, what did you think?" he asked when he turned to me.

My mouth split open with a huge smile, "I loved it!"

He threw his arm over my shoulders, and we made our way towards the path. "Glad you enjoyed it." He placed a kiss on my temple.

We stayed quiet as we walked; holding hands and following the running water to the place where we had once sat, the rock ledge where we had confessed our love to one another, the memories bittersweet with all that had passed in the intervening months.

After we got settled on the rocks, Mitch tucked me into his side and rested his head against the top of mine. His heart beat steadily in his chest, and the sound of birds filled the air around us. The water gurgled over the rocks, and we both remained silent.

"I didn't think I would ever see you again, Corey," he whispered into my hair right before he kissed my head.

"I know." I pushed away enough so that I could observe his face. "I know you were hurting, Mitch. I saw some of it after the accident."

"What did you see?" His hand played with the ends of my hair on my back. I loved the almost-tickling sensation of his fingers' movements.

"I was at the funeral."

His brows rose, and his hand stopped moving. "You were there? Did you talk to me?"

"I did."

His hand resumed the movement along my back, "I felt you. I heard you, only, after a while, I thought I had imagined it. When you disappeared after that, I thought the pain had produced the sound and feelings."

My head found its way back to his chest. "No, I was there. You needed my strength."

"I did." He kissed the top of my head again. "I need you."

For a while we didn't talk. "Mitch, I need you to understand that what happened was meant to be, and you can't blame yourself for it."

He pulled away and put his hand under my chin to lift it. "You can say that all you want, but I still feel responsible. You are so important to me, and I had promised you I would keep you safe, but I didn't."

"Mitch, honey, it was my time, my destiny to die that day." I thought briefly about how Brock had made the call a bit early, and I decided not to tell Mitch that part.

"I can't accept that. Your destiny was with me. What am I supposed to do now?" he asked, hurt threading his words.

I sighed, "I don't know."

CHAPTER 61 ~ MITCHELL

*W*hen Corey just popped in on me, I was more than surprised. Happiness filled the emptiness of the past half year.

When she wrapped her arms tightly around me, I knew exactly where I wanted to take her. The drive to the creek was smooth, and for once, I didn't have to pretend that she sat behind me. I actually felt her body tucked tightly to mine.

The smiles she gave me put light back in my heart. The kisses she placed on my lips ignited me with a peace that I didn't know could be felt.

I almost forgot that she was dead. Her body felt so real, her scent drifted around her and completed me.

When our conversation turned back to her death and the promises I had failed to keep, we both tensed.

"I can't accept that. Your destiny was with me. What am I supposed to do now?" I felt like I was being a whiney child, but I had to know what happened now.

I felt her sigh as she spoke, "I don't know."

"Neither do I." I turned my head away from her. I didn't want her to see the pain on my face.

"Mitch, can you just be happy that we have these few moments together?" She put her hand under my chin and turned my face back to hers.

"But how long are we going to have them, Corey? Do I have to die to be with you forever?" Shock crossed her face as the words left my mouth.

"No! Mitch, it isn't your time to die. Please don't say those things."

"Why not? I want to be with you, Corey. If I were dead, we could be together. Maybe you should have let Joe kill me." The thought of dying didn't frighten me, not as much as the thought of living without her did.

She pushed away from me, "Mitch, stop! Don't talk like that. You are going to die, but not now. You have a long life to live—and what about Beth and Chase?"

"What about them?" I challenged back to her. "Chase isn't mine, wait —" he stopped talking and stood up, "you don't want me with you because of Brock. Is that it?" I felt the anger pump in my veins as the thought occurred to me.

She stood up and faced me, "Mitch, your brother has nothing to do with this."

"He doesn't, does he?" I spun away from her, wiping my hands over my head. "Tell me you don't care about him." I waited tensely for her to speak.

"Mitchell, you are making more out of this than there needs to be. Of course, I care about Brock, but it's not like you think." I felt her hand on my back and shrugged it off.

"It's not what I think!" I snorted a laugh, "Not what I think."

She stepped around me and grabbed my forearms to hold me still. Her grasp was stronger than I imagined it would be.

"Mitch, there are things that you just don't understand, a lot of things that you don't know about. Brock is my Garda. He watched over me and protected me for years. He didn't pick me, he was assigned to me. This is just destiny that we all came together the way we did."

"Destiny?" I couldn't hold back the hard laugh, "Are you buying your own words, Corey?"

She stepped back as if I had slapped her. "Yes, I do believe in destiny, Mitch. I believe in fate, I believe in things happening for a reason. What's wrong with that?"

What was wrong with believing in fate? I hung my head, as I tried to calm myself down.

"I'm sorry," I stepped closer to her and put my hands on her hips. "I'm sorry. I just miss you so much, and I don't understand where things go from here. Seeing Brock with you was a shock."

She put her hands on my chest, "I know. You need to speak with him. There are things that he needs to tell you, things that he needs to explain to you." Her eyes were pleading with me as she spoke softly to me.

"Maybe someday, but not right now." I pulled her into my chest and held her.

"Just think about it, okay?" she whispered into my chest.

"I will." My stomach growled loudly just after the words left my mouth, and we both laughed.

"Looks like you need to eat." She pulled away and I glanced around us, darkness had begun to settle in. I hadn't even noticed.

"Do you eat?" I asked her as I took her hand, and we started walking away.

"I sure do, and I would love a hamburger." She winked at me, and I pulled her close to wrap my arm around her waist.

"I think I know just the place." By the time we got back to the motorcycle, the sky was getting really dark.

We climbed on and hit the road. She snuggled up to my back again, and I tried not to think about what would happen in our future. Instead, I concentrated on the bike and the feel of her arms around my waist.

I felt her sigh deeply behind me. I took one hand off the handlebars and reached down to squeeze her hands that lay against my stomach.

I glanced down at our hands touching for only a moment, but when I lifted my head back up, two headlights were coming straight at us.

CHAPTER 62 ~ BROCK

For the first time since Coralenna had joined the Realm, I felt that we had peace between us. The fact that she didn't judge me for what had happened but instead seemed to sympathize with what I had done made me feel almost inadequate in her presence. What an incredible woman she was.

I sat next to Billy, he was one of my newer charges, and he needed some direct assistance from me. I glanced over at him and, while he was drunk, he appeared to be doing alright behind the wheel of the car.

I leaned my head back on the seat and stared out the window. The stars were coming out in the heavens above, and I smiled. I closed my eyes as I remembered the sincere expression on her face.

When Billy made a noise beside me, I turned from the window to see him messing with the buttons on his dashboard console. He punched one preprogrammed button after another on his radio, taking his focus off the roadway while he did.

A sound registered in my mind just as a flash of light struck the windshield. A motorcycle was coming straight towards us. The fact that a crash was imminent was not my concern. The real concern was that the people on the bike were Mitch and Corey, and Corey was in a mortal body.

Without another thought, I phased out of the car to Corey and yanked her from the bike and into the level above just a split second before impact.

The shocked expression on Corey's face as she met mine sent a pulse down my spine. My arms encircled her tightly and her hands had gone to my waist.

We stared at each other. One electrical burst through my body quickly became two and then three. Her mouth opened, and she dropped her head back as if it were too heavy to hold up.

If I felt them, then she felt them, too, and they were quickly becoming overpowering. I glanced to my left just long enough to see a motorcycle wedged under the front of a car and a body lying on the side of the road. Before I could realize what the scene was, both Corey and I phased back to the Realm.

CHAPTER 63 ~ COREY

*Y*anked from the serenity I had felt while riding behind Mitch, my body was suddenly a minefield. My nerve endings burned through every inch of my body. A surge traveled with each beat of my heart.

I barely saw Brock's face in front of me, his features contorted in a similarly painful way as mine. The random thought that my body would combust into a bright fireball twisted through my mind.

My head dropped back, and I felt myself falling. The landing was soft, but the body that ended up on top of mine was anything but.

"Coralenna," a husky pain-filled voice reached my ears, and I struggled to open my eyes as the intensity rushed through me. Brock's face came into view as my lids opened into slits.

His jaw was clamped tightly, and the urge to kiss his lips to relax him filled my mind. My hands reached for his face, sliding over the hot skin of his cheeks and into the hair on the sides of his head.

I pulled his lips to mine, the urge a sudden need that filled me from the bottom of my toes to the top of my head. Our lips met, and colors exploded behind my eyelids. I heard him groan as he slid his hand around the side of my ribs and pulled me tighter to him.

The kiss deepened, both of us allowing this insane hunger to sate the other as our tongues tangled and our lips crushed against one another's.

The pain started to recede and pleasure slowly replaced it. His body called to me, and mine responded. There were no thoughts, no questions to ask. There was only the need to feel what we had.

My arms slipped over his shoulders, pulling his body as close to mine as it could get, but not sating the need to feel him.

His lips left mine and traveled down to my throat, my pulse raced under his touch and my eyelids blinked heavily. Stars filled the sky above me. I closed them again, wanting only to feel the passion we had together.

As he kissed my neck lower, I turned my head to allow better access and cracked open my lids again. With a start I jerked, and Brock lifted his head.

Fifty or so people stood watching us. I gazed around and realized we were lying on the beach in the Realm—and we had an audience.

"Some privacy, please," I whispered, and while Brock started to laugh, we phased from the beach and landed on the bed in my quarters.

"Better?" he said as he stroked my face.

"No," I pulled his head down to mine, his lips just a fraction of an inch away, "now it's better." He closed the distance between our lips, and all other thoughts melted from my mind.

PART 8

The Decision

CHAPTER 64 ~ BROCK

The pain sliced through me, and I struggled with the feelings that grew in me. Corey would be upset that the connection was being made against her will.

With her under me in the sand, I felt every inch of her body touching mine. She shifted and reached for me. Afraid to do anything wrong, I allowed her to lead. There was no hesitation when our lips met. The strongest emotions I had ever experienced burst forth in me, arching like rainbows around my heart.

I pulled away from her lips only long enough to attach them to her neck. Her startled jerk had me lifting my head. We had an audience, and more would come. This was a huge moment in the Realm. The connection of two spirits into one, a total consuming and twisting of their lives together, it had not happened in several years, and many had only heard of such a thing.

I understood their wanting to watch as our bodies joined physically and mentally, this was a beautiful thing, but as Corey begged quietly for privacy, I realized that was exactly what I wanted also.

Her blue eyes sparkled in the soft light of the moon as it came through the window, "Better?"

"No," she replied as she pulled me closer, "now it's better."

With just a slight movement, I closed the gap and took her lips again. Joy filled me as I released the fear that we would not connect, that it could have all been a lie.

Ribbons swirled like satin around our bodies as with each kiss, each touch, her memories invaded my mind. Her feelings, her likes and dislikes wound over and into me. Everything about me would be pouring into her, I knew. When our connection completed, there would be no lies between us. We would know each other better than we did ourselves.

Corey pulled my shirt over my head, running her hands over my shoulders to cup my face. "Brock," she whispered as she raised herself up to take my lips again.

After kissing her, I needed to know one thing, and I pulled back, "Corey, are you alright?"

Her drawn brows displayed confusion for only a moment, then a slow sensuous smile spread out over her lips and her brow smoothed out. "I'm wonderful, the pain is gone now." She touched my bottom lip with her thumb, and I kissed it gently.

"There will never be pain again, Corey." My mouth returned to her neck and nibbled. A soft sigh wafted into the air and we allowed ourselves to join on the wings of passion and fly high into the heavens.

We made love over and over, and I had never felt as content and fulfilled as I did now.

We snuggled beside one another, and I tried to keep thoughts of what had happened to make this event transpire out of my mind.

"I'm hungry," she spoke as her head lay on my chest, her hair fanned out around her. My fingers tangled in her soft locks.

Laughter rumbled through my chest, "I thought I had sated your hunger."

She laughed and lifted her head, "One of them, but with the workout we just had, I could use some nourishment."

She rolled back on her elbow to view me better, pulling the sheet up to cover herself gracefully.

"I love your eyes, the color is so unique," she whispered as she reached out a hand to caress my cheek.

My hand rested over hers, "I love you, Coralenna."

"I know." She smiled almost wistfully and pulled her hand away, "I felt it. I felt everything."

"That was pretty intense, wasn't it?" I cleared my throat and sat up against the headboard.

"Intense? No, I'd call it earth-shattering." Her hand rested over my chest, her finger gently tickling the hair that grew there. "Why were people watching us?"

With a quick glance around the room, I turned back to her. "There has not been a strong connection in a long time, since I first came here. It is an amazing thing, and everyone understands how powerful it is. They all wanted to watch it, to share in the joy."

"Doesn't that seem kind of freaky?" she asked hesitantly.

Laughter shook the bed, "The first time I saw it, I was so entranced, I couldn't look away. It was one of the most beautiful things I had ever seen, but when we were on the beach, the only thing I wanted was privacy with you."

"I'm glad. That's all I wanted, too." She placed a kiss on my chest and then threw the sheet back to climb out of bed. "I'm taking a shower and then getting something to eat."

"Do I get to join you?" I teased as she paraded naked to the bathroom door.

She called out over her shoulder, "No. If you join me, we will never get to eat."

My shoulders felt like a tremendous weight had been lifted off of them. Things were finally falling into place, everything except what had happened to Mitch.

I climbed out of the bed and phased to my quarters where I turned on the water for my own shower. Corey hadn't mentioned Mitch once since we'd connected. Did she not remember what happened? If she didn't remember, what was going to happen when she did?

The weight that had appeared to have been lifted suddenly felt like it hung over my head.

This was the first time we had been apart since the connection, and I felt like something major was missing, like a limb had been cut off. After a quick shower, I pulled some clothes on and phased back to her.

CHAPTER 65 ~ COREY

*W*hen Brock phased from the bedroom, I felt it and shivered. He was only one floor away, I knew he went to his own quarters and yet I felt alone. Would it always feel that way when we were apart now that we had connected?

Connected—wow, how had it happened? I couldn't remember us having a conversation. I don't know who reached out to whom, or what we were doing when it started. The feelings had slammed down on me so quickly, taking my body by complete surprise.

The peppermint shampoo I used tingled my scalp, reminding me of the penetrating burning I had felt all over my body earlier. The pain had come to an end when we had started kissing and had been replaced by incredible elation. The knowledge I had gained during the connection made me better understand Brock in a way I had never known another person.

The bathroom was steamy when I finished my shower, and I dressed quickly and went to the kitchen. What should I make? I wondered as I pulled open the fridge. I had no idea what he liked to eat, but just as the thought crossed my mind, I realized that I did.

I pulled out some lunch meat and closed the door. Inside a cabinet I pulled out rye bread and took out four pieces. Back in the fridge, I pulled out the mustard and mayonnaise. I didn't like mustard, but I knew for a fact that he did.

Brock phased back to my quarters just as I was about to slice the sandwiches. I could relax. The sensation of being alone dissipated, and I felt whole again.

Brock pulled out a stool from the counter bar and sat down, his brown hair darker since it was still wet and brushed back off his face. I pushed his plate over to him. He lifted the top slice of Rye and smiled.

"Makes things a whole lot easier to know exactly what you like." We shared a smile, and I slid onto the stool next to him and dug into my sandwich. Ham and cheese had never tasted so good. "So, what now?" I mumbled with my mouth full.

He reached for the napkins that stood in a chrome holder on the counter, placing one next to my plate and wiping his mouth before he casually shrugged.

"I have no clue. I guess we just go back to doing what we were doing before."

With another bite in my mouth, I thought about what he said. After I had swallowed, I turned to him; I wanted to ask him something, but I didn't know how.

"What?" he muttered around the food in his mouth. He set his sandwich down and returned my gaze. "What's on your mind?"

"When you went to your quarters, did you notice anything strange?" I bit my bottom lip, waiting for his reply.

He smirked and picked up his sandwich, "You mean like I was missing my right hand?" He took a big chunk of his sandwich and peered at me from the corner of his eye.

So he had felt the same thing. "Yeah, like that." I reached for my own food.

"Yep, I felt it. Why do you think I came back here without drying my hair?" He pushed the last piece from the first half of his meal into his mouth.

"Oh, that's right, you're Mr. GQ. I know that about you now." I threw my head back and laughed, trying not to choke on my food.

"I'm not that bad," he said as he tried to swallow and almost choked himself when he laughed at his own words.

"We'll see about that, I guess." I set my sandwich down and wiped a small glob of mayonnaise off my fingers onto my napkin. "Will we always feel strange being apart?" I changed the subject back to the more important issue.

The muscles in his jaw moved up and down as he finished chewing. "I'm not exactly sure, but I think yeah."

"So how do we deal with that? I mean, we both have different charges, and won't we want time apart?" Brock raised an eyebrow. "Not that I want any time away from you right now, that's not what I'm saying. I'm just saying if we are here for eternity, won't we get tired of each other?"

Brock leaned over and placed a small kiss on my lips, "Corey, I've been with you for years already, and I can't imagine not having you around me now."

"Yeah, we'll see how you feel in another forty years." I turned back to finish my sandwich.

He laughed beside me and picked up his second half. We spent the afternoon snuggled on the couch, listening to music, and talking about the things we knew about each other, trying to better understand what some of them meant.

Around dusk, Montgomery phased onto the balcony where we stood watching the sunset.

"Well, you two look happy." He had a bottle of champagne in his hand. He raised it up to us, "A little toast to our new couple?"

Montgomery's arms opened wide, and I stepped into them, giving him a tight hug. "I'll go get some glasses. Is David coming?" I glanced over my shoulder as I walked to the sliding door.

"Afraid not, he's busy watching over someone right now." His voice held more tension than I had ever heard from him, but he had his back to me, so I went inside to get the glasses.

When I came back with the glasses, Brock seemed as tense as Montgomery. "What's going on?"

"Nothing you need to worry about right now, my dear." Monty started to untwist the metal cage over the top of the cork, and dropped it on the

313

side table. With two thumbs under the cork, it took little pressure to pop it. Champagne bubbled up and over the side of the bottle. He poured the three glasses and set the bottle down.

"Here's to the new and incredible couple." He raised his glass high and we all clinked them together. Brock and I exchanged smiles over our glasses. Just as the champagne touched my lips, David appeared.

"You have to come now. He's trying to cross over."

CHAPTER 66 ~ MITCHELL

*M*y brain had shut down, and when consciousness started to click back into place, I found myself deep in the dark recesses of my mind. I thought my eyes were open, yet I could not see anything. My heart beat slowly in my chest, I heard it inside my head, but I couldn't feel it.

There was only silence around me. I felt like I was all alone inside a sound proof dark chamber. I tried to move, but my limbs would not listen. Frustrated, I allowed the darkness to swallow me again.

I noticed beeps, high-pitched ones that I wanted to swat away from me, yet once again my body would not comply with my mind. Dry air tickled the inside of my nose, and I wanted it to stop, but there was no way to make it go away.

Mumbled words twirled around me in the air, but they meant nothing to my ears. Confused by all these feelings, I searched for the darkness and moved back into it.

A third time I found myself on the fringes of life. My body would not respond when I asked it to. I could only listen, and the hollow words spoken beside me mentioned coma and paralysis. They couldn't be talking about me, could they?

I went off to find the dark silence once again, finding more peace there.

The beeping continued, a shuffling sound over the floor was muffled in my ears. Something touched the tip of my left finger. Something else touched my right hand, and I could feel a swirl of movement over the skin. Was someone touching me?

The sound of a door opening reached me. A masculine voice spoke, "Mrs. O'Reilly, the test results just came back."

"Was there anything different?" a soft worried feminine voice answered.

"Not really. There is very little activity in his brain. We will continue to monitor him, but I'm not sure if things will get better." The male voice sounded as if it were closer.

"But there is activity, right?" her voice was garbled.

"Yes, a slight amount, but his brain had some major swelling, and we aren't sure if he is going to come out of the coma. It is a good sign that he can breathe on his own, but you have to prepare yourself for the fact that he might never come out of this."

The sound of muffled crying reached me, and I succumbed to the peaceful place I had found earlier.

In my secluded darkness I could walk, I could see, although there was nothing, nothing but memories, recollections of my life, of my family—and of Corey.

Where was she? The last thing I remembered, she had been on the back of my motorcycle. A car had come around a bend, and I'd had no chance to avoid it. Just before the crash, it had felt like she had been torn from behind me, or had that been because of the crash?

She was an angel, right? So she couldn't be killed again, could she? Could something have happened to her? If she was alright, wouldn't she be here with me?

Maybe I needed to go look for her. I turned in the darkness and started to walk. I did not know which way to go, I only knew to follow my mind's path.

If I had counted the steps, maybe then I would have known how far I had traveled before the space in front of me started to lighten. My feet moved just a tiny bit faster.

From just beyond the light, a shadow appeared. I squinted to try and see it better. My steps slowed as the figure emerged and moved towards me.

The light silhouetted the figure, and I knew the movement and lines of the person coming towards me.

"Corey, you came for me."

CHAPTER 67 ~ BROCK

*C*orey had asked if things would always feel strange when we were apart, and I had no idea how to answer her. There were so few connected couples in the Realm that I had never thought to ask about it. Maybe I should have taken the time to find one of them and ask them.

We could do that together.

With the sun setting in the glorious sky, I held her in my arms. The contentment we shared was quickly brushed aside when Montgomery arrived.

Since I was connected to him, I knew something was going on, and when Corey stepped away to get the glasses, he filled me in.

"What's going on? Where is David?"

He glanced to the door before answering. "David is with Mitch, he's watching him, but it's not good."

"How bad is it?" I leaned back against the railing, crossing my arms over my chest.

"He's in a coma, and he is showing very little brain activity. He keeps coming forward and moving back. We're not sure which way he's going to go. It's not time for him to come here."

My jaw clenched. How was Corey going to react to this? She didn't seem to recall what had transpired.

Corey came back onto the balcony, and we raised our glasses in a toast. The news that Montgomery had shared with me put a slight damper on the celebration, and the appearance of David completely dashed any further thoughts of a good time.

"You have to come now. He's trying to cross over." David's face was alarmed, concern evident in his voice.

Montgomery set his glass down and turned to David, "Are you sure?"

"Yes, I felt him descend back and he's going deeper. He came around just about the time they were talking about how bad he was."

"Who are you guys talking about?" Corey eyeballed David and Montgomery cautiously.

I dropped my head down to my chest, took a deep breath, and then lifted my chin. "Mitch."

Confusion and fear raced across her face, piercing my heart, "What's wrong with Mitch?"

"She doesn't know?" David's voice rose an octave in surprise.

As Coralenna answered, I shook my head, "Know what? Tell me what's going on!"

Before I could answer, Montgomery stepped in front of her and took the glass out of her hand, setting it down on the table. He took both of her hands into his and stared her in the eye.

"You don't remember the accident, Coralenna?" he questioned softly. I knew that he was trying to comfort her by touching her, but her entire body was tense, I felt it.

Her hair swished around her shoulders and she shook her head hard.

"Coralenna, Mitch was in a motorcycle accident. He's in very serious condition."

The croak of her voice could barely be heard, "How serious?"

"Serious enough that he is trying to come home, but it's not his time, and you need to stop him."

"Oh my God," she pulled away from Montgomery and sat down in one of the gliders. "How am I supposed to stop him?"

"Yeah, how is she supposed to stop him, he's on a level that we can't reach. We can't enter a comatose person's mind." We all turned to David as he spoke.

Montgomery glanced at me and stepped over to Coralenna, squatting down beside her, he placed his hand on her knee. "Well, I have an idea."

Coralenna's face was stricken with emotion, "What?"

"David's right. We don't have the ability to cross over to that level, but you two might be able to."

"What do you mean?" Coralenna flicked a glance at me then stepped in front of Montgomery.

"Now that you two have connected, you have a strength that is beyond what we normally have. I have heard of another couple who were able to use their power together to cross over for something similar to this."

"But Mitch would freak out if he saw Brock. That might cause more trouble if he shows up with me." Coralenna sat up straighter in her chair.

Montgomery stood back up, "He might not have to cross over with you. Just being close enough might give you the strength to move over into that level."

Corey stood up quickly, "Then we have to try it." She tore her gaze from Montgomery's face and focused on me sternly. "Did you know about the accident?"

It was only a matter of time till that question was asked, I knew. "Yes, and you did too."

"Me?" her voice rose. "How could I have known? I've been here, wrapped up in your arms this whole time, the whole time Mitch has been lying in a bed dying, and you knew!"

"Corey, you were at the accident scene," I said slowly.

Her eyes started flicking back and forth in an effort to remember.

"You were riding on the back of the motorcycle with Mitch. I pulled you off right before he crashed."

She continued to jet her eyes around and then her feet began to shuffle and she turned in circles. Her expressions were changing so quickly, I was afraid to speak again.

She sucked in a sharp breath and stopped moving, and I knew she had remembered. Her head spun around to face me. "Why did you do that? Why did you take me from him? I could have helped him!"

Her anger was understood, and I worked hard to remain calm as I replied, "Coralenna, you were in a mortal body. If you had been in that crash, you could have been injured or killed."

"What? I'm already dead! Please explain to me how you can die again?"

With the use of my back muscles, I pushed off the railing and moved closer to her. I saw her shoulders straighten, and her jaw clamp down, but she didn't move away.

"Sweetheart, your mortal body could have been killed, and then your soul would not have been able to return here. That's why we have always said it was so dangerous for you in the living arena."

"But what about Mitch?" she started to tear up. "Couldn't you have saved him, too?"

"We can't change destiny. We can only guide people. What happened to Mitch was meant to happen. I just couldn't let anything happen to you." My voice lowered as I spoke, and I lifted my hand to slide my knuckles over her cheek.

A single tear slipped out and I caught it with my thumb. "We'll help him, Corey, I promise we will do everything we can."

Her nod was jerky, but she circled her arms around me and put her head on my chest. For a few moments, I held her tightly. David cleared his throat behind us.

Coralenna and I pulled apart, but kept one arm around each other's back.

"We need to go," David said meaningfully.

"Let's go save my brother." I tipped Corey's face up and kissed her lips lightly. We phased while still holding each other.

CHAPTER 68 ~ COREY

*W*hen they said Mitch had been in an accident, guilt rained down on me like a load of bricks. Here I had been happy and safe in Brock's arms, and Mitch was fighting for his life.

How I had not remembered the accident was beyond me. When Brock mentioned it, I wracked my mind to find the pieces of the puzzle that would fit together. Using my own memories that I had tucked deep inside, and the ones that I had acquired from Brock, I relived the whole incident.

The fear that Brock had felt right before it happened and the sound of the crash around us as our bodies ignited, I had thought were from our connection.

I wanted to be angry at someone, but hearing what Brock told me about dying a second death calmed the heated threads in my head and heart. From his memory, I knew he had only pulled me to protect me, to save me. How could I fault him for that?

As I stood against his strong chest and felt the love he had for me, I knew I had no right to be angry with him. He loved me, and he would do anything for me.

Now we had to do everything that we could to save Mitch.

We phased to his hospital room. The pale blue walls displayed shadows from the machines hooked up to him. One small light was on over his bed, reflecting towards the ceiling rather than directly on him.

His entire body was practically covered in plaster, one whole leg and half of the other one. Tubes and wires were connected to every part of his chest; nose and arms were visible around the bandages.

I choked on a sob and buried my head in Brock's shoulder. He held my head tightly to him, and I heard him clear his throat. Tears rolled down my cheeks, and as I leaned back to wipe them off, I saw Brock wipe his own cheek.

"Where's Montgomery?" I turned, but only David stood in the room with us. Beth sat silently in the chair beside Mitch's bed, her eyes closed, but I knew she wasn't sleeping.

"I don't know. I'm sure he'll be here in a minute," Brock said from beside me.

"We can't do this without him. We don't know what to do!" The words rushed out of my mouth.

"Relax, my dear," Montgomery landed beside me and patted me on the arm. "I needed to make a pit stop and make sure we were doing it right."

Relief that he had shown up was short-lived as the monitor in front of us started to beep rapidly.

"Coralenna, you need to go," Montgomery said beside me.

"Go where? I don't know what I'm doing!" My body shook with fear.

"You and Brock need to be touching him and holding hands yourself. You can do it from here, you don't need to be in the living arena, but you do need to all be touching."

We moved to Mitch's side. I placed my hand over his shoulder while Brock touched the visible skin of his thigh.

Beth sat up in her chair and studied the monitors, alarm on her face.

"Focus, Corey, you need to focus on Mitch. Go inside his mind, find him. He's in the dark someplace searching for the light." The heart monitor began to slow; my hands grew damp.

"Go, Corey, find him," Brock's strained voice came from beside me as I focused all my energy into Mitch. It took a moment, and then I found the small piece of his mind that appeared to be working.

I contained a sob as I felt the inside of his battered body. How could he recover from his? Dear Lord, please help me, I prayed as I moved towards the single area of his mind.

CHAPTER 69 ~ MITCHELL

"Corey, you came for me."

The most beautiful sight in the world stood before me.

"Hello, Mitchell." Her voice sounded like musical notes to my ears, tinkling in the darkness around me. I smiled and reached for her.

She slipped into my arms, and I held her. "I'm so glad you're alright. I was worried about you."

She pulled back so she could see into my face. "I'm fine. You don't need to worry about me. We need to worry about you, though." She cast a glance around, "It's so dark here, take me someplace else."

"Let's go into the light." I pointed behind her and she shook her head.

"No, take me someplace nice, take me to the river." Her smile melted my heart. I would do anything for her. The image of the river and the rocks along the banks came to mind, and there we were.

"Wow, that was kind of cool." Birds were singing in the trees and the water was rushing over the rocks. The sun was high in the sky, but the trees blocked out the strongest of the rays. "Is this better?"

"Much better, Mitchell," she paused and ran her fingers over my cheek. I snuggled into her palm as she cleared her throat, "Mitchell, you need to go back, you can't stay here with me."

Surprised that she would say that, I stared at her for a moment, "No,

I'm right where I want to be, with you." I leaned forward and put a soft kiss on her lips.

She stepped back slightly and put her hand along the side of my face, "Mitch, you can't stay. You have to return."

Frustration edged my voice as I countered, "I don't want to. I want to be here with you."

"Honey, I know you do, but it's not your time. You have a family that needs you and a long life to live."

"I'm ready to leave them. I want to come up to heaven with you," I said adamantly.

"But what about Chase? What about watching him grow up? What about Beth? Do you want to leave her all alone? I know you love her. You need to go back to your family. They need you now more than ever."

What about Chase? I would miss watching him play baseball and all the things he accomplished in school. I'd miss his graduation and the day he would get married. Could I give up those things?

While things were better with Beth, could we fix everything and share a happy life, or would I always be wishing I was with Corey?

I turned away from her and moved to the edge of the rocks, staring into the running water.

"Mitch, time goes by so fast, and you don't want to miss a minute of it. You have the chance to go back, to be a part of your son's life. He needs you."

"But he's not my son!" I spun around on her and stared at her hard.

"Yes, he is. You have raised him. You are the only one he knows as a father. You can't tell me that because a mistake was made all those years ago that you are going to hold that against him, or against Beth for that matter."

I didn't want to leave my son, and I knew that Beth loved me. Could I leave them alone? If it had been anybody other than Brock, it wouldn't have mattered, but this was my own brother.

"Wait, you don't want me with you because you want to be with Brock." I stepped closer to her, the anger that had started to recede grew back threefold.

"You don't know the whole story about what happened with Brock and Beth. He was—"

"And I don't want to know! I don't care! He's not my brother! My brother wouldn't have done that to me." I crossed my arms over my chest, feeling the need to protect myself.

"Mitch, you need to listen to me, please. Just listen for a moment."

"Whatever, Corey, what?" I turned away from her again and scrutinized the water.

"Mitch, Brock was very ill. He didn't know it at the time, but he had a brain tumor."

My head turned slightly toward her, "He what?"

"He had a very large brain tumor." She stood still, watching me, the sun shining down on her hair. I thought about her words for a moment before I turned back to the water.

"That's no excuse," I blurted out.

"No, you're right. It's not. He made a bad choice that night, but the tumor was large enough that it caused major problems with his personality and the way he dealt with things. Shortly after, he found out about the tumor. The tumor was inoperable, he was going to die."

My head hung down. My brother had cancer and never told me.

"When Beth told him she was pregnant, he already knew he was dying. He made Beth promise not to tell you because there was no way he could ever be a father to the child, and that was his odd way of making up for what he had done. The tumor is what killed him."

"No," I turned back to her, "he died in an accident. They never said anything about a tumor."

"They were wrong. The police saw a man killed in a car accident and never questioned it, but he was coming back from chemotherapy and had a problem. He crashed because of the tumor."

I blinked and then blinked again. He had been sick, and I never knew.

"So you're saying that because of the tumor, he did what he did?"

"Yes, it changed his personality. I know that doesn't excuse it, but that's the truth. I'm sorry you had to hear that from me, I wish that he could have told you himself." She paused for a moment. "Someday, you will need to speak with him, learn to forgive him and Beth."

I thought about what she said, but I wasn't sure how to forgive them. "How do I do that?" My arms fell to my sides as I thought about it.

She walked to me and took my hands in hers, gently squeezing them, "You just let it go, you just believe in what you have, and you forgive them. Brock gave you a gift from God. Don't turn your back on it."

For the first time, Corey looked like a real angel as the sun shone down around her, and she just glowed. How had I been so lucky to have someone like this in my life?

"If I return, will you leave me?"

She picked up each of my hands and kissed the backs of them one at a time.

She shook her head and smiled, "No, I'm never going to go away. I'm your Garda, and I will always be with you in some way. You may not see me, but I'll always be right here." She placed her hand on my heart.

"You promise?" I placed my hand over hers on my chest.

"I promise. You will always have my love, Mitchell."

"Okay, but can you tell me one more thing before I go?" My heart started to beat a bit faster thinking about never seeing her again, never holding her again.

"Sure, anything." She took her hand from my chest and laced her fingers with mine.

"What's going on with you and Brock?" I tried not to sound angry, but I wasn't sure I succeeded.

She threw her head back and laughed, "Oh, that is so complicated, Mitch."

"Does he love you?" I whispered when she stopped laughing and brought her attention back to my face.

She grew serious, "Yes, he does."

I swallowed and forced myself to keep eye contact with her, "And do you love him?"

She paused, taking a moment to think before she answered, "I care for him deeply. Is it love? I don't know. It's not what you and I shared, but, I think in time, I will grow to love him."

My head bowed at her words. I had hoped the answer would have been no, but who was I to tell her whom she should love and whom she shouldn't.

"Mitch, he's my destiny," she whispered. "Are you ready to go back now? Beth is waiting for you; she's really worried."

"Can I hold you one last time?" I was torn. I didn't really want to leave her, but if she said this wasn't my time, then I had to believe her.

"I wouldn't have it any other way." She pulled me into her embrace, and we stood there for a long time. The sun shone down on us, the breeze gently tossed the ends of her hair, and the birds sang softly in the trees. To me, until the day I died, this place would be my heaven.

When we finally pulled apart, she tipped her head up and kissed me one last time. The kiss was one of the softest we had shared, one of promise but also of goodbye.

"Take us back, Mitch, it's time to go home," she whispered.

I gazed at her, "I love you, Corey."

"And I will always love you, Mitchell," she murmured softly.

I closed my eyes and found myself alone in the dark once more. A moment of fear struck me, but I felt her presence calling to me, and I reached for it.

Very slowly, I felt myself coming back. The high-pitched beeping in the room reached my ears, and the cold air filtered in my nose. I fought to open my eyelids, and for the first time, they started to respond.

They fluttered softly, and I struggled to keep them open. I knew someone stood over me, but I could not see who. After a few more tries, I was able to get them to open, and I blinked to clear the fuzzy image.

Beside my bed, leaning slightly over me was Corey.

"Welcome back, Mitch," she said with a smile.

CHAPTER 70 ~ BROCK

The sight of my brother lying in the hospital bed tore at my heart. Corey buried her head into my chest. I understood why because that was exactly what I wanted to do: hide.

As Corey touched Mitch's shoulder, I silently prayed that what we were about to do would work. The Maker had said to believe, and that was what I would do.

Even though Coralenna's hand was in mine, I felt her slip away from me. I gasped for air as loneliness settled around me. I struggled to reach for her and searched for her energy pattern, finally finding it as it wove through Mitch's mind.

Every part of his body was destroyed, and his mind was the worst. How hard he must have struck the pavement to cause that much damage. I struggled to stay strong and not turn away from what I was seeing. She had so much more courage than I did to face this.

When she reached him, I could hear her words, and when they moved to the stream, I could see it all through her internal sight. She loved him so much, but she fought to make him understand that his life was here and not above.

Tears ran down my face as she stood there and explained to him what had happened all those years ago. It should have been me explaining it, but she did it for me. She removed a burden from my past and took it upon herself to right it. My love for her grew with each word.

I even found myself snickering when she threw her head back and laughed at our connection. The seriousness of her tone gave little doubt to the fact that she did truly care for me, and that one day I would win her love. For now, I would be satisfied to have what I had with her.

The moment Mitch decided to come back, I knew that we had succeeded. I left her mind just before she went into his arms, giving them a last moment together to say goodbye. They both deserved that.

Joy passed through my entire being when Corey slipped back into her body. I squeezed her hand and thanked God for putting such an incredible woman in my existence.

"Brock, I need you to keep hold of him, I want to try something before he starts to come back."

At a loss for words, I stared at her in awe of her radiant beauty. She focused again and squeezed my hand tightly. I felt her slipping back to Mitch, and panic teased my mind.

"Relax, Brock, I need to pull your energy to do this."

Steeling myself for God knew what she was about to do, I felt her draw on my inner strength. I focused on her and finally realized what she was doing, she was repairing his brain.

When she shifted back into her body once more, I felt how weary she was. She had drained herself and pulled a lot of my energy out, too.

Her soft smile turned towards me, "We did it."

Mitch tried to blink, and we all held our breath. David and Montgomery stood at the end of the bed, one with his arms crossed tightly, chewing on his bottom lip while the other fisted his palms by his side.

Mitch finally opened his eyes and blinked slowly into Corey's face. The barest of smiles touched his dry cracked lips.

"Welcome back, Mitch."

I checked on Beth, she was sitting very still. *Beth*, I called out softly to her and her eyes sprang open.

She saw Mitch's eyes open. Corey moved back as Beth took position next to his bed.

"Oh my God, thank you! Thank you! Mitch, honey, can you hear me?"

She touched his face gently, and I glanced at Corey to see tears running down her cheeks. Beth was wiping the tears from her own face as quickly as she could, but more kept appearing.

Mitch moved his head slightly to acknowledge her.

"Oh, Mitch, I thought I'd lost you. Don't you ever do that again. Promise me you won't ever do that again! I need you too much."

Mitch turned his head slightly to Corey, she winked at him. He turned his face to me, and we watched each other for a moment. A tear rolled down towards his ear. My vision immediately blurred with moisture.

His head tipped ever so slightly, and I reached out to touch his leg, gently squeezing above his knee. He closed his eyes as another salty drop slipped out.

Beth had turned away and was calling for the nurse, missing the silent exchange.

As the door burst open and multiple people entered the room to check on Mitch, Corey turned to me, "Let's go home, I'm exhausted."

I wrapped my arm around her and used my other hand to wipe the tears off her face. "Yeah, let's go home."

With one last look at Mitch, we phased back to the Realm.

CHAPTER 71 ~ COREY

his had to have been one of the most emotional and exhausting days I had ever had, alive or dead. When Brock and I returned, we both fell into each other's arms and were sound asleep in moments.

When we woke, we were summoned to the Maker. He was happy with our abilities to bring Mitch back and for healing him. He told us that while we had the ability, we weren't to use it lightly.

The only reason he had allowed us to use the power was because, first, he wanted us to test our strengths, but also because the accident that put Mitch where he was had ultimately been our fault and not part of his destiny.

Had Brock been paying more attention to his charge and not consumed in thoughts of me, he would have been able to stop the crash.

Just as if I hadn't been so consumed by my desire to be with Mitch, I could have assisted Mitch in averting the danger that came around the corner.

We both understood that we had erred, and we stood closely together, my back and shoulder against his chest while his hand rested on my hip and we accepted responsibility.

The Maker had also told us that my decision to help Mitch return had secured my position in the Realm and that of a Gardaí. My faith, belief, and loyalty would never be tested that way again.

Once we left there, we spent all of our time side by side. My feelings grew for Brock each day, and I knew that I loved him. He was a strong man, a man made of principle. Even though he'd once made mistakes, I knew what kind of man he really was deep inside.

Brock took me with him to see his charges. We had learned that since it was painful to be apart, we would share the responsibility between us of the people we were to protect.

Some were to be protected to come join us, while others were watched over and guided so that they would eventually enter heaven.

Mitch was still my responsibility, well, our responsibility, actually. We stopped in to watch his progress and laughed when he smiled at the doctors that kept repeating what a miracle his survival was and how well he was recovering.

Beth seldom left his side and usually only because he forced her to go spend time with Chase and get some rest. He was released from the hospital a week after he woke up with a medical report stating he should fully recover.

Many times when Mitch was alone, he would talk to me, and once in a while say something meant for Brock. We didn't answer him, but he still knew we were there.

Brock had moved into my quarters permanently right after we returned. Being together was just easier. I would now see the door knocker on the outside of our front door and smile. My yin and yang were finally back in tune with each other.

A month after Mitch was released from the hospital, Brock and I were watching a movie, snuggled on the couch in our home. I felt the stirrings from below and listened carefully.

"Do you feel it, too?" Brock said quietly in my ear as my head rested back on his shoulder. I nodded.

"Should we go? It's been a little while since he called out to us."

I tipped my head up so I could see his face, "I'd like that."

"Yeah, me, too." He tweaked my nose, and I sat up. We listened for the call and followed it. Brock and I were a little surprised when we landed at my gravesite.

Mitch stood balancing himself on crutches while Beth stood to his side, extremely nervous. Her hands gripped a bouquet of my favorite lilies.

"Corey, are you there?" he spoke towards the sky, and Brock and I smiled at each other. "Corey? Brock? Can you guys hear me? I need to talk to you, please."

Hello, Mitch. His shoulders relaxed slightly as he heard my internal response.

"You're there. Can you come forward, I'd like to talk to you in person, please?" he twisted his neck left and right, searching for me.

Beth's face seemed to pale more, and her hands strangled the flower bundle.

I peered over my shoulder at Brock. He shrugged.

I let go of Brock's hand and took a step forward, allowing myself to only be seen by Mitch. The smile that lit his face warmed my heart.

"How are you?" We stood about six feet apart as I spoke.

"I'm good, no, I'm great now." He glanced at Beth and I followed. Her forehead was wrinkled as her eyeballs darted around.

"Mitch, can you see her?" she whispered.

"You can't see her, Beth?" She shook her head quickly and took a step closer to him.

When he turned his attention back to me, he asked, "Corey, can you show yourself to her?"

"Why?" I was not opposed to it, but I wanted to know why this was important to him.

"She has something she would like to say to you, please." I contemplated the two of them for a moment. I sent Brock a reassuring smile over my shoulder when I felt him tense and took another step forward that would bring me to the living arena.

Beth gasped, and Mitch reached out to grab her arm when she stumbled back. She took a deep swallow and stepped forward to be even with Mitch.

"Hello, Beth." The breeze tickled my skin. I forgot how different things were once I stepped into this level.

"Hello, Corey," her voice shook as she spoke.

"There is nothing to fear, I'm not going to hurt you." I smiled to show her I was sincere.

"I know that. If you were, you would have done it when Mitch was in the hospital." She raised her chin up as if she expected me to challenge her words.

"If it had been his time, then yes, I could have, but he has many more years here, with you and your family." I saw moisture begin to pool.

"Thank you. Thank you for not taking him from me." A tear ran down her pale cheek. I stepped closer to her and saw her shoulders stiffen.

"Relax, Beth, I promise I'm not going to hurt you." I stood in front of her, searching into her frightened face. She was a strong woman, and some residual guilt reared its head in me for what I had done to their relationship. "I'm very sorry for the pain that I caused you."

She glanced away from my face and swallowed shakily, "Thank you, but you don't need to apologize. If it wasn't for what Mitch shared and lost with you, I might not have ever gotten him back."

I slid a quick peek at Mitch. He hung his head for a moment and then looked back up at me solemnly.

"You have an incredible husband, Beth, and I know that you two will get through everything and have a wonderful, happy life together." I reached out and touched her arm. What I felt coming from her startled me so much that I jerked my hand back and glanced at Mitch.

Mitch was confused at my reaction, "What's wrong?"

I moved to stand in front of him, "Mitch, I know you might not want to see Brock, but I need him to come forward for a minute."

Beth sucked in a breath and put her hand to her mouth.

Mitch turned to her, "Beth, it's alright." He turned back to me, "That's fine. I'd like to speak with him myself."

Beth was shaking her head back and forth slowly, and Mitch turned back to her, "Beth, I've already told you that I forgive you, and now I have to tell him I forgive him."

Tear after tear rolled down her pale cheeks, but she nodded slowly.

340

"Do you really forgive me, Mitch?" While we had watched Beth, Brock had stepped over. Beth hitched in a tight breath and pushed her hand tighter to her mouth.

Brock stepped beside me, instinctively resting his hand on my back. Mitch noticed the gesture, straightened his shoulders, and refrained from making a comment.

"Yes, I do. When I got back home, I had Beth go up in the attic and pull down that box of stuff that I got from your house. If I had taken the time before instead of getting angry at the letters I saw, I would have seen the medical records you had stored in there." He eyed Brock carefully. "I assume you left them there so I would know the truth."

"Yes, that is exactly why I left them there." I felt the tension in Brock's body rise just before he spoke again, "I owe both of you an apology, especially you, Beth. I should have never allowed that to happen that night."

Beth's hand slowly lowered from her mouth as she bounced between the two men's faces.

Mitch glanced at Beth, the side of his mouth tipping up, "Let's just call it even and move forward."

Beth nodded and faced me, "I think you told Mitch that Chase was a gift from God, well I believe he really is. Because of the accident, Mitch may never be able to have kids of his own."

Sorrow pierced my heart to know that I might have caused that, but at the same time I knew I could do something.

Brock spoke up from beside me, "Chase is your child, Mitch. He might have been fathered by me, but we share the same blood, and there is no one else in this world that I would want to raise him."

Mitch blinked his eyes rapidly. "Thank you, Brock," Mitch whispered.

"Beth, I need to take your hand for a moment, and I need Brock to take your other one, okay?"

Beth was immediately alarmed and stepped back from us.

"Please, don't worry. We aren't going to hurt you." Her alarmed face turned straight to Mitch. He seemed concerned but told her it would be alright.

I reached for her hand and grasped it tightly. Brock stepped up beside me. *What's going on, Coralenna?*

Just wait, you'll see. I said silently to him and reached for his hand, clasping it. Brock put his hand out to Beth and she reached out to take his. I closed my eyes, focusing on what I had felt earlier.

No way— Brock shivered as he felt what I had earlier.

"We're gonna fix that." I poured my energy into Beth, focusing on the dark mass that grew in her body. Brock sent energy into her, too, and we dissolved the mass completely.

When I opened my eyes again, Brock was smiling down at Beth. She moved her gaze between the two of us. "What did you do?"

Beth, shh, it's just me, Corey, I whispered into her mind. *When you go back to the doctors, the lump will be gone. You don't have to worry about that now. Focus on your family because you're going to have a lot to take care of soon.*

Beth broke down in sobs, and I pulled her into my arms. I saw Mitch share a small smile with Brock as he laid his hand on Mitch's shoulder. "It's gonna be alright now, brother, it's gonna be alright."

EPILOGUE

Mitchell

I sat in the hospital room, smiling. How much our life had changed over this last year, so much anger, so much love, and so much life.

Beth told me a week later when she came in crying from visiting her doctor that she had had a large lump in her left breast, but now the cancer was gone. She stood in my arms, and we both cried and thanked God for what He had given us.

Two months before today, I gave a final deposition in court concerning the incidents in which Joe had tried to implicate me. Shortly before my day in court, Joe had disappeared, and no one knew where he was.

I knew that I needed to watch my back, he wasn't like Corey, and I had my suspicions that he played for the southern team, but since the day at the cemetery, I had not seen Corey or Brock to ask.

"Here, can you take her?" Beth asked from the hospital bed, and I reached over and carefully picked up my daughter, Rebecca Corey. I tickled her soft skin with the tip of my finger while a wail came from Beth's arms.

"Guess Mathew Brock is hungry again, huh?" I chuckled as she tried to adjust him to her breast.

"I'm sure he is, he already eats more than Chase, and he's only a day old."

I watched her feed our son and thought about how lucky I had been. That night that I had come home angry and upset, and Beth and I had made love on the kitchen floor had been the night these two had been conceived.

"Do you think they know?" Beth interrupted my thoughts.

I studied my little newborn daughter and then glanced at my son, wondering the same thing.

They're beautiful, Mitch.

Tears pooled in my eyes as I looked up to see Corey and Brock standing in the corner of the room, both radiant and smiling.

"Yeah," I forced myself to hold it together, "yeah, they know."

Beth scanned the room and then turned her attention back to me, "Good."

If Corey had not stopped me that night in the parking lot, and I had not gone home to Beth and made love to her, these two incredible gifts would not be here. Only a short time later when my accident occurred, my ability to have children disappeared.

What I had done earlier that night was wrong, but Corey stopping me, well that was just destiny—just pure and simple destiny—and that is what I would always believe.

Corey

"You do know that you changed the course of their lives, right." Brock nuzzled my ear as we stood in the room and watched Beth and Mitch cuddle and feed their children.

"I didn't change their destiny. I saw her future when I touched her. She would have beaten the cancer, but it would have been a long and dangerous road while she carried those two."

"I think it's pretty cool that they named them after us."

I twisted my neck so I could look up at his face. He stood directly behind me with his arms wrapped around my waist. "Yeah, it's pretty cool. Let's go home, Brock. It's time to leave these two to their lives for a while. They won't need us until those two get bigger."

"Alright," he gave me a quick kiss and smiled down at me.

"How about we play hide and seek?" I grinned mischievously.

His eyebrow rose quizzically over his left eye, "Okay, if that's what you want. You go first."

I phased from his arms and waited for him to follow. When he arrived in our bedroom, I was leaning back on the pillows of our bed. "It sure is a shame that we don't land in the same place."

Brock burst out laughing, remembering the time something similar had been said. With two steps, he dove onto the bed and into my arms, right where I wanted him to be.

The End

MORE BOOKS BY STACY EATON

Paranormal Romance:
My Blood Runs Blue
Blue Blood for Life
Garda ~ Welcome to the Realm

Domestic Violence – Crime - Suspense:
Whether I'll Live or Die
Barbara's Plea
You're Not Alone

Romantic Suspense:
Liveon ~ No Evil
Second Shield
Distorted Loyalty
Six Days of Memories
Finding the Strength
Second Shield II: The Return

Contemporary Romance:
Tempt Me Too

Mistletoe & Cocoa Kisses

The Heal Me Series
Fan Fiction based off of
Melissa Foster's Remington Series
Cured by Love, Heal Me Series, Book 1
Revived by Love, Heal Me Series, Book 2
Mended by Love, Heal Me Series, Book 3

Celebration Series:
Tangled in Tinsel, Book 1
Tears to Cheers, Book 2
Heathens & Hearts, Book 3
Rainbows bring Riches, Book 4
Sweet as Sugar, Book 5
Making Mom Mad, Book 6
Sparklers & Spankings, Book 7
Raffles to Rattles, Book 8
Flirting with Fireworks, Book 9
Working Under Wheels, Book 10
Masquerading at Midnight, Book 11
Blessings and Beans, Book 12
Velvet and Vows, Book 13

The Sometimes Series:
Sometimes You Win
Sometimes You Lose
Sometimes You Play The Game

Pleasure Your Fantasies Series:
Mistletoe Fantasies (2017)
Whispered Fantasies (2018)

ABOUT THE AUTHOR

Stacy Eaton began her writing career in October of 2010 and as each year goes by, she releases more and more novels. Stacy recently took an early retirement from law enforcement after over fifteen years of service, with her last three in investigations and crime scene investigation.

Stacy resides in southeastern Pennsylvania with her husband, who works in law enforcement, and her teen daughter who is working toward her second degree black belt in Tae Kwon Do and on the choral and cheerleading squads at school. She also has a son who is currently serving in the United States Navy.

Stacy is very involved in Domestic Violence Awareness and served on the Board of Directors for her local Domestic Violence Center for three years. She continues to volunteer with them when she has time.

Be sure to visit www.stacyeaton.com for updates and more information on her books.

www.ingramcontent.com/pod-product-compliance
Lightning Source LLC
Chambersburg PA
CBHW020326180626
46812CB00001B/69